W9-BTA-547

Diary of a Waitress

Diary of a Waitress

The Not-So-Glamorous Life of a Harvey Girl

Carolyn Meyer

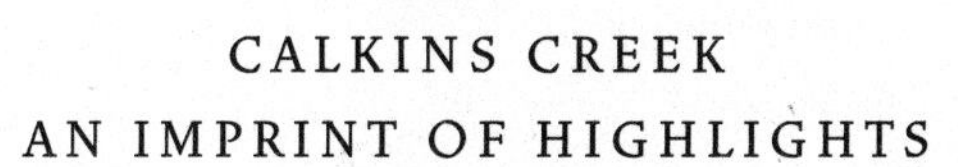

CALKINS CREEK
AN IMPRINT OF HIGHLIGHTS
Honesdale, Pennsylvania

Calkins Creek
An Imprint of Highlights
815 Church Street
Honesdale, Pennsylvania 18431

Printed in the United States of America
ISBN: 978-1-62091-652-0
Library of Congress Control Number: 2014948477

First edition
The text of this book is set in Fairfield Light Std and Futura Std.
Design by Robbin Gourley
Production by Margaret Mosomillo
10 9 8 7 6 5 4 3 2 1

Remembering my mother, Sara Knepp Meyer,
pianist and flapper
1909–1979

This diary and a silver fountain pen
engraved with my initials were given to me
by my grandmother, Margaret Preston Blair,
in celebration of my graduation from
Leavenworth High School, Leavenworth, Kansas,
May 22nd, 1926.

KATHERINE AMELIA EVANS

Tuesday, June 1st, 1926

I MADE TWO IMPORTANT DECISIONS TODAY: ONE, TO apply for a position as a waitress, and two, to begin my career as a journalist.

This is not the path to my future that I expected or dreamed of, but this is how it came about.

My father broke the news this morning at breakfast. I love that phrase, "broke the news." You can almost hear the drumroll as somebody important steps forward and makes an announcement, and everyone gasps. But Daddy just laid aside the morning paper and said, "I'm awfully sorry to tell you, Puss, but you won't be going away to college this fall as we planned." He sipped coffee, not looking at me. "I hope you're not too disappointed."

I stared at my father, my knife hovering above a second slice of toast, ready to spread on the apple butter. *Not too disappointed?* My throat went as dry as that toast. "Why?" I croaked.

I'd thought it was settled. I even knew what courses I'd take: English composition, beginning French, world literature, ancient history, biology.

"Sometimes things change. Things we don't have any control over." He sounded a little wobbly. "The store hasn't been doing as well as it used to. Business is slow. I hoped it would turn around, but it hasn't. I'm sorry, but I just don't have the money to send you." He glanced at me, then picked up his paper again. "I understand that McMeen's is hiring sales girls in their shoe department. I know the manager, Mr. Kauffman. I've already spoken to him about you."

I couldn't believe what I was hearing. "You want me to sell shoes?"

"Just temporarily, until things improve at the store. It won't be forever, Puss—only for a year or two."

Don't call me Puss! I hate that nickname. Practically everyone calls me Kitty, except my immediate family: Daddy, Mother, and my brother, Howie. It was Howie who started this Puss business. "You know—*Kitty* just sort of led to *Puss*," he explained. Only my grandmother still calls me Katherine. Gramma Blair says nicknames make a person seem common.

My shattered dreams lay among the eggy plates and toast crumbs. *Selling shoes! Spending my life trying to please persnickety old ladies with stinky feet.* I wanted to know more—*had to* know more. But there was no chance to ask questions. Mother, who'd left to call Howie to come down for breakfast and hadn't been present for Daddy's announcement, returned to the table, sighing.

"Your lazybones of a son still has not stirred, Howard," she said, but she said it lovingly. Even when she calls him a lazybones, my mother speaks lovingly of my brother. She apparently didn't notice that my life had just practically come to an end. "He must have stayed out quite late last night."

Until two a.m., I thought sourly, but I didn't mention that I'd heard him entering his room through a window by way of the porch roof. Howie is Howard Russell Evans, Jr., age nineteen and a junior at the University of Kansas in Lawrence, where until about ten minutes earlier I'd been planning to begin my freshman year in September.

"What about Howie?" I growled, and my mother looked at me, startled, as though she was surprised to see my grumpy self still at her breakfast table.

My father's nose was buried in his newspaper again. Graceful as a dove in her summer kimono, Mother rose to refill Daddy's cup.

"What do you mean, 'What about Howie,' dear?" she asked.

I waited for my father to say something, but he didn't. He just turned a page.

"Daddy says business is bad and we can't afford for

me to go to college this fall, after all," I muttered, trying to sound reasonable and succeeding only in sounding petulant. "Even though I've already signed up for my classes. So I'm wondering about Howie. Is *he* going back in September?"

"Well, *of course* he is, Puss," she said. She poured coffee into her own cup, added a splash of cream, and stirred in half a spoonful of sugar before taking a sip. "It's very important for him to finish his degree so he can go out into the world and be a successful businessman, maybe even take over your father's business, build it into something *big*." She glanced toward Daddy, his hand reaching out from behind the paper to pick up his cup.

"His grades are terrible, Mother," I argued. Surely she'd listen to such logic. "Howie just likes to spend time with his fraternity brothers and his girlfriends. I'd do much better than he does!" I added desperately.

"Darling, I know you'd earn excellent grades—we're so proud of you, you know that! But someday you'll marry a nice young man and have a family, and you don't *need* college for that. Howie does. He's *going places*."

It was pointless to argue, I knew, but I couldn't help myself. "What if I don't marry, Mother? Or not for a long, long time? Or what if I do marry and have seven children and my husband *dies*?" I said dramatically. "I need to be able to support myself."

That last prompted my father to abandon his paper

and stroke his little mustache and murmur, "Now, Puss . . . now, Puss." He stood up and put on his linen suit jacket, dropped a kiss on my mother's upturned forehead and ruffled my hair. He then picked up his Panama hat on his way out the front door to walk twelve blocks to the corner of Fourth and Shawnee, to Evans & Son, Fine Men's Clothiers Since 1909. The "& Son" part refers to my brother, who will presumably someday take his place behind the stacks of shirts, racks of silk neckties, and drawers full of socks and gloves and handkerchiefs that my father sells—although not enough of them, as I had just learned, to send me to college.

My brother Howie picked this moment to saunter in. Devilishly handsome, tall and athletic, the kind of boy that girls follow like fleas follow a dog, he was dressed for golf in his stylishly baggy plus fours. He's a caddy at the country club and even gives a few lessons. As soon as he appeared, my mother leaped up and positively *raced* to the kitchen for the privilege of serving him his breakfast.

Howie dropped into a chair across the table, yawning and raking his fingers through his mop of wavy brown hair, and grinned at me. "You arguing again? I'm telling you, Puss, you should be a lawyer, you'd knock 'em out cold, that's for darn sure."

"And what chance do I have of becoming a lawyer or anything else," I snarled, "when I'm not even going to college to study to be a journalist, which is what I've always dreamed of being! And I'll have to sell shoes!"

To my own disgust, I burst into noisy sobs and rushed out of the dining room, as I heard my brother asking, "Jeez, what did I say to set her off like that?"

I AM ALMOST SEVENTEEN, a year younger than most of my classmates, having skipped fifth grade. I was the salutatorian of my class and the class secretary. I would have been valedictorian, but Ned Freed, the smartest boy in the Class of '26, pulled A-pluses when I had only A-minuses in chemistry and physics. I won first place in an essay contest about Carry Nation, who used to go around Kansas smashing up saloons; the prize was a wristwatch. I was also the editor of both the *June Bug*, our yearbook, and the *Patriot*, the school paper that came out every two weeks during the school year. Actually, Phil Rayburn and I alternated: the first semester Phil was editor of the *Bug* while I was associate editor, and when I was editor of the *Patriot*, he was my associate. Second semester we switched roles. It was a perfect arrangement.

It probably goes without saying that I am crazy about Phil Rayburn, and it would be logical for him to be crazy about *me*, given that we have so much in common, both wanting to become journalists. But no—Phil is crazy about Elizabeth Pipher, who had some dumb assignment on the *June Bug* staff, in charge of snapshots. Elizabeth is very musical, and sings and dances and plays the piano and had the lead in the senior play, *Contrary Mary*. She also has dimples and other physical attributes too numerous to mention. A lot of people think she's stuck up because of all that. Elizabeth just strings Phil along, and he's fool enough to let himself be strung. They went to the senior prom together, and the senior picnic, and I ended up going with Jimmy Bedwell (some people call him Bedwetter, of course) and having a miserable time and probably making Jimmy—who is very nice and deserves better—miserable, too.

I intended to change all this when I went away to college to study journalism, which is what Phil Rayburn plans to do, and he would realize then that I am his soul mate. But my father has just announced the end of my dreams of one, going to college, and two, becoming Phil Rayburn's soul mate and traveling the world together as journalists. Who could have a soul mate who stays in Leavenworth, Kansas, selling *shoes!*

I flung myself on my bed and wailed for a while, attracting the worried attention of O'Reilly, our Irish setter. But I've never been able to sustain that kind of high emotion. I washed my face and dressed and went downstairs, which was now empty and quiet. I could hear Mother in the kitchen with Betty Jane, the girl who comes to help out, making a list of groceries to be ordered.

The dishes had been cleared away from the table, napkins put back in their silver rings. Only the morning paper was still where Daddy had left it on the sideboard, open to an Evans & Son Clothiers advertisement for a special sale on neckties and linen handkerchiefs.

I picked up the paper and smoothed it out. Then my eye fell on an advertisement next to Evans & Son Clothiers. Beneath an illustration of a smiling girl in a prim black dress and white apron pouring coffee for a well-dressed man, with a sketch of a locomotive in the background, was this:

WANTED

Young women 18 to 30 years of age,
of good character, attractive and intelligent,
as waitresses in the Harvey Eating Houses
on the Santa Fe Railroad in the West.

Good wages with room and meals furnished.

No experience necessary.

To apply, write to:
Miss Alice Steele
c/o Fred Harvey Company
Union Station, Kansas City, Missouri

I read the advertisement again, laid the paper back on the sideboard, then picked it up and read it a third time.

I know about Fred Harvey and the Harvey Houses. Mr. Fred Harvey once lived here in Leavenworth, in the big stone mansion over on Olive and Seventh Street, a dozen blocks from our house. He started a chain of eating houses in railroad depots, serving first-class meals. After he died—which was before I was born—his son took over the business. Fred Harvey's wife, Sally, stayed in their mansion until she died, and since then one member or another of the family has lived there. When my mother was a girl, she knew the Harvey family. She talks about going to Mrs. Harvey's house for luncheons before she married Daddy, and she has hinted that those fancy luncheons were something she gave up by marrying somebody who sells men's clothes for a living.

There are a lot of Harvey Houses—I have no idea how many—along the Atchison, Topeka & Santa Fe Railroad, all the way out to California. My father took our whole family to the Harvey House in the new Union Station in Kansas City when it opened in 1914, but I was only five and I remember hardly anything about it. He and Mother go there for special occasions, and Mother plans for days beforehand. Daddy says the food is the best you'll find anywhere, and Mother has even mentioned the waitresses, known as Harvey Girls. "So polite and well trained!" she said.

No. 6. MILLER'S VIEWS.
FRED. HARVEY EATING HOUSE AND S

A FE STATION, CHANUTE, KANS.

I studied the advertisement in the *Leavenworth Times.* Then I came up to my room, sat down at my writing desk, and composed a letter to Miss Alice Steele of the Fred Harvey Company, in which I claimed to be eighteen years of age. Everyone says I look older. In my graduation picture, taken with my hair up for the first time—I'd decided not to wear my eyeglasses for the picture and have kind of a foggy expression—I *do* look older. Besides, I will turn seventeen at the end of July, so it's not really that much of a lie, just a year, and I think that hardly matters. I stated that I graduated second in my high school class, that I am neat and orderly in my habits, that I am ready to learn and able to work hard (I'm not absolutely positive about that, but I feel sure I can). Then I added with a flourish that I was ready for the adventure of travel and ended, "I intend to become a journalist someday, and I'm sure my experiences as a Harvey Girl will give me a lot to write about."

I did not know how to assure Miss Steele that I was of good character, but I can't think of anyone who would say that I'm not.

I addressed the envelope and sealed it, "borrowed" a two-cent stamp from a secret drawer in Mother's desk, walked to the corner of our block, and dropped my letter in the letterbox.

Now I'm having second thoughts. I wonder when I'll receive a reply. And what I'll do then.

Wednesday, June 2nd

I HARDLY SLEPT AT ALL LAST NIGHT. MISS STEELE should receive my letter today. If she answers it today, maybe I'll have her letter tomorrow. Waiting for a reply is turning me into a wreck. If she says no right off the bat, I'll die of disappointment, but if she says I have to come in for an interview, I'll be even more nervous than I was for *Contrary Mary*, and I didn't even have the leading role.

I had to tell somebody, so I walked two blocks to Maudie Albright's. Maudie and I have been friends since childhood. Our favorite thing has always been to go down by the Missouri, watch the boats moving upstream and down, and dream about the adventures we'll have some day. But Maudie doesn't talk much anymore about having adventures. She's taking a secretarial correspondence course and is learning to type and plans on getting a job in an office if she doesn't get married first. So far she has no prospects for a husband, but she can type *the quick brown fox jumps over the lazy dog* fairly fast and mostly accurately.

"It uses all the letters in the alphabet," she explained. I didn't believe her at first, but I checked, and she's right. Still, I have a hard time imagining tomboy Maudie as somebody's secretary.

We sat on the swing on the Albrights' front porch. "You're nervous as a cat on a griddle," Maudie said, eyeing me curiously. "What's going on?"

That was all it took for me to spill the whole story: that I wouldn't be going away to college, and that I'd sent a letter in answer to the newspaper ad, applying for a job as a waitress. "I'll save my money and go to college later on and become a writer."

Maudie seemed doubtful. "Gosh, I don't know, Kitty. I'd be nervous, too. What if they send you to work somewhere far away?"

"That's the whole idea," I said. "I'm hoping for the Grand Canyon or somewhere out West." I probably sounded very calm and assured, but the truth is I've never been away from home for more than a couple of days.

Maudie's blue eyes grew big and round. "Aren't you afraid of Indians? I hear there's plenty of them out there."

I hadn't even thought about Indians!

There's a shelf of encyclopedias in Maudie's living room, and we pulled them out and found a painting of the Grand Canyon like the reproduction that hangs in the Leavenworth train depot. Does it really look like that—all gorgeous reds and dramatic purples? What must it be like, not just to visit such a place, but to live there, to be a part of it? The Albrights also have an atlas with maps of each state, and Maudie and I pored over maps of Texas and California, but the longer I thought about it, the queasier I felt. Just looking at those maps made me homesick. What if I go there and hate it and I'm miserable? I was beginning to think sending the letter to Miss Steele was probably a mistake.

Maudie turned practical. "What are you going to wear to the interview?" she asked. "And how are you going to get there?"

I hadn't thought about that, either. Maybe I won't even be asked to come for an interview. I'm probably getting all worked up for nothing. But Maudie is sure I'm going to be hired. "You're smart, and you know how to talk to people—not like me, getting all tongue-tied."

We decided that if I'm to go for an interview—and that's a very big "if"—I'll take the streetcar to the city, and I'll tell Betty Jane and Mother that I'm spending the day at Maudie's.

"This is so exciting, Kitty! I'm just glad it's you and not me! But if you're hired, what are you going to tell your parents? Your mother would have a fit."

"I'll figure that out later," I assured her, trying to sound much more confident than I felt.

Thursday, June 3rd

One minute I wish I could call back that letter I wrote, telling myself it was a huge mistake to think I could become a Harvey Girl, and the next minute I convince myself it's the best idea I've ever had. Either way, I'm jittery. Mother and Daddy don't seem to notice a thing, except for Mother telling me not to bite my fingernails.

"I thought you'd broken that habit years ago," she said, tapping her own carefully manicured nails on the table. "You'll never be able to get a manicure if you don't stop."

I've never had the slightest interest in having my nails done. That is entirely my mother's notion. But it would make a better impression if I quit biting them.

Friday, June 4th

Oh my Lord. I'm to go for an interview on Tuesday. That's four days from now.

I had been sitting on the front porch with O'Reilly,

waiting for our mailman, Mr. Pratt, not wanting Mother or Betty Jane to be the one to pick up an envelope addressed to me and ask questions.

"Letter for you today, Kitty!" Mr. Pratt called out and handed me a long envelope with "Fred Harvey" printed in elegant blue script in the corner. I dropped the rest of the mail on the hall table and tore upstairs to my room, so nervous I forgot to use the elegant silver letter-opener engraved with my initials that my Aunt May sent me for graduation, and just ripped open the envelope with my thumb.

I am in receipt of your letter applying for a position as a Harvey Girl. Please come for an interview on Tuesday, June 8, at 11:00 a.m. I shall expect you at that time unless I hear from you to the contrary, by letter or by telephone.

It was signed *Alice Steele, Director of Personnel, Fred Harvey Company.* I wonder if Miss Steele typed the letter herself or if she has a secretary, somebody like Maudie.

I sat down on my bed to catch my breath and read it again.

Of course I will go to the interview. There's no harm in that. I probably won't even be offered a job. I have no experience, although the advertisement says experience isn't necessary. But *still.* I'd lied about my age; I won't be seventeen for six more weeks, and the ad specifically says "young women 18 to 30." What if Miss Steele asks for proof? If she wants to hire me, will I have to get my father's permission? And if I do, will he give it? What will he say? What will *Mother* say?

I ran over to Maudie's and showed her the letter. She was very excited for me. "How can you be so *calm?*" she wanted to know. But I don't feel calm at all. I'm still biting my nails. Maudie wants me to rehearse what I'm going to tell them, but I can't do it. I'm afraid that would jinx it for sure.

I just wish this were over.

Sunday, June 6th

I'VE DECIDED TO WEAR THE SAME OUTFIT TO THE interview that I wore to church this morning: navy blue pleated skirt, white middy blouse with blue trim, blue straw hat, blue patent leather purse, and white gloves. It will make me look like a person of good character, which is now in doubt since I'm sneaking off for my appointment and lying to Betty Jane and Mother, telling them I'm going to Maudie's. And if Miss Steele asks me about my age, I'll have to lie again. I'm not used to lying. She'll know.

I plan to be on the nine o'clock streetcar to Union Station.

Tuesday, June 8th
Union Station, Kansas City, Missouri

My new life is about to begin. I've been hired. I leave day after tomorrow for Emporia for training to become a Harvey Girl.

Feeling a little woozy—I didn't realize it would happen so *fast*.

More later. The streetcar to Leavenworth is here.

So excited I can hardly breathe!

Later Tuesday
Leavenworth

This is how it happened.

First, I nearly missed the streetcar this morning because it started to sprinkle and I had to rush back for an umbrella, and then I ran into Betty Jane, who said it seemed funny that I was all dressed up in my Sunday clothes just to spend the day with Maudie, and I invented a story about going to visit Maudie's grandmother. Another lie. I am not a person of good character.

It took an hour for that darn streetcar to make I don't know how many stops in Kansas before it crossed the river, made more stops in Missouri, and finally arrived at Union Station. I kept my gloves on, even though it's hot, so I wouldn't bite my nails. But I was there in plenty of time. I had at least an hour before my appointment with Miss Steele.

Union Station is like a cathedral, soaring to a painted ceiling hung with three enormous crystal chandeliers and a gigantic clock near the cavernous waiting room. It just takes your breath away. I had time enough to wander through the shops—a drugstore, a toy shop, a perfume shop selling little glass bottles of scents from all over the world, a bookstore with miles of shelves, a candy store with a display of mouthwatering chocolates. And a gift shop that sells Indian curios from out West, where I definitely hope to go someday!

I went into the Fred Harvey lunchroom to see what it was like. I can say this: it's huge. It must seat a couple hundred people. The gleaming counter is black marble. Enormous gold and silver urns stand against the back wall. There's nothing like it in Leavenworth—nothing even half that size.

I slid onto a swiveling seat at the counter and pulled off my gloves. They'd somehow gotten smudged on the streetcar. A smiling girl, looking cool and crisp in a black uniform and starched white apron, came to take my order. *So that's a Harvey Girl*, I thought, because I'd never actually seen one, and wished I had the nerve to ask her some questions. I ordered coffee—which I honestly don't like and hardly ever drink, but it seemed like the grown-up thing to do—and a piece of coconut custard pie. I'd been too nervous to eat any breakfast, and now my stomach was rumbling. That would certainly make a poor impression.

The waitress brought me a very big piece and explained that Fred Harvey eating houses always serve not just a slice but a full quarter of the pie. I was poking at the meringue when two girls came in and sat farther down the long counter. One of the girls was well dressed, nothing out of the ordinary—I took her to be a local girl—but her friend, oh my! A flapper if ever I saw one, in a long-waisted dress with a skirt so short it barely covered her knees. Her blond hair was bobbed and she had bright-red cupid's-bow lips. She ordered coffee black, as though she drank it every day, and her friend had milk and strawberry cake. I wondered who they were, because they seemed an unlikely pair. "An odd couple of ducks," my father would say.

I kept an eye on the big clock. As the hands moved closer to eleven, the two odd ducks prepared to leave. I paid my bill, remembered to slip a dime under the saucer for a tip, smiled back at the Harvey Girl behind the counter, and walked out into the vast atrium at the same time as the two girls. I hadn't thought to ask the waitress for directions to the elevator or the stairs, and I must have looked about as dumb as a stump, because the flapper turned to me and said, "I'll bet a nickel you're going the same place we are—to see Miss Steele!"

I nodded, a little surprised. What about me made her think I was going for an interview?

"Well, then, come with us. We'll take the elevator."

The flapper was the talkative one. She said her name was Cordelia Hart, and the other girl was her cousin, Violet. Violet wanted to be a Harvey Girl, and Cordelia, who was visiting from Reading, Pennsylvania, came along for moral support. "Vi is just so determined! Anything to get away from home, huh, Vi?"

Violet nodded and studied the marble floor. "I'm sort of nervous," she murmured, and Cordelia squeezed her arm and guided her toward the elevator. Violet couldn't have been any more nervous than I was.

The uniformed operator pulled back the folding gate and opened the elevator door on the second floor. A door with FRED HARVEY—PERSONNEL lettered on the frosted glass loomed across the hall. Cordelia brazenly pushed open the door and marched in. Violet followed her, and I trailed along behind.

Several girls sat stiffly in a row of chairs as though they were in Sunday school or waiting to see the school principal, and they glanced up as we entered. A woman in a polka-dot blouse at a desk with a telephone took our names and verified our appointments. They were at ten-minute intervals. "That doesn't seem like much time," I said, mostly to myself.

"Time enough for Miss Steele," the receptionist said briskly. Without looking up she pointed down the hall. "Ladies' washroom is that way," she said.

I fled to the washroom and peered in the mirror above the sink. I looked a mess. Should I keep my gloves on for the interview, or not? Was it better to wear dirty gloves, or no gloves at all? My hair was damp and tangled under my hat, my skin was pale and sickly, my glasses had gotten smudged—should I wear them or not? I look better without them, but I see better with them. I stuck the gloves in my purse, washed my face, dragged a comb through my hair, wiped my glasses, and went back to the reception room.

Violet sat alone. When she turned to look at me, I saw that her eyes were red-rimmed and her cheeks streaked with tears. She shook her head sadly. "I wasn't even in there for the whole ten minutes, and Miss Steele said, 'I think you're best suited for some other line of work.' Now Cordelia is talking to her, and she didn't even send a letter."

The inner door flew open and Cordelia sailed out, beaming. "I'm hired!" she crowed.

The other girls all turned and gaped at her. "But

you didn't come here for an interview!" Violet cried.

"Miss Evans?" the receptionist was saying. "Miss Steele will see you now."

Miss Steele was tall and thin with a narrow face, short dark hair, and large teeth. She was dressed in a smart tailored suit. Her desk was perfectly neat, and my letter lay open in front of her. "Be seated, please, Miss Evans."

I perched on the edge of the chair, feet together, purse balanced on my knees.

"If you will, Miss Evans, please tell me why you think you have the qualifications to become a Harvey Girl." She leaned her elbows on her desk and made a steeple of her fingers, watching me.

I can't remember exactly what I said. I thought of the smiling girl in the lunchroom, bringing me a piece of pie that I barely touched, the gleaming coffee urns behind her, the starched linen napkin at my place, the sugar bowls and cream pitchers and glass water jugs arranged just so along the counter, and I said something about believing I would take pleasure in giving good service to customers. I admitted I had no experience as a waitress or in any other job. I prayed silently she wouldn't inquire about my character or ask my real age.

"And what do you expect to gain from the experience of being a Harvey Girl?"

I swallowed, mouth dry as dust, and said I dreamed

of someday becoming a journalist and writing about interesting people and places, adding that I hoped being a Harvey Girl would help me realize that dream.

Was that a ridiculous thing to say? Had Violet said something just as dumb, and that's why she was sitting in the reception room with tears streaming down her face? And what in the world had Cordelia told Miss Steele that had persuaded her to hire a flapper with bobbed hair?

Miss Steele looked me over carefully. "And you are eighteen years of age, correct?"

I said I was.

"In that case, Miss Evans, I'm pleased to offer you a position as a Harvey Girl with a contract for six months, beginning the eleventh of June." Then she rattled off a lot of information. I hardly heard a word she said.

"Everything is spelled out in this contract." She pushed an envelope across the desk and asked if I had any questions. I shook my head.

She handed me a pen, and I signed *Katherine Amelia Evans*. My hand was shaking. The signature didn't even look like mine. Miss Steele wrote her name below mine and blotted them both.

"Good!" For the first time Miss Steele smiled at me. "I am an excellent judge of character," she said, "and I am sure you will do very well with us."

She told me to speak to the receptionist about the proper size uniform. I'm to leave for Emporia on

Thursday, two days from now, and start my new life as a Harvey Girl on Friday.

"Welcome to the Fred Harvey Company, Miss Evans." She rose and reached out to shake my hand. Mine was hot, sweaty, and trembling. Hers was cool, dry, firm. I walked unsteadily out to the reception room, where several anxious faces peered up at me. Cordelia's and Violet's were not among them.

"Miss Landis!" the receptionist called out. "Miss Steele will see you now."

A tall, big-boned girl in a flowered dress that fit all wrong moved hesitantly toward the inner door. I smiled at her encouragingly. "Good luck," I whispered. "It's not so bad."

In a daze I gave the receptionist my measurements for a uniform and took the elevator down to the main floor. "I've been hired!" I told the operator. "I'm going to be a Harvey Girl!" He tipped his cap and congratulated me. I walked out of Union Station and into the bright sunlight. *Kitty Evans, Harvey Girl.*

Impulsively I ran back to the lunchroom. The same waitress looked up and smiled. "Your pie—" she began, but I interrupted whatever she was going to say. "I'm going to be a Harvey Girl!" I said, so loudly that a couple of customers turned to look. I wanted to tell everybody! The waitress gestured as if she was applauding, and I hurried away.

I'm embarrassed to say I even told the streetcar conductor. I waited until we were on our way to open the packet with the train ticket to Emporia and an information sheet. I'm glad to have it all written out, because I don't remember much of what Miss Steele told me.

You will receive thirty days of training, for which you will receive no pay.

If your training is completed successfully and you are accepted as a Harvey Girl, you will be sent out on the line to a Harvey Eating House wherever you may be needed.

You will be paid fifty dollars a month plus room and board.

Uniforms are provided.

You will share a room with another Harvey Girl in a chaperoned boarding house, and you will comply strictly with all the rules and regulations.

You agree not to marry for the duration of this contract.

At the end of your contract you will be given a ticket home, at which time you may enroll for another six months to a year.

Good luck, and welcome.

Signed, Fred Harvey

I've told the elevator operator, the waitress, and the streetcar conductor, but now I'm going to have to tell my parents. I had an hour on the streetcar back to Leavenworth to figure out what I'm going to say, and I still don't know. What if they forbid me to go?

Still Tuesday the 8th

THE RAIN THAT THREATENED ALL DAY SUDDENLY CAME down in buckets as I was walking up Fourth Street from the streetcar stop. A horn honked, and the Bedwell Lumber & Millwork truck pulled up beside me with Jimmy Bedwell behind the wheel. After graduation he went to work for his dad's lumber company, and driving the truck is probably the part he likes best.

"Give you a ride home before you drown?"

I hadn't talked to him since the senior prom, which in my opinion was an unmitigated disaster. (*Unmitigated* is one of my favorite words.) It was pouring, and my umbrella was practically useless. I hesitated for less than a second and then climbed in beside him.

Jimmy is not bad-looking and he's intelligent and polite, but he's *short*—probably three inches shorter than I am. Not that it's his fault, but it's too darn awkward to dance with a boy who's that much shorter. And when he brought me home after the prom and tried to kiss me, it was even worse.

Now he looked me over before he put the truck in gear. "You're all dressed up. You'd look really good if you weren't half-drowned." He was grinning like a fool.

I made a snoot at him. "Thanks," I said.

The truck lurched forward. "To tell the truth, you look good no matter what, Kitty. I was wondering if you'd like to go to a picture show at the Rialto on Saturday night. Charlie Chaplin in *The Gold Rush*. It's supposed to be real good."

Jimmy's mother plays piano while the films are showing at the Rialto, and he always gets in free.

On Saturday I'll be over a hundred miles away in Emporia, but I couldn't tell him that before I'd even told my parents. So I said, "I'm sorry, Jimmy, but I have other plans," and watched the disappointment spread over his face like a rash. "Maybe some other time."

Jimmy dropped me off at Maudie's. She squealed when she saw me. "What happened, Kitty? Tell me everything!"

"I'm a Harvey Girl," I said, and we both burst into tears. I'm not sure why.

The rain had stopped when I walked home, skirting the puddles, and quietly entered the house. No one was around—Mother was "resting her eyes" as she does every afternoon, Daddy was still at the store,

Betty Jane had gone for the day, and I guess Howie was at the country club.

Now I'm in my room, worrying about how to tell my parents what I'm going to do. O'Reilly is with me, head on paws, giving me a sympathetic doggie look, as though he knows I'm in a quandary (another of my favorite words) and would help if he could.

Mother has just rung the little bell to let us know that dinner is ready. O'Reilly recognizes the signal and leaps up, all eagerness. I, less eager, prepare to follow him downstairs.

After dinner Tuesday

THANK GOODNESS THAT'S OVER. WHAT AN ORDEAL!

I waited until we were eating dinner—breaded pork chops—and picked the moment when everybody had a mouthful to announce that I'd made a decision.

"Oh? And what's that, Puss?" Daddy asked, and Mother glanced up. Howie poured cream gravy on his baked potato.

"I'm going to become a Harvey Girl. I went for an interview this morning, and I was hired."

Mother dropped her knife and fork with a clatter. "You'll do no such thing!"

Howie stifled a snort of laughter, Daddy stared at

me as though he couldn't believe his ears, and Mother let out a little scream and covered her mouth with her napkin. Then they all started talking at once, asking questions but not listening when I tried to explain.

Mother's voice cut through the others. "You are not going, Kitty. It's simply out of the question. A *waitress!* You are not that sort of girl. They have terrible reputations! The lowest of the low! You might as well have just told us you intend to become a . . . a saloon girl!"

"I'd certainly like to hear a little more about it," Daddy said. "Who talked you into this, and why have you convinced yourself to go through with what sounds to me like a very poor idea?"

I gripped the seat of my chair and concentrated on staying calm. I assured my father that no one had talked me into anything. I reminded him that he'd told me I won't be going to college this fall, as we'd planned all along. "You suggested I get a job selling shoes," I said. "I think being a Harvey Girl will be more interesting."

"You are much too young to leave home!" Mother cried. "You're scarcely more than a child! Do they even know how old you are?"

"Mother, I'm practically seventeen!" I declared, and I heard my voice go shrill.

Things slid downhill from there. I was determined not to get mad, and if I did, then not to show it, and if I showed it, at least not to do something really dumb, like cry.

So, of course, I ended up getting mad and showing it and crying anyway. Mother insisted I was ruining my life and had given her a terrible headache, and it was all *too much.* Daddy just kept telling us to please calm down. O'Reilly watched us worriedly from under the table.

Finally Daddy said, "I suppose you'll have to learn the hard way," and Mother said, "You're ruining your life, and you're ruining mine, too!" But they did not forbid me, which I suppose they could have.

Howie kept a straight face but winked at me. I wish I knew what he was thinking.

Now I'm wondering how will I get through tomorrow, with Mother and Daddy so upset and me feeling like I want to throw up.

I've studied the list of rules Miss Steele included in the packet.

Uniforms must be absolutely spotless
at all times.
No jewelry.
No makeup.
Nails short and clean. No nail polish.
Hair pulled back and fastened with hairpins.
Black stockings and black shoes only. Must be
kept clean and polished.

Black shoes. The only black shoes I have are the ones I wore to the senior prom with Jimmy, and they hurt my feet. Tomorrow I will ask Maudie to go with me to McMeen's shoe department where, thank goodness, I will *not* be applying for a job, and I will buy my Harvey Girl shoes.

Wednesday, June 9th

MOTHER SAYS I'M A SELFISH, THOUGHTLESS DAUGHTER and my selfishness has made her ill. She lies on the sofa with wet tea bags on her eyes, which are swollen from crying, and fans herself.

Daddy looks sad and worried, but he did pat me on the shoulder before he left for work this morning and said, "If this is what you want to do, Puss, then I won't tell you that you can't."

Gramma Blair came by at lunchtime, shook her head, and said, "I never thought I'd live to see the day that a granddaughter of mine would be so *common*." Then she turned to Mother and asked, "Is her father actually allowing her to do this? She'll be ruined!"

"Apparently so." Mother dabbed at her eyes with a handkerchief.

Betty Jane is doubtful. "You're gonna be homesick, I promise you that," she said. "Bet money you'll be home again before the first month is out, and glad to be here, even if all you'll hear from your momma is 'I told you so.'"

Maudie and I went shopping after lunch, and after I'd tried on half a dozen pairs of shoes and finally bought one, we walked down by the river and watched the boats.

"I'm going to miss you, Kitty," she said, tossing a stick out into the current. "You're so brave. You've always been so daring."

I wasn't feeling at all brave or daring, but it was nice to hear her say that, and I promised I'll write whenever I can.

The big surprise was Howie. He came to my room while I was packing and sat down on the foot of my bed. "All I've got to say, Puss, is good for you! You've got spunk! Get out and see the world!" Then he looked at me *very seriously*, which he never does. "You're darn lucky, you know that, Kitty? You're breaking out of here!" He said that he's expected to come back home after graduation and go in the haberdashery business with Daddy. "You think that's what I want?"

I stared at him. "Isn't it?"

"*Heck,* no!" Howie jumped up and started pacing. "Ever since eighth grade I've wanted to be an actor! Go to the city—Chicago, or even New York—and get into theater."

That was a surprise. "I've never heard you say anything about being an actor."

"I don't talk about it," Howie said. "You can imagine how Mother and Father would react, so please keep it under your hat." He struck a solemn pose. "'Cowards die many times before their deaths; the valiant never taste of death but once.' Et cetera, et cetera." He dropped the pose. "Shakespeare. *Julius Caesar.*" He sat down again, his head in his hands. "What about you, Puss? What do you really dream of doing?"

For the first time I felt that somebody in my family actually cared about what I wanted in my future. "Being a writer," I said. "I thought you knew that."

"Well, imagine that!" Howie slapped his knee. "Look, the folks are pretty upset about this. But I'm all for it! You need a ride to the depot tomorrow? I don't have anything scheduled until eleven. I'll be glad to drive you."

I accepted his offer, even though I think he just offered because he feels guilty that he's the one who gets to go to college.

Thursday, June 10th—On the train

My big adventure is about to begin.

I took one last look around my room—the three-quarter spool bed with the pink-and-white quilt Gran Evans made for me before she died, the old desk that Daddy found at a farm sale and painted white—and wondered when I'll sleep here again. After one more check in the mirror above the dresser, I smeared a bit of Vaseline on my lips with the tip of my little finger. *Do I look eighteen?*

Mother was reclining on the sofa when I went to say good-bye. "If you're not careful, you could easily become a disgrace to your family," she said, dabbing at her eyes. The tea bags hadn't done much good. "I hope you realize that."

Daddy hugged me, told me that if I need anything at all I'm to be sure to let him know, and slipped me five dollars. Then Howie carried my suitcase out to his elderly Model T Ford to take me to the Leavenworth depot. I turned to look up at my bedroom window as we drove away. O'Reilly was lying on the porch, tail thumping, and that's what almost made me cry.

Breakfast wasn't sitting well. I've never traveled any farther than Kansas City by myself. Now I'm on my way to a strange city, going to work in a place I've never seen, signed up to do something I never even thought about until a few days ago. What if I can't do it? What if I hate it?

Howie parked the Ford near the depot. "I promised you when you turned sixteen I'd teach you to drive, and I didn't do it," he said. "I'm sorry, Puss."

"It's all right," I told him and forced a smile. "Maybe when I come home."

We were waiting on the platform for the local to Topeka, where I have to change trains, when a shiny black Packard sedan pulled up and a silver-haired man stepped out and unloaded two suitcases, a small trunk, a valise, and a hatbox from the backseat.

"That's R. Cameron Fuller, president of the bank," Howie said. "I caddy for Mr. Fuller out at the club."

The passenger-side door of the sedan opened, and out stepped Cordelia Hart, looking for all the world like someone whose picture belonged on the cover of a magazine or in the society pages of the newspaper. No sign of Cousin Violet. Mr. Fuller deposited her baggage on the platform and kissed her cheek. "Bye, Uncle Cam!" Cordelia trilled.

Then she noticed us. "Hello, Kitty, hello!" she called, waving happily. And when I introduced her to my brother, she smiled and batted her eyes, and my brother flashed his lopsided grin, which girls seem to fall for.

The train pulled in, whistle blasting, brakes screeching, steam belching. Howie gallantly offered to put all of Cordelia's luggage onto the train for her. I carried my own suitcase.

The conductor hollered "B-o-a-ard!" and Howie jumped off. The train began to move and Howie stood on the platform, waving.

Cordelia decided we should sit together. I was so nervous my stomach was churning, but she looked completely calm, cool, and collected, as if taking off across the country to some unknown place were the most ordinary thing in the world.

"Your brother is certainly very handsome!" she said. "You'll have to tell me all about him."

After I answered her questions about Howie—where he went to school, what he was studying—I didn't have much more to say. But Cordelia did.

Her parents are divorced, she confided, and that shocked me, because I don't know anybody who's divorced, and now her mother is married to a rich businessman. Lorenzo Hart made his fortune in cement, for building bridges and so on. "My mother married him for his money," she said.

Cordelia had taken piano lessons since she was seven, and after she finished boarding school, she went to Philadelphia to study at a conservatory of music. But at the end of May, Lorenzo informed her that she

wouldn't be going back to the conservatory, because she would just end up getting married anyway and there was no point in spending all that money for nothing. *Pretty stingy for somebody who's rich,* I thought, but I didn't say so.

"He has a husband picked out for me," Cordelia said. "Walter is the manager of Lorenzo's cement factory, and he is probably the dullest, stuffiest person I have ever met."

Walter wants to get engaged, Cordelia said, and her mother is already talking about a wedding. Cordelia decided to come out to visit her cousin to escape from her mother and Walter. "Vi found a newspaper ad for the Harvey Girls, and we joked about what a madcap adventure it would be to work as waitresses and see the Wild West. Then I was hired and Vi wasn't, and now she's mad at me. But here I am, a Harvey Girl! Isn't that the craziest thing?"

I agreed that it was, and for a while we gazed out the window at the scenery. Not that there was much to see—once you leave the beautiful hills around Leavenworth, Kansas is just miles and miles of prairie. I was chewing my fingernails again and remembered how Mother was always trying to persuade me to stop. Suddenly I missed her. It's Thursday, so she's probably getting her hair done.

I wonder if Phil Rayburn will notice that I'm gone.

Jimmy will, even if Phil doesn't. It's nice to know that somebody besides Maudie will miss me.

I quit gnawing on my fingernail and thought about what Cordelia had said, that deciding to be a Harvey Girl is "the craziest thing." *Maybe it's the dumbest, too.* Whatever made me believe I could be a waitress? And not just any waitress, but a Harvey Girl! I'm not at all like Cordelia. I'll bet it hasn't even entered her mind that she might not make it.

Still Thursday—another train

WE GOT OFF THE TRAIN IN TOPEKA. TWO REDCAPS carried Cordelia's baggage down to the platform and deposited it near the track for the Emporia train. She was busy fishing coins from her purse to tip the porters when I noticed the girl in the flowered dress I saw last week in Miss Steele's office. A sad-looking older couple and a handful of younger kids plus a tall, skinny fellow in overalls were gathered around the girl. The mother and the kids were crying, and the fellow in overalls held the girl's hand and bent down to whisper to her. The father watched them, stony-faced.

A little while later the train to Emporia chuffed

into the station, and there was a general rush to board. Cordelia climbed on, carrying her hatbox, and claimed a pair of seats. I was right behind her. The redcap followed with Cordelia's bags and went back for her trunk.

I glanced out the window in time to see the boy in overalls hugging the girl tight. She was hanging on to him for dear life. But the conductor was calling "Board!" and the girl pulled away, grabbed a battered suitcase held together with a leather strap, and jumped onto the train. The conductor swung up behind her and the train started to move, jerking hard and throwing her off balance so that she nearly fell. Tears were pouring down her face.

"Now there's a case of misery if ever I saw one," Cordelia said, and in a flash she rushed to help the girl, insisting that she sit with us.

The girl's name is Emmaline Landis, but she asked us to call her Emmy. Her whole family drove in from their farm in a wagon to see her off. "I'm on my way to Emporia. I'm to be a Harvey Girl," she said shyly.

"Well, so are we!" Cordelia announced. "So we may just as well get acquainted." Little by little Cordelia drew her out—the big family, older ones married and gone, younger ones still at home, Emmy somewhere in the middle.

"That tall, good-looking lad in overalls?" Cordelia asked. "Is he your brother?"

Anyone could see that he wasn't.

Emmy blushed. "That's Carl. He's my beau, and he didn't want me to leave. He's afraid I'll meet some new fella and forget all about him. He wants me to stay on the farm and get married."

She doesn't look any older than I do, and I can't even imagine getting married so young. Cordelia asked Emmy what *she* wants.

"Well, that's what I want, too—but meantime I have to help out my folks. I thought about looking for a job at the five-and-dime store in town, but I saw the advertisement for Harvey Girls, and I thought, *That's* for me. Pap had been saying I needed to get a job, but when I went and found one, then it was a different story. He thinks I'll go snobby on them. The preacher at our church has Mam convinced I'll end up among people of bad character and fall into sin."

People of bad character! Does that include girls who lie about their age?

"But are you in love with Carl?" Cordelia demanded. "Madly, passionately, head-over-heels in love with him?"

Emmy shrugged. "I like him well enough, I guess."

"*Like him well enough!*" Cordelia snorted. "*Well enough* wouldn't be half good enough for me, and it shouldn't be for you either, Emmy." You'd think she'd known Emmy for years and could dish out advice that wasn't asked for.

Emmy didn't seem to mind. "Carl's the only boy I've ever gone with. I imagine you've been with a whole bunch of fellas, Cordelia."

Cordelia gave her a *look*, but Emmy either ignored it or didn't see it, and we found something else to talk about.

Late Thursday, Emporia, Kansas

So here I am in Emporia.

When the train pulled in late this morning, Emmy and I helped Cordelia down with her luggage, there being no redcaps in sight. My stomach was churning again as the train left us standing on the platform with the hot sun beating down. We dragged our bags into the shade under an arched portico.

A small, round-faced woman in a black uniform and a spotless white apron came out to greet us. Her name, she told us, is Beatrice Porter, and she's the head waitress and also the dormitory chaperone. She's a lot older than we are—close to thirty, I'd guess—with sharp features and eyes set a little too close together. She wears a big silver pin with the number ten on it.

Beatrice eyed Cordelia's pile of luggage. "I'll have a busboy carry it up for you. Unpack only what you need and store the rest in the baggage room."

Cordelia began to protest. "But I'll need all my things!"

"Not for a while, you won't," Beatrice said firmly. "You'll be much too busy." She pointed to the depot, two wings with steep pitched roofs on either side of a center section. "Harvey Girls stay over there in the east wing, kitchen helpers in the west wing," she explained. The second floor of the main section is for hotel guests.

Beatrice marched off toward the east wing, not bothering to see if we were following. Cordelia grabbed the valise and the hatbox, and we hurried along the platform behind her. She led us up two flights of creaking wooden stairs to our rooms under the eaves.

Cordelia and I are sharing a room; Emmy will be in the room next door. Her roommate was downstairs, working the lunch counter. When I saw our little room with the two beds, a single bureau, and a narrow wardrobe painted white, I could not imagine where we'd put everything.

Beatrice was rattling off information. "Uniforms are in the wardrobe: one to wear, one in the laundry, two in reserve. If you spill something on it, you must go up to your room and change immediately. They'll be washed for you, but you're responsible for starching and ironing. Try them on to make sure they fit and are the right length: exactly eight inches from the floor, no more, no less. No chewing gum. Read the rules for hair and makeup," she said, looking hard at Cordelia's crimson lips. "You start tomorrow with the morning shift, six a.m. Be down for breakfast by five. Questions?"

"Yes, ma'am. What does the number ten mean on your pin?" Emmy asked.

"That's the number of years I've been a Harvey Girl," Beatrice said, and for the first time she smiled.

She pulled a watch from a small pocket and checked it. "The eastbound train is due here for lunch at eleven twenty, the westbound at twelve forty-five, if they're running on time," she said. "Today you'll observe the Harvey service, and after the passengers board, you may have your lunch." She paused and then added, "The manager is Mr. Shaeffer. He's a stickler for detail, as you'll soon find out."

Beatrice clumped down the stairs, and Cordelia flung herself dramatically on one of the beds, moaning, "I've never starched and ironed a darn thing in my life!"

I haven't done much of it either. Back home, Betty Jane always does our laundry.

"That's one thing I *do* know how to do," Emmy said. "Guess you two are about to learn."

Cordelia jumped up and yanked open the doors of the wardrobe where our uniforms hung like a flock of crows. A tag with our name on it is sewn into each one. A sign posted on the wardrobe door lists the rules. Cordelia read them aloud:

No rubbish of any kind may be thrown in the toilets.

Bathtubs must be thoroughly cleaned after using.

Loud talking and laughing in rooms and halls should be avoided.

Employees must be in their rooms by 10:00 p.m. unless given special permission by manager to remain out longer.

"There's lots more," she said and banged the wardrobe door shut. "This place is as strict as my boarding school! Maybe even worse!"

I suggested we try on our uniforms. I like the idea of wearing a uniform, because it makes everything seem more official. Cordelia says it's just another reminder of boarding school, which was not her favorite place.

Emmy went down the hall to examine herself in the full-length mirror outside the bathroom. She came back grinning, and spun around for us to admire. "This is the first dress I've ever had that Mam didn't make for me. Most of my clothes were made out of remnants from the dry goods store, except for my church dress. And that's a real bathroom, too!"

Cordelia raised one eyebrow and Emmy, looking embarrassed, explained, "I'm used to an outhouse and bathing in a washtub in the kitchen on Saturday nights."

I took my turn at the mirror down the hall and liked what I saw: The black dress came almost to my ankles with long sleeves buttoned at the wrist, a white collar starched stiff as cardboard, and a little black bow tie. A white bibbed apron nearly as long as the dress wrapped around to button in the back. After years of having my straight brown hair in plaits, I was happy when Mother decided I was old enough to wear it in an updo. I would never have the nerve to bob my hair like Cordelia's.

I smiled at myself in the mirror and a Harvey Girl smiled back.

Cordelia was still fussing with her apron. "Will you look how long this uniform is? And whoever heard of wearing an outfit like this in summer? We'll roast alive."

She grumbled that she might just look for somebody to turn up the hem for her, maybe an inch at first, then more later on when they realize how much better it looks. I reminded her what Beatrice said: Eight inches from the floor, no more, no less.

"What's she going to do—measure?" Cordelia asked scornfully.

We changed back to our traveling clothes and went downstairs. The long hoot of a whistle signaled the approach of the 11:20 eastbound train. The conductor had telegraphed ahead with information on how many to expect in the dining room and the lunchroom next to it.

"Three minutes!" the manager called out. A thin

man with thinning hair and an even thinner mustache, Mr. Shaeffer stalked through the dining room, pointing out a little smear here, a stray crumb there—a stickler for detail, as Beatrice said—and the waitresses rushed to fix things. The busboy trotted out to greet the train and sounded a brass gong with a mallet as the passengers climbed off.

The crowd surged in, the manager directed them to their seats, and the waitresses moved confidently among the diners, briskly taking orders and pouring drinks. Fifteen minutes after they were seated, the diners were enjoying their main course, and a relaxed-looking and smiling Mr. Shaeffer was strolling among the tables. At twenty-two minutes, the desserts were being served.

Eight minutes later, the passengers laid aside their linen napkins and settled their bills, and when the whistle blew they were ready to board. It had all been accomplished in thirty minutes, the exact time allowed for the locomotive to take on coal and water. I couldn't imagine how the girls did it. And always smiling! I couldn't imagine how I was going to do it! What if I dropped a tray, or spilled soup in somebody's lap?

Even before the train left the depot, the busboys had cleared away the dirty dishes, and the waitresses were polishing the marble countertop and resetting the tables. Mr. Shaeffer made another inspection, growling orders, and the place began to fill up again, this time with local people: cowboys in chaps, railroaders in overalls, businessmen in suits, and a few women wearing hats and gloves and leading young children by the hand. Everyone greeted the waitresses like old acquaintances. The pace slowed a little, but not much. The westbound would arrive soon.

Beatrice directed us to seats at the lunchroom counter, and a waitress brought menus. Her name is Frantiska, which she pronounces "Fran-*teesh*-ka," but everybody calls her Franny K. She speaks with an accent and has a mole on her upper lip, like a beauty mark. Even before Franny K. took our orders, Cordelia was asking where she's from.

"Moravia, part of Czechoslovakia," she said; her father came over to work in the coal mines. "You're the new girls?"

We said we were.

"One of you is supposed to room with me."

Emmy said, "That's me."

I settled on the veal loaf, mashed potatoes, and cauliflower. I thought I was hungry, and the food was good—delicious, in fact—but after a few mouthfuls I couldn't eat any more. I felt queasy again.

"What happened to your last roommate?" Cordelia asked Franny K. Cordelia would make a good journalist. She's certainly not afraid to ask questions.

Franny K. shrugged. "Quit. Could not take all the

rules, everything always having to be perfect. Queen Bea weeds them out fast."

"Queen who?" Cordelia wanted to know.

"Beatrice, but we call her Queen Bea. Not to her face, though. What she says, goes. Follow the rules, and everything is fine. But just don't try to pull a fast one."

I wondered what it was that Franny K.'s former roommate couldn't take, if she had tried to pull a fast one, and if so, what it was.

Franny K. picked up my half-empty plate and glanced at me. "Was everything to your satisfaction?" she asked, and I assured her it was fine.

She must have guessed how I was feeling. "You'll do all right," she said. "You'll catch on real quick. Everybody helps everybody."

The lunch crowd was thinning out, the locals going back to work. The Harvey Girls whipped through the dining room, setting up for the 12:45 westbound. The whistle had barely sounded when the busboy was on his way out with his mallet and gong and the process was repeated.

Franny K. shooed us away from her counter to make room for the new customers. "Go for a walk and see the town," she said. "You won't have much chance after today."

Friday, June 11th

EMPORIA DOESN'T SEEM LIKE A BIG TOWN—NOT EVEN AS big as Leavenworth. Railroad tracks run through the center, and a wide street parallel to the tracks ends at the cattle pens at the western edge of town where the pavement stops. You smell the cows before you see them.

We walked north, then east, away from the depot, past the *Emporia Gazette* next door to the post office, and stopped under the marquee of the Strand Theater to look at the posters.

NOW SHOWING

THE GREAT K & A TRAIN ROBBERY
STARRING TOM MIX AND HIS HORSE, TONY

That made me think of Jimmy Bedwell. He's a fan of Western movies and especially of Tom Mix. He says when he gets his own car he's going to name it Tony, after Tom's horse.

Emmy was studying a poster for Mary Pickford in *Sparrows*, with organ accompaniment. "That's my cow's name," Emmy said.

"Sparrows?" Cordelia asked, and Emmy said, "No—Mary Pickford."

Cordelia said she hoped Emmy had a bull named Douglas Fairbanks, Jr., and that made Emmy laugh. We all thought the two movie stars made a perfect couple.

We linked arms and kept walking, stopping to look in the show windows of Newman's Department Store. What Cordelia saw didn't impress her.

"At Wanamaker's in Philly they use dress mannequins to show off the clothes," she said, and told us how she used to go to concerts in Wanamaker's Grand Court, which has the largest pipe organ in the world.

Emmy couldn't understand why anybody would want a great big pipe organ in a department store when all you need to buy is a pair of work gloves or a sunbonnet. And Cordelia couldn't understand why anybody would want to buy a sunbonnet.

"Who wears them?" Cordelia asked, and Emmy snapped right back, "Mam does, when she's hoeing beans."

Our exploration continued past the Broadway Hotel, which looks brand-new, and a lot of small shops and big churches. We ended up on the campus of the teachers college, where there are green lawns and benches beneath big shade trees. Cordelia kicked off her shoes, peeled off her stockings, and buried her toes in the grass. Gramma Blair would have said that was common, so I didn't do it, even though I wanted to.

Emporia is up-to-date and modern—the streets are paved, and buses have replaced the old electric streetcars—but Cordelia acts as though she just woke up and found herself at the ends of the earth.

"Not much to see in this hick town," Cordelia complained. She's gone from excited to dismal in no time flat.

Emmy disagreed. "Compared to where I come from, this is the big city." She turned to me. "What do you think, Kitty? Hick town or big city?"

I shrugged. "It seems nice enough," I said. What I didn't say: *But it's not home.*

Later Friday

THE THIRD FLOOR IS STIFLING. THE WINDOWS ARE OPEN, but not a breath of air stirs. While we were gone, the busboy brought up Cordelia's trunk and two suitcases, and now there is hardly room enough to turn around. We decided to unpack. Franny K. was taking a nap, and Emmy didn't want to bother her.

"I'll unpack later," she said, and sat on one of the beds in our room. "I don't have much."

Cordelia brought about five times as many clothes as I did. We've agreed to share space in the wardrobe fifty-fifty, and each of us has two drawers in the bureau.

Even if she stores most of her things in her trunk, she'll still need more space.

The big black hatbox had Emmy's attention. I don't think she'd ever seen such a thing, and the notion that a person would have so many hats that she would need a special box to keep them in seems outlandish to her. The hatbox now sits on top of the wardrobe, and Cordelia has shoved her two suitcases under her bed and talked me into letting her put the valise under mine. We dragged the trunk into the hall for the busboy to take down to the baggage room.

Our wardrobe is crammed with Cordelia's stylish dresses, like the one she was wearing at the interview with Miss Steele. They're shorter than any of my dresses, hardly cover her knees, and are cut straight with no waistline. Her chest is naturally flat, she says, but she wears a bandeau that laces at the sides to flatten it even more.

"The boyish figure is in," Cordelia explained.

My mother would not be pleased to know that my roommate is a flapper. And wouldn't she have a fit if she knew I'm dying to be a flapper, too!

Saturday, June 12th

First day as a Harvey Girl.

What a scramble this morning, to give everyone a chance in the bathroom when there are eight girls who have to be down for breakfast at five a.m. and on the floor by six. Not *at* six, but *by* six. There is a break after the westbound train stops, and then we must be back at our places when the evening trains come. Franny K. says it's a good idea to take a nap, but I'm too excited to sleep.

There's an awful lot to remember. Queen Bea says that by the time our training is done we will have learned all the positions in the lunchroom and dining room, so that we can be moved around as we're needed. She has started me out as a "drink girl," and for that I have to learn the cup code. Here's how it works:

The tables are set with a cup and saucer at each place along with silverware and a starched napkin that stands up like a tent. The waitress who takes the order places the cup so that the drink girl knows what to pour. If a customer orders coffee, the cup sits in the saucer. But if someone asks for milk, the cup is turned upside down *beside* the saucer. The cup is upside down *on* the saucer with the handle pointing one way for black tea, another way for green tea, a third way for

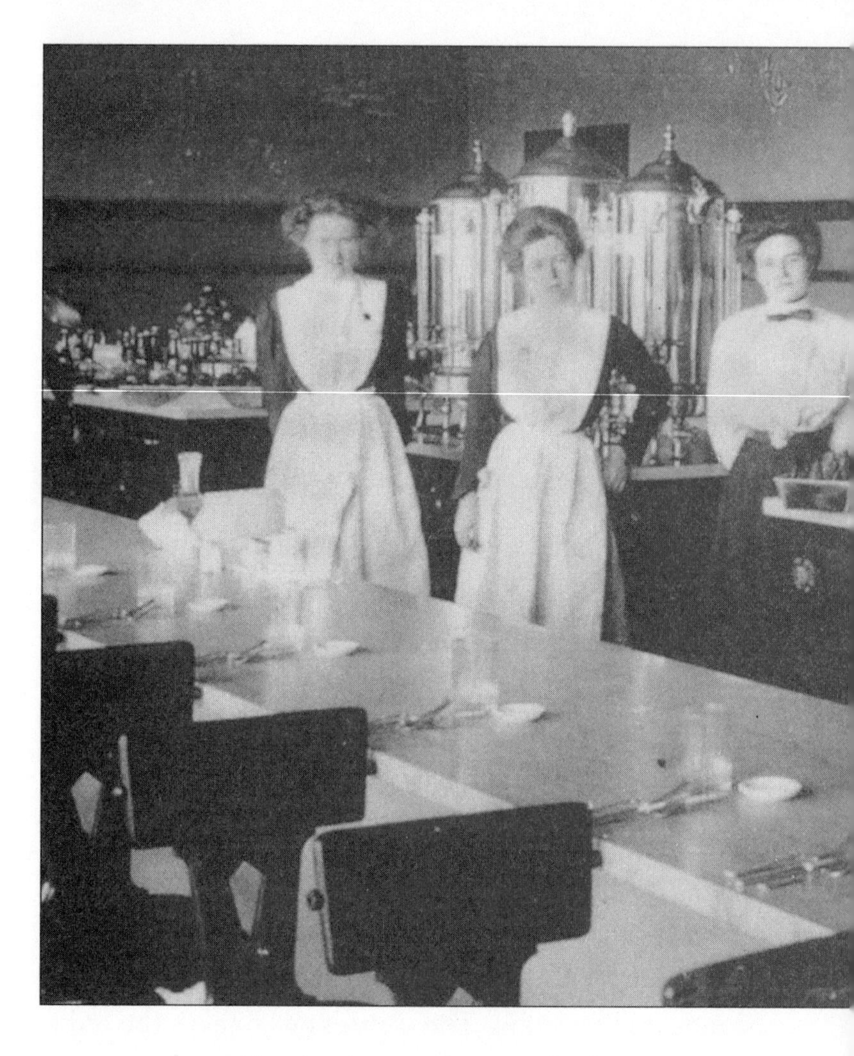

orange pekoe. For iced tea, the upside-down cup is tilted *against* the saucer.

I was hoping all my customers would order coffee, but it didn't work out that way. Everybody wanted something different. The only mistake I made was with the iced tea—I forgot to bring the lemon slices.

We were told that Mr. Harvey was always very particular about the coffee. The coffee beans are brought in from Boston and ground here in the kitchen. There are two big urns in the dining room and another two in the lunchroom. Every hour you have to dump out every drop of coffee from one of the pair, clean it, and make a fresh batch. An hour later you empty the other urn, so that no cup of coffee has been brewed more than two hours earlier. Heaven help you if Mr. Shaeffer spies a fingerprint on one of those urns! So you polish and polish. The silverware, too, and the sugar bowls and cream pitchers. We're not allowed to sit down, even when we're not busy. There's always something that has to be done.

"No lollygagging," Mr. Shaeffer said.

"It's the Harvey Way," Queen Bea said.

Cordelia said under her breath, "There's probably a Harvey Way to brush your teeth."

Tuesday, June 15th

PEOPLE IN EMPORIA GO OUT FOR DINNER AFTER CHURCH on Sunday, just like back home. Gramma Blair always takes our family to the Mansion House, her favorite restaurant in Leavenworth. I usually have the baked ham, and Howie makes a point to order roast beef "rare and bloody," which Gramma Blair says is barbaric and will someday give him a bad stomach. I remembered that as I was rushing around on Sunday, filling cups, trying not to make another mistake.

I'd gladly stay a drink girl, except that drink girls

don't collect any tips, but yesterday, just when I was feeling fairly confident about the cup code, Queen Bea moved me behind the lunch counter.

"When you finish your thirty days here and go out on the line, I want to be sure you can handle any position in any Harvey House. Clear?"

She always talks that way. She gives an order or explains something, and ends it with "Clear?"

I was in a panic the first time I had to take a customer's order, keep everything straight in my head without writing it down, and report it to the kitchen. One order is fine, two are all right, but what about remembering orders from four people?

Franny K. says I worry too much. "After Mr. Shaeffer has threatened to fire you a couple of times for the smallest little thing and Queen Bea has bawled you out good and proper, your memory will improve." It's good to be there with Franny K. She doesn't get rattled, and she helps explain some of the peculiar things we have to learn.

For instance, when you put the three pats of butter on the customer's bread-and-butter plate with a special little fork, you must make sure to leave a fork mark.

"Why?" I asked Franny K.

"So the customer sees for himself that we don't touch the food with our dirty hands."

At the end of our shift, she and I climbed upstairs

for a few minutes' rest before the dinner train arrived. My feet hurt. I didn't have a chance to break in my shoes before I wore them on the floor, and that was a big mistake. I could hear the water running in the bathtub. Cordelia, probably. She always manages to call first dibs on a hot bath. Emmy had gone to see if any mail had come for her. All I wanted was a chance to sit down.

"I was watching you today," Franny K. said. "You'll do fine, but I'm not putting any money on your friend."

I paused outside my door, hand on the knob. "Which friend?"

"You can tell Emmy's used to getting up at the crack of dawn and putting in a day of hard work, but Cordelia is used to having other people do things for her. Which one would you bet on?"

"I'd bet on both of *them*," I said. "Right now I'm just not so sure I'd bet on *me*."

Wednesday, June 16th

Fifth day. I'm tired. Twice yesterday, and once again today, I came close to bursting into tears. I will never remember all the things we have to remember. I will never learn to do everything the Harvey Way. Things happen so fast, there's no time to catch your breath.

I rush to take orders and deliver them to the kitchen, the orders are filled quickly, then I serve the customers their food. The kitchen is a madhouse: chefs hollering, assistant cooks and helpers and salad girls all working at breakneck speed.

Meanwhile, Mr. Shaeffer glides among the tables, soothing customers who worry that the train will leave without them or they'll have to leave half their meal behind. Nervous Nellies, he calls them. He tells them that everything will be taken care of to their complete satisfaction, reassuring them: *There is no need to rush! No need to gulp down your food! Plenty of time to relax and enjoy your meal! No Harvey patron has ever missed his train.*

The drink girl pours; I serve the first course, remove the plates, bring the second course, remember to smile; more butter here, an extra roll there; offer dessert, replace a dropped napkin, present the bill.

Then the whistle blows, bills are settled, and off they go, saying *Best meal I ever had.*

I look beneath the saucer. There's usually a dime to drop into my apron pocket, but there's no time to count, because we're getting ready for the next train, the next customers.

Saturday, June 19th

ONE WEEK DOWN, THREE WEEKS AND TWO DAYS TO GO for my training. Everything is a blur. At the end of each day I just want to collapse. It's hard to keep up with my diary.

I'm up at five, throw cold water on my face, put on my uniform, race down to the staff lunchroom. The kitchen people have been at work for at least an hour. They feed us a big breakfast—oatmeal, eggs, pancakes if we want them—because we can't be sure when we'll have a chance to eat lunch. I think of my mother with her one boiled egg, single slice of dry toast, and one cup of tea. She doesn't believe in big breakfasts. She'd be shocked to see how much I eat.

Then the workday begins. First comes the breakfast rush, and we're busy until around nine o'clock when businesses open and the managers and clerks leave. A steady stream of railroad men starts to arrive and continues all morning. Then we begin getting ready for the eastbound. Electric fans whir in the dining room, but in the kitchen it's fiercely hot, and noisy, too—pots banging, cooler doors slamming, knives whacking, waitresses calling out their orders, cooks hollering, "Hot stuff! Coming through! Pick-up Table 4, Table 7, Table 13!"

But out where the customers are enjoying their meal, everything is calm and pleasant, efficient but never rushed. They'd never guess the frantic pace on the other side of those twin swinging doors, one in, one out.

Tomorrow after the Sunday crowd finishes, we will have the afternoon off, and I will welcome the chance to look back over my notes and see if I've left anything out. Or maybe I'll just sleep.

Sunday, June 20th

MR. SHAEFFER CHANGED HIS MIND. WE WERE SHORT-handed and the "new girls"—that's Cordelia, Emmy, and I—were told we had to work all day. Only Franny K. and the others who have been here longer got time off.

Emmy didn't seem to mind. "On the farm we never had a day off in the summer—just in the winter. There's always something to do. Sunday church was the only time we weren't working. Besides, here we'll earn tips."

Cordelia objected a great deal. "It must be against some law or other, how hard they work us," she complained. "I am so tired I don't know my own name! And who can get a decent night's sleep with the freight trains roaring through at all hours? I never thought I'd see the time when a long soak in the tub was the best way to spend a Saturday night."

The job is a lot harder than I expected. I think of Maudie, sitting at her typewriter and practicing *the quick brown fox*. Maybe she has the right idea. Maybe I should have stayed in Leavenworth and gone to work in the shoe department at McMeen's. Or learned to take shorthand and be a secretary. It might not have been so bad after all. At least I'd be allowed to sit down occasionally.

But I am determined. *No quitting*, I tell myself. *Stick to it, Kitty!*

In the end Mr. Shaeffer relented and gave us a few hours off. I bought some picture postcards at the newsstand across from the dining room and sent one with a photo of the depot to Mother and Daddy: *Having a fine time learning to become a Harvey Girl. Miss you and hope to hear from you soon. Love, Kitty*

Then I wrote to Maudie: *I am not a quick brown fox or a lazy dog, but I'm a Harvey Girl—almost, anyway. Write to me! Love, Kitty*

I debated sending a card to Phil Rayburn, but I couldn't think of anything clever to say to him. He probably doesn't even know I left Leavenworth. Jimmy Bedwell would appreciate it more.

Hi Jimmy—Greetings from Emporia. The Great K&A Train Robbery *is showing here. Too bad I don't have time to see it. Your friend—Kitty, the Harvey Girl*

Wednesday, June 23rd

MAIL! IT'S FROM DADDY, WRITTEN SUNDAY AFTERNOON. The weather is hot and humid, not much different from here. He reported what the sermon was about and what they had for dinner at the Mansion House. He said the roses are blooming in Mother's garden and she's won second prize from the garden club. Mother is busy planning the Fourth of July picnic they host every year in our backyard.

It will be a special one this year, the 150th anniversary of the signing of the Declaration. Sure do wish you'd be here for it, Puss.

Business has been picking up, but I guess not enough for me to go to college this fall, although he didn't say. Howie, who's giving golf lessons when he isn't working at the store, said to be sure to say hello to my friend Cordelia. Gramma Blair sent her love.

At the end of the letter, Mother added a P.S. *I hope you're being a good girl, as always, and not spending time with people who aren't the right kind. O'Reilly misses you and hopes you'll come home soon. Love, Mother*

Daddy enclosed a dollar bill, which will come in handy until I start earning a regular wage. Daddy calling me Puss usually annoys me to death, but for just a minute it made me homesick. Deep down, stomachache-y, wish-I-was-there-right-now lonesome for him and Mother and Howie. I miss my own room with my own desk, and I miss Betty Jane's dessert she calls "apple brown Betty Jane." I miss O'Reilly. I wish I could take a walk down by the Missouri with Maudie and watch the riverboats go by.

I was wallowing in all the things I was missing when I noticed Emmy watching me with a worried look. "Feeling blue?" she asked, and I admitted that I was, a little.

"Me, too," she said, and that surprised me, because Emmy isn't the sort who ever seems really up or really down.

She still hasn't heard from Carl. Bill, the manager of the newsstand, lets us know if there's anything for us when the mail is delivered. Every day Emmy hovers around while he sorts it, but so far, nothing.

"It's a real busy time on the farm right now, and he's not good at writing," she said. "Carl is not what you'd call a scholar. He always said I was wasting my time, having my nose in a book. He *did* promise he'd write to me when he could, though," she added wistfully. "He'll get around to it, I'm sure."

We climbed to the third floor, Emmy went into the room she shares with Franny K., and I went into mine. Cordelia wasn't there, and sometimes that's a relief. It's easier to write in my diary when I'm alone.

There are letters almost every single day for Cordelia from Walter, who would be her fiancé if she'd let him, and quite a few from her parents as well. She tosses them away without bothering to answer.

"Walter pleads and Mummy and Lorenzo order me to come home to Reading. I wrote them as soon as I decided to be a Harvey Girl, before I left Uncle Cam's, and I explained that I'd be undergoing *intensive* training and couldn't possibly engage in any correspondence until it's finished."

I've noticed that when we have a break after the lunch rush and again after the dinner rush, Cordelia disappears into the kitchen, and about fifteen minutes later she comes back. What is she doing? Yesterday I decided to find out. I took my time refilling the sugar bowls, and when the coast was clear I went into the kitchen. The dishwashers were scrubbing pots and the helpers were sweeping up. No Cordelia. One of the boys saw me looking around and gestured with his thumb toward the back door.

I heard the low murmur of voices outside. Behind a hedge of sprawling bushes I saw Cordelia, surrounded by the baker and a half-dozen cooks in white hats, all puffing on cigarettes. I backed away, hoping I hadn't been noticed. Now I'm worried. If Mr. Shaeffer or Queen Bea finds out, she'll be duck soup.

She has already been in trouble once. Every day before the morning shift, Queen Bea lines us up and rubs a cloth over our faces to make sure we're not wearing any rouge or powder. Cordelia knows better than to do the cupid's-bow lips, but she figured she could get away with a dab of powder on her nose and a touch of rouge on her lips.

"I feel naked without it," she said. "Anyway, who's going to notice?"

Queen Bea noticed, and Cordelia received a lecture and a face scrub.

I think she likes to see if she can get away with breaking the rules, or bending them a little. Sometimes I wish I could be more like her. Bold! Maybe not a flapper, exactly—I don't have a boyish figure, for one thing, and I don't have the nerve to bob my hair or roll my stockings below my knees, or even pretend to smoke. But just to *feel* bold, even if I don't act that way.

Thursday, June 24th

EMPORIA SEEMS LIKE A NICE, PEACEFUL PLACE, LIKE Leavenworth or Atchison or any other Kansas town I've been to, but yesterday it was a whole lot different. Even the waitresses who've been here for a while say they've never seen anything like the numbers of people who drove into town or came by train. Both the dining room and the lunchroom were filled to capacity all day long, and we were run ragged.

"Must be a big convention," Franny K. muttered.

The Ku Klux Klan came to Emporia to hold a big rally, and this morning at breakfast, that was all anybody could talk about. People were saying that about four thousand KKK marchers had arrived from all over Kansas and other states, too. The mayor didn't want them to parade through town in their white robes and their spooky white hoods. The police chief said there was a city ordinance against marches by masked men, but a district judge overruled the mayor and the chief and wouldn't let them interfere with the parade.

I was serving two policemen at the lunch counter, regulars who come in for breakfast every morning and always order the same thing.

"Everybody in Emporia turned out to watch," a

ruddy-faced patrolman we call Officer Dan told the man sitting next to him. I was busy with several other customers, but I kept an ear open and heard most of it.

Masked men in white robes marched four abreast in groups, carrying banners for whichever town they represented. They headed up Merchant to Twelfth Avenue, then across to Commercial, pretty much the same route Cordelia and Emmy and I took the day we arrived. They ended up at Fremont Park only about a dozen blocks east of the depot and sang patriotic songs and listened to speeches until almost midnight.

"You could probably hear them clear over here," Officer Dan said when I set down his cinnamon bun and refilled his coffee cup. "The park's not that far away."

I thought I'd heard something, but I didn't tell him I was too tired last night to care what was going on.

"They gathered at the bandstand and put up a cross with electric lights on it and listened to some crazy preacher for over an hour." He poured cream into his coffee until it was almost white. "We were just glad they weren't burning a cross, like the Klan does some places."

One of those places was Leavenworth. I remember when we found Klan leaflets in our front yard a couple of years ago, and we heard reports of a cross burning. Daddy seemed pretty upset about it. He said some of the most important people in our town supported the Klan, but others were against it.

"Why were they marching?" I asked the policeman. Engaging in conversation with customers is against the rules, but my curiosity as a future journalist was winning out over my duties as a Harvey Girl.

"Because they hate colored people, Catholics, and Jews."

Gramma Blair is dead set against the mixing of the races, and my mother once told me it would be better not to invite the Jewish girl in my class to our house, but they believe that Klan members are low-class and go too far. Howie is much more outspoken: "The Ku Klux Klan is a bunch of ignorant skunks," he'd said when we heard about the cross burning near Leavenworth.

Officer Dan's friend said he was sure William Allen White, the editor of the *Gazette*, would write an editorial about it. Mr. White and the mayor and the police chief and a lot of other people don't want the Klan here.

Someone else at the counter spoke up and reminded Officer Dan that when Mr. White ran for governor a couple of years ago on an anti-Klan platform, it didn't go over well. "White says the KKK makes Kansas look bad. He's right, but he lost the election, and that's a pity."

The policeman polished off his cinnamon bun, put on his hat, nodded to the other customers at the counter, and left. I picked up the dime under his saucer, and I began thinking about the people I'd waited on yesterday. Howie was right—they were a bunch of ignorant skunks, even if one of them *had* left me a quarter.

Saturday, June 26th

Today was my first day serving in the dining room, and I was petrified. At a table for four, I'm to start with the ladies, oldest first, and then move on to the gentlemen, remembering exactly what each one ordered. On my first order, two of the people changed their minds, just when I thought I had it all straight. I arranged the cups for the drink girl and dashed out to the kitchen, where everything was going a mile a minute, to give my order to the cook.

"Quit mumbling!" the cook bellowed. "Might as well be talking Chinese if you don't speak up."

I took the orders at the next table and put them in—shouting this time—carried out a tray with salads for both tables, poured our special dressing from a little pitcher over the chunk of lettuce until the customer said *Stop,* and used the special fork to place the pats of butter on the bread-and-butter plates. Then I made another dash to the kitchen for the main dishes, hoisted the heavy tray onto my shoulder, and carried it into to the dining room, remembering to smile even though I was scared I'd lose the whole thing in one tremendous crash.

Among my first customers were a grumpy old fellow

and his wife, a sad-faced woman in an ugly green hat. Just the two of them, so it should have been easy. He ordered the Fried Flounder with Tomato Sauce and his wife asked for the Chicken Croquettes with Cream Sauce. I served their dinners, and the grumpy man immediately began to complain. He insisted that the fish wasn't fresh. "I can tell from the smell. Old fish!"

As we'd been taught, I apologized and offered to bring him something different. "Our steak smothered in onions is excellent, sir," I said. "Our regular customers say it's one of their favorites." I made that part up.

"If I wanted steak, I'd have ordered steak in the first place! Fried flounder is on your menu, and fried flounder is what I expect!"

I raced back to the kitchen with the "old fish" and told Klaus, the Viennese chef. Practically all of the chefs are from some foreign country and can be hard to understand with their funny accents, especially when they're busy. Klaus grabbed a clean plate, piled on a big piece of fish, ladled tomato sauce over it, and arranged a sprig of parsley next to the boiled potatoes. "Tell him I prepare it myself, just for him."

Back I went with the new plate, and Mister Grumpy made a big show of sniffing the fish. "Much better," he said. "But I distinctly told you not to put tomato sauce on it."

He hadn't said a word about tomato sauce, I was sure of that, but I apologized again and asked what

I could do to make it right. He grumbled that he supposed if he was going to get back on that train without going hungry, he'd just have to eat it. Meanwhile his wife kept poking at her chicken croquette, not saying a word.

"I hope your meal is satisfactory, ma'am," I said, which is what we're supposed to say after they've had a few minutes to taste it.

"I don't much care for chicken," Ugly Green Hat said, giving the croquette another jab.

Then why did you order it? I wanted to ask, but instead I asked sweetly if there was something else she'd like.

She looked at me with sad eyes. "I'd love two poached eggs, four minutes."

Desserts had gone out to most of the other diners, and the drink girl was refilling cups. The gong would sound in twelve minutes, and the eastbound train would be ready to leave the station.

The assistant cook rolled his eyes, cracked a couple of eggs with one hand, dropped them into a pan of simmering water, and turned over the four-minute timer. I delivered a piece of fresh melon and a raspberry sundae to another table and trotted back to the kitchen to pick up Ugly Green Hat's poached eggs, perched cozily on buttered toast triangles.

She gazed unhappily at her eggs and poked the yolk with a fork. "They're not right," she said. "I asked for four-minute eggs. These are still wobbly. I can't eat a wobbly egg."

I assured her that I had seen him turn over the timer, just as she'd ordered. I thought she must enjoy poking her food.

"But they're not the way I ordered them!" she cried. Her face had turned bright pink, and she looked close to tears.

I was close to tears, too.

Mr. Shaeffer came over to see what the problem was, apologized *again*, and told Mr. and Mrs. Grumpy there would be no charge for their meals. They proceeded to devour every bite—he even mopped up the tomato sauce with his bread—and took two slices of chocolate cake with them to the train, which they made on time. There was no tip left beneath the saucer. Not a surprise.

As the train was pulling out, Mr. Shaeffer spoke to me. "I'll tell you what Fred Harvey used to say, Kitty: 'It is our business to please cranks. Anyone can please a gentleman.' You just had your first taste of a crank."

"Two of them," I said.

Sunday, June 27th

BESIDES CORDELIA AND EMMY AND ME, THERE ARE seven other Harvey Girls. Five of them are almost finished with their training, and if they're approved they'll be sent out on the line to another Harvey House for six months to gain more experience.

One of the five, Ruth Ann, may not make it. Mr. Shaeffer yells at her at least once in every shift. He prowls around like a hungry tiger, ready to pounce on the slightest imperfection—a glass that isn't set precisely at the tip of the knife, or a little spot on a white apron, a spot so tiny no normal person would notice. But Mr. Shaeffer is no normal person, and he noticed right away and bawled her out for not changing it immediately. That was last week.

"He has it in for me," Ruth Ann wailed, but Queen Bea told her that if she would just pay attention and concentrate on doing things right, she wouldn't find herself in hot water.

The rule—"the Harvey Way"—is that orange juice must be squeezed fresh each time it's ordered. But Ruth Ann decided to save time by squeezing a few oranges when she had a free minute and sticking a pitcher of juice toward the back of the cooler where it wouldn't be noticed.

Johnny, one of the busboys, saw what she was up to and warned her. "Don't be a dumb bunny! If Mr. Shaeffer catches you, he'll fire you on the spot."

Ruth Ann just shrugged. Johnny won't be mean and tell on her, but nothing gets by Mr. Shaeffer. I'm holding my breath.

I'm holding my breath about Emmy, too. Franny K. says her roommate is homesick and misses the farm.

We'd dumped the old coffee from one of the big silver urns and were fixing a fresh batch. "I don't think it's the *farm* she misses. I think it's the *farmer*—Carl," I said.

"She writes to him every single night," Franny K. whispered. "But he hasn't written to her even once. Would it kill him to send a postcard?"

I said I thought we should do something to get Emmy's mind off Carl and cheer her up. Franny K. said we could all probably do with some cheering up, but then she nudged me. "Later—Shaeffer's giving us the eye."

The manager was suddenly looming over us. "If you ever get done with your conversation, girls, I'm sure you can find something useful to do." He pulled a fat gold railroad watch from his pocket and checked it. "The eastbound is due in twenty-seven minutes."

When he'd gone, Franny K. whispered, "I'll tell you what time it is—time to start having some fun!" She hurried off to grind the coffee, and I tackled a stack of starched linen napkins back from the laundry and began folding them the Harvey Way.

Monday, June 28th

Having a little party was Evelyn's idea. Evelyn has been here the longest next to Queen Bea. She has a round face and deep dimples, as if somebody poked two fingers into a ball of yeast dough, and a laugh that starts down in her belly.

Cordelia perked up when word of a party started going around. After we finished up the dinner service yesterday evening, I went down to the baggage room to help her get some things from her trunk. She dug out her ukulele and located a peach-colored sleeveless dress with a six-inch fringe around the bottom and a row of fringe across the chest.

"I'm going to get dolled up," she said. "This will be swell."

I was stuck wearing my middy blouse and skirt, the same old thing I wore to the interview with Miss Steele that was also my church outfit, and Cordelia wore her shimmering flapper dress and looked absolutely stunning. It would have been easy to dislike her, but then she showed me how to put her little metal mask over my mouth to paint my lips in a cupid's bow. I looked like a Sunday school teacher with a flapper's mouth, but it was better than doing nothing.

She sat on her bed and tuned the uke. "My dog has

fle-e-eas," she sang, tightening the pegs. "That's a trick for remembering the pitches of the four strings, G-C-E-A," she explained when she saw me looking puzzled. "Too bad they don't have a piano, or I'd provide some real entertainment." She strummed a few chords, and then her fingers took off.

Pack up all my care and woe,

Here I go, singing low.

Bye, bye, blackbird.

Cordelia jumped off the bed and ran out into the hall, playing and singing.

Where somebody waits for me,

Sugar's sweet, so is he.

Doors flew open up and down the hall, and heads poked out—Franny K. and Emmy, Evelyn and Ruth Ann and the four other girls I haven't gotten to know well yet.

Bye, bye, blackbird!

Soon all the girls had come to find out what was going on. No sign of Queen Bea, which was surprising. She must not have been in her room, because you'd have had to be deaf not to hear the racket.

It didn't take long for the cooks and busboys to collect under our windows and holler at us to come down. The party was under way.

"Let's go, gals!" Evelyn commanded, and we trooped downstairs and out to the stone terrace near the bushes where the cooks sneak off to smoke cigarettes.

Cordelia knows all the hit songs, and we sang along: "When the Red, Red Robin Comes Bob, Bob, Bobbin' Along" and "Five Foot Two, Eyes of Blue." Still strumming her uke, she began dancing the Charleston, motioning us to follow her as she kicked, swiveled, and fast-stepped. Evelyn and Franny K. and some of the others fell in line and imitated her steps. I'm not generally one to try things in front of everybody until I've practiced, but I joined in anyway.

"Come on, Emmy!" Cordelia called. "You, too, Klaus!"

Emmy stood off to the side, hands tucked under her armpits, and shook her head. Our Viennese chef was leaning against a tree, watching. "I would rather waltz," he said, poker-faced.

The more Klaus protested, the more Cordelia insisted, and eventually she talked him into it. He caught on fast, adding a few flourishes of his own.

But there was no persuading Emmy.

I quit worrying about what my feet were doing and danced. "Now you're on the trolley!" Cordelia yelled.

Emmy was trying frantically to catch my attention. Then I saw why. Mr. Shaeffer stood at one door, Queen Bea at the other, both watching silently. There was no chance to alert the others. Everybody was having too much fun.

"It's ten minutes after ten o'clock, past your curfew," Queen Bea announced. "The party's over."

Tuesday, June 29th

Glory hallelujah! Carl finally wrote Emmy!! At first I was glad for her, but now I'm not so sure it's a good thing. She's a mess.

Carl explained that he wrote the letter about a week after she left and then forgot to mail it. I know she's happy to hear from him, but his letter upset her. The preacher is causing trouble, still telling Emmy's mother that Emmy will end up among people of bad character and fall into sin. The preacher has been telling Carl that waitresses are really just prostitutes, hanging around as the customers get off the trains and offering them their favors in exchange for money.

"And Carl believes him!" Emmy said. Her face was puffy and her eyes were red. "*The lowest of the low,* he says." Carl wants her to quit and go home before her reputation is ruined and everybody in her town finds out she's a waitress.

Cordelia was outraged. "Queen Bea keeps her beady eye on us from the minute we drag ourselves out of bed in the morning until we're ready to drop fifteen hours later. It's ridiculous for that dumb preacher to say such awful things about girls who work as hard as we do!"

Emmy sighed. "Wish you could make Carl believe that."

Monday, July 5th

THE 150TH ANNIVERSARY OF THE SIGNING OF THE Declaration of Independence has been celebrated for almost a week all across the country. President Coolidge, who was actually born on the Fourth of July, announced that he'd plant a willow tree, like the one in George Washington's yard, and read out the names of the signers in Christ Church in Philadelphia.

Back home my parents are throwing their annual Fourth of July party. Daddy has hung the American flag on our front porch. Betty Jane's sister is helping with the potato salad and the shortcake with a red-white-and-blue theme—strawberries, blueberries, and vanilla ice cream. I'm sure Daddy has complained about paying forty cents a pound for sirloin steaks, on top of the expense of hiring a man to come and cook them, as he does every year. Mother no doubt had a long conversation with Jake, the colored man who takes care of our yard, to make sure the garden is looking its best even though there hasn't been much rain this year. The punch bowl is set up on the porch, Daddy joking it would be nice if they had some rum to put in the punch, but that's out of the question since Prohibition went into effect six years ago—unless you know a bootlegger. Howie has probably finished shucking the sweet corn, and about now Mother is reminding him to run down to the creamery to pick up the ice cream.

I thought I'd be feeling homesick again, but I've been too busy all day to give it more than a few minutes of consideration while I was brushing my teeth, and again when I was shining my shoes. I wonder what Maudie is doing. I've had one letter from her, neatly typed with only a couple of mistakes, telling me that she's applied for a few jobs and had an interview at the Sexton Funeral Home. They offered her a position in the office.

I don't know if I want to be around dead people all day long. But the starting pay is pretty good, and Mr. Sexton says there's a chance for advancement. He didn't say exactly what that would be. When are you coming home? Every time I see Jimmy Bedwell he asks if I've heard anything more from you.

She mentioned seeing Elizabeth Pipher at the Rialto Theater with Phil Rayburn, and that piece of news didn't exactly improve my mood.

It's a patriotic time here at the Emporia Harvey House, too, and probably at all seventy-five Harvey Houses along the Atchison, Topeka & Santa Fe Railroad from Chicago to California. Cupcakes with little paper American flags planted on top are given out to every customer. At the main office at Union Station in Kansas City, someone sees that the menus are changed regularly and rotated so that a traveler who eats at a Harvey House in Arizona one day has a different choice in California the next. But this Fourth of July is special, and for a full week our menus have been special, too, with patriotic names for some of our dishes—Paul Revere Pot Roast, for instance, and Liberty Bell Lettuce Salad.

We were busy with no let-up all day. Because it's a holiday—today is the legal celebration of Independence Day, bank and post office closed—we didn't have the usual customers coming by on their way to work, but a lot of folks who had picnics yesterday must have decided to treat themselves to a meal in a restaurant today. The trains still ran east and west, and diners still expected to be served a three-course meal in thirty minutes. There was a parade through town, with marching bands and floats sponsored by different organizations. If you went out on the station platform, you could hear the music in the distance, but we had no chance to see any of it.

I stuck a calendar on the door of the wardrobe, and every day I draw a line through the date, counting down to when we'll finish our training here and be sent out on the line to who-knows-where. June 11th was my first day, and July 11th will be my last. Six more days, and then what? It's possible that Queen Bea will decide I'm not Harvey Girl material and tell me to go home. Or maybe she or Mr. Shaeffer has already discovered that I'm not eighteen and won't even be seventeen until July 29th.

Cordelia said I shouldn't worry, that I look older and act mature for my age. "Besides, you're a good waitress. You never gum things up. You follow all the rules."

Cordelia was lying crosswise on her bed, swinging her legs. Emmy came in, and Cordelia moved over to make room for her. Emmy had news: Ruth Ann's been given her walking papers.

That wasn't exactly a surprise. "Poor Ruth Ann!" Cordelia said. "Back to a chicken farm in Iowa!"

"Sometimes I think it wouldn't be so bad to be sent home," Emmy said.

"Sounds perfectly ghastly to me," Cordelia said. She sat up and began filing her nails with an emery board. "I don't care if I never see Reading again."

Tuesday, July 6th

FIVE DAYS UNTIL OUR MONTH IS UP, AND THE DARNEDEST thing happened! Mr. White, the editor of the *Emporia Gazette*, came in for lunch as he does practically every day—always between trains, never when we're busy serving our train customers. He's a stoutish man, wears a bow tie, and has a round, pleasant face that makes me think he'd be very nice to work for. Sometimes he has somebody with him, the mayor or some other important person, but usually he's alone, and he always sits at the same table. We all know that's Mr. White's table. Queen Bea almost always waits on him—until today.

"He asked for you to be his waitress," she whispered.

I must have looked dumbfounded.

"Yes, you. Now go."

I smiled and greeted him the way we'd been trained: "Good day, sir. What may I get for you?"

He rattled off his order—navy bean soup, chicken salad, banana cream pie, coffee—and then he added, "Please tell me your name."

None of the customers has ever asked me my name. We are all just Harvey Girls, and they usually call us "Miss" when they call us anything at all.

When I told him "Kitty Evans," he wanted to know if that was Kitty for Katherine with a K, and I said it was.

"'Katherine' was my daughter Mary's middle name." He studied me, head to one side, rubbing his chin, and I thought he looked sad. "You remind me a lot of her."

"I do?" I must have sounded like a real dumbbell, but I didn't know what to say.

He nodded and asked me how old I am.

That just about floored me, because I hated to lie to him, but telling the truth might also get me into trouble with Mr. Shaeffer or Queen Bea. When I hesitated, making up my mind, he filled in the blank himself.

"I'll guess that you're about seventeen, am I right?"

"Yes, sir."

"My Mary was just your age when she died. Knocked off her horse," he went on. "That was five years ago."

He pulled a wallet out of his inside pocket and opened it to show me his daughter's picture, a pretty girl with her hair drawn back in a single braid. "My Mary certainly wanted nothing to do with those flappers." He said she refused to wear her hair up, even when her mother wanted her to, and wouldn't think of having it bobbed. "Liked to wear riding clothes—it was hard to get a dress on her."

He smiled and put the picture away. She'd been assistant editor of her high school annual that year, he said, and in line to be editor the next year.

I blurted out that I'd been editor of my high school yearbook, and of the school paper, too, explaining how Phil and I had alternated jobs. I hadn't planned to tell him any of that, and I was aware of Mr. Shaeffer watching me curiously. We weren't supposed to have conversations with customers, but on the other hand, this was William Allen White.

"Perhaps I should take your order to the kitchen, sir," I said.

"You do that, Kitty," Mr. White said, "and we'll talk more later. I have some questions for you."

I raced to the kitchen and called out Mr. White's

order in a firm voice. Then I did my best to be patient with a family that came in with two young children, and none of them had any idea what to order because they had never been here before, and it was the wife's birthday. The regulars always make up their minds quickly, but this family had questions about every blessed item on the menu. I tried to answer, and when they asked for a few more minutes to consider, I hurried back to the kitchen to pick up Mr. White's navy bean soup and chicken salad.

"Now, Kitty, I know you're busier than a one-armed paperhanger," Mr. White said when I brought his order, "but I want you to tell me why you decided to become a Harvey Girl. Sounds to me like you should be headed for a career in journalism."

I couldn't help grinning. I told him that's what I plan to do, but first I want to see a little bit of the country and save up money for college.

He took a small white card out of his pocket and laid it on the table. It had his name, *William Allen White, Editor, Emporia Gazette,* in neat black letters, with the address and a phone number. "Get in touch with me when you've worked it all out and you're ready to be a newspaperwoman."

I thanked him and put the card in my pocket.

He tapped his forehead. "Remember," he said, "think like a journalist. Be observant. Be a good listener, and learn to eavesdrop—you can learn a lot by listening to people when they're not aware of it. Your eyes and ears are your best tools. And keep notes. Make it a practice to write everything down."

After Mr. White picked up his hat and left, I found a silver dollar under the saucer, the biggest tip I've gotten, and maybe the biggest I'll ever see. But his business card and the conversation we had are even more valuable.

Wednesday, July 7th

WE WERE FINISHING SERVICE FOR THE NOON WESTbound when the mailman delivered a batch of letters for the Harvey House staff. In the bundle was a notice for Miss Cordelia S. Hart: a package, registered and insured, was being held for her at the Emporia post office. She'd have to go there to sign for it and pick it up.

"Oh, lord," Cordelia groaned. "I'm dead on my feet, it's at least a hundred and two in the shade, I'm dying to take a bath, and the last thing I want to do is walk to the post office to pick up some darn package. And who'd be sending me a package, anyway? My birthday isn't until October."

I said I'd go with her. To be honest, I wanted to walk by the office of the *Gazette,* just to take a peek inside and see what a big newspaper office looked like. After observing me in deep conversation with the editor, Queen Bea told me that William Allen White is very well known, and won a Pultizer Prize for journalism. He is friends with lots of famous people and even knew Teddy Roosevelt.

I didn't tell her he'd left me his business card, which I'm keeping in my diary.

As soon as we'd cleaned up and everything was ready for the dinner trains, we had two hours off. Cordelia and I changed out of our uniforms and headed for the post office.

It was hot, and Cordelia complained. But this was Kansas in July—what did she expect? "Isn't it hot in Reading, too?" I asked, and she admitted I was right, it was miserable in Pennsylvania this time of year, but if she were at home she'd be cooling off in the plunge pool at the country club.

I had considered not saying anything about my conversation with Mr. White, but it was too exciting to keep secret. As we hopped from one shady spot to the next along Merchant Street, I told her the whole story, repeating what Queen Bea had said about him being famous and winning an important prize for his editorials.

"You are so darn lucky!" Cordelia sighed. "You're

not even seventeen yet, but you have this idea of what you're going to do someday, who you're going to be. A journalist! Not like me, just drifting along and waiting for life to happen."

"You've been saying you want to go to California."

She shrugged. "California is just a dream. I really have no idea *what* I'm going to end up doing."

Cordelia signed for a big box that turned out to weigh next to nothing. The return address was Walter Vogel's. She decided she'd lug it back to our room and open it there.

We tried to find a shady side of the street, but there wasn't one. Sweat trickled down my back, soaking my shirtwaist. I took a turn carrying the clumsy package while Cordelia dabbed at her forehead with a wilted handkerchief. I was almost as curious as Cordelia about what could be in that box.

Back in our room, she tore off the brown paper wrapping and found a smaller gift-wrapped box inside it, and then a smaller one inside that, then another wrapping. "Walter probably thinks he's being clever," she said. "What a dope." She finally made her way down to a small blue box with gold lettering: *Bailey Banks & Biddle.*

"That's a jewelry store in Philly. I'll bet Walter sent me some expensive thing I don't want." She sighed. "Poor Walter! I haven't written him since I've been here, except a couple of postcards. He just doesn't understand!

He's as devoted as an old dog, and about as exciting."

She sat on her bed, surrounded by torn wrappings and empty boxes, and stared at the blue box. Such suspense! I wondered if she was ever going to open it.

Finally Cordelia took a deep breath and removed the lid. Inside the blue box was a very small velvet-covered cube. Anybody could guess what was in it. It *had* to be a ring.

She groaned. "Oh, lord."

It *was* a ring—and not just any ring, but a huge diamond surrounded by tiny sapphires. A little envelope was tucked next to the velvet ring box.

Cordelia opened it and read the card: *To Cordelia, my dearest future wife. All my love, Walter.*

It made her furious. "What a boob!" she fumed. "Of all the stupid things to do—mailing me an engagement ring! We're not even engaged!" She jumped up and began pacing around our room, which was not easy, given its size. "He knows darn well that I simply do not want to get engaged—not now, and probably not ever!"

She was sure her mother was in on it, thinking that a big diamond—"a hunk of glass," she called it—was all it would take to make her jump on the next train back East, get married, and turn into a nice little wife who plays bridge with the girls every Wednesday and cooks a pot roast for hubby's Sunday dinner.

I had no idea what to say to all this. Finally I asked

her what she was going to do.

"I'm going to California!" she cried fiercely. "I've made up my mind—I'm going to be a pianist. I'll get a job playing in a swanky cocktail lounge in some ritzy hotel in Hollywood, or something even better. You just watch! Cordelia Hart is going to be somebody and have fun doing it!"

Cordelia, who an hour earlier had no idea about her future, was now imagining herself in Hollywood. She took a deep breath. "I guess that answers your question, doesn't it, Kitty? I'm going to tell him *No*!"

I can't imagine how I'd react if somebody sent me a diamond the size of a cherry. I probably wouldn't be able to keep my mouth shut for five minutes. I asked her if she wasn't even going to try it on.

"Nope," she said, and to prove it, she shoved it into a drawer next to her underthings and banged the drawer shut. "I'm going to mail the darn thing back to him tomorrow. Such nerve! Should I go downstairs right now and ask to use the telephone and call him, do you think? Or should I write him a letter?" She looked at me helplessly. "What would you do?"

"Write to him."

"I'm a terrible writer! Nothing I try to say ever comes out the way I want it to," Cordelia complained. Then, *bingo*, a bright idea: I could write it for her! She'd tell me what she wanted me to say, and I'd figure out the best way to say it. She even offered to pay me—"Your first professional assignment as a journalist!"

I said it would be kind of the reverse of *Cyrano de Bergerac*. Cordelia looked at me blankly, and I explained that it's a play about a Frenchman named Cyrano with a big nose. Cyrano wrote love letters for his handsome friend to send to Roxane, the girl Cyrano was secretly in love with.

This made no sense to Cordelia, who claimed she wasn't any good in English classes, since all she ever cared about was music. "So will you do it for me, Kitty? Please?"

I agreed to write the letter, if she'd let me try on the ring. That was the only pay I was willing to accept.

Which is how I came to be sitting here on my bed, flashing a gorgeous diamond on the third finger of my left hand, trying to find the right words to tell poor Walter Vogel that I cannot accept this lovely ring, and I am returning it by registered and insured mail, and I'm terribly sorry that I can't marry him but I will always care for him as a friend.

Thursday, July 8th

Cordelia was copying my letter onto Harvey House stationery she picked up at the newsstand, when there was a tap on the door. I sat on my hand to hide the ring. Emmy poked her head in, saw the mess of wrappings and boxes, and looked at us with a big question mark on her face.

"Go ahead and show her, Kitty," Cordelia said.

I flashed the diamond, and Emmy's eyes grew big as eggs. "Is it real?"

"It's real, all right," Cordelia replied. She ended the letter with a flourish and stuck it in an envelope. "Walter sent it to me, and I'm sending it back. You want to try it on?"

Emmy shook her head, backing away as if it were something dangerous that might explode. "You're sending it back? You don't like it?"

"The ring is fine. It's Walter I don't want," Cordelia said, and told Emmy the story.

If Emmy thought Cordelia was crazy, she didn't let on. Cordelia packed the ring and the letter in the Bailey Banks & Biddle box (I love that name—so alliterative), and this afternoon the three of us walked to the post office and mailed the ring. It was like a ceremony, with Emmy and me as witnesses.

I'm betting that in a few days, depending on how fast the mail travels, there'll be a telegram, maybe even a long-distance telephone call, from Walter. Emmy thinks Cordelia will change her mind. I disagree. Cordelia won't give in; I'd bet on that, too.

On the way back to the Harvey House we stopped off at the drugstore, ordered cherry phosphates—Cordelia's treat—and drank a toast.

"To my disengagement!" Cordelia said, raising her glass.

We were halfway through our fizzy drinks when Emmy, who'd been unusually quiet, even for her, asked if I'd do her a big favor—write a letter for her to copy and send to Carl. "Something to make him see that waitresses aren't at all what he thinks."

How could I say no?

Cordelia found a used envelope in her handbag, and I asked the pimply-faced soda jerk, who'd been hanging around, gaping at us, if he would lend us a pencil. He handed over a chewed yellow stub and went back to swishing a damp rag over the marble counter.

Dear Carl, I began. Then I stopped to ask Emmy if she wanted to make it more affectionate: *Dearest Carl*, or *My darling Carl?*

She shook her head. "*Dear Carl* is fine."

I was so happy to get your letter. I hope you've been getting my letters, too. If you have, you know that I've made friends with some wonderful girls, and we're all working hard to learn to be first-class waitresses. Being a Harvey Girl is not a job, it's a profession—that line was Cordelia's suggestion—*and one to be proud of. I hope that you'll be proud of me, too, and that you will not listen to the poisonous opinion of Preacher Bledsoe. He doesn't know anything about Harvey Girls.*

In a few minutes I'd roughed out a first draft, and Emmy said she'd copy it over later tonight.

"You're a really good writer, Kitty," Emmy said solemnly. "Someday you'll have a great career."

Cordelia raised her half-empty glass. "To Kitty Evans, professional writer of the future."

We slurped up the last of our sodas, making rude noises with our straws. The soda jerk stared at us.

Later Thursday

TWO DAYS OF TRAINING LEFT, AND I'M NERVOUS AS A cat on a griddle, as Maudie likes to say. I haven't made any major mistakes, so I'm pretty sure I won't be told that I'm not up to the Harvey standard and not cut out to be a Harvey Girl. But I'm nervous about where I'll be sent next. Franny K. says it's possible I could be kept here in Emporia. I wouldn't mind—I'm used to it, I'd still be in Kansas and not too far from home. Queen Bea has taught me everything I know and makes me do my best, and I've gained respect for Mr. Shaeffer. I was a little bit afraid of him at first, the way he stalks around, ready to pounce, but now I see that he's a lot more housecat than tiger.

Also, if I stay here, I'll get to know Mr. White. But my goal is to see more of the world, or at least a piece of it. I think if I asked Mr. White, he'd advise me to move on. But where to? That's the big question. What if it's someplace I hate—some place *putrid*?

I'm not sure what Cordelia will end up doing. Until that diamond ring arrived in the mail yesterday, I thought she might decide she'd had enough, that being a Harvey Girl is much harder and not nearly as exciting as she had expected. It turns out that she has a tough spirit, as tough as Emmy's.

Cordelia doesn't mope, period. There've been times when I've felt blue and wondered if I made a mistake leaving home, but Cordelia never seems to have any doubts at all. If she does call it quits, it won't be because she yearns for Pennsylvania, but because she has a better idea.

Friday, July 9th

Since our first day here, Queen Bea has told stories about surprise visits from supervisors. Back in the 1890s, Mr. Fred Harvey himself used to show up unannounced. The next train might be steaming down the track, the kitchen in a frenzy, the girls at their stations ready to spring into action, but if Mr. Harvey found the least little thing that wasn't up to the Harvey standard, like a cup with a tiny chip on the handle or silverware that wasn't lined up precisely, he'd grab a corner of the tablecloth and give it a yank, and everything would come off with it.

Queen Bea admits she hasn't seen anything this dramatic, but even after Mr. Fred Harvey died, supervisors used those stories to keep the staff on their toes. About once a year or so, a rumor circulates of smashed dishes and flying silverware at some Harvey House along the line, although nobody can ever say exactly where. Mr. Shaeffer is a perfectionist—just like Mr. Harvey. So whenever a train is due, whether it's eastbound or westbound, passenger train or freight, he is prepared. If a supervisor shows up here, Mr. Shaeffer is not going to be caught out.

"Does it happen often?" Emmy asked. "A supervisor coming here?"

"Often enough," Queen Bea said.

Today we saw it with our own eyes.

The eastbound train was running fifteen minutes late. That meant we'd have even less time than usual to clear and set up for the westbound. It was a really hot July day—hot even for Kansas—and among the crowd stepping off the train was a man in shirtsleeves who was expecting to have his meal in the dining room. Men are permitted to wear shirtsleeves at the lunch counter, but in the dining room they are required to wear coats. Queen Bea greeted the gentleman and reminded him politely of the coat rule. She led him to the closet where Mr. Shaeffer keeps a selection of high-quality alpaca jackets in a variety of sizes and invited him to pick a coat from the rack.

He objected. It was too darn hot to wear a jacket, and he was darned if he was going to bow to such a darn stupid rule. Queen Bea didn't back down. Her voice was crisp and firm. The rest of us rushed around, trying to do our jobs.

Mr. Shaeffer intervened immediately. He offered the man a complimentary beverage and dessert if the gentleman would understand that this was a hard and fast rule and agree to comply. "Otherwise, sir, with great regret, I shall have to refuse you service."

Mr. Shaeffer won the battle. The gentleman—I didn't think he was much of a gentleman—grabbed the coat Mr. Shaeffer offered, grudgingly put it on, and was shown to a table. Emmy's table! There he was, still grumbling and grouching, and she had to run even faster, because the argument had used up more than five minutes of the thirty. He would probably complain about the food, and everything else, too. But Emmy is imperturbable.

He must have been the first person in the history of the Emporia Harvey House who didn't like our famous Thousand Isle salad dressing. A quarter of a head of lettuce was already at his place, and Emmy's job was to pour the dressing over it from a little pitcher and then to leave the pitcher on a saucer so he could help himself to more, if he wished. He said she'd poured too much and sent the lettuce back to the kitchen. She replaced it.

Next, he wanted more gravy for his roast turkey, and Emmy brought it. He said his coffee wasn't hot enough, and she took his cup away and came back with a fresh one. He asked for another pat of butter; Emmy served him two, with fork marks on both.

I had my own table to take care of—nice people, happy about everything—and watched Emmy out of the corner of my eye. How was she going to serve him his peach pie and ice cream before the whistle blew? But Emmy kept calmly doing what she was doing, without looking the least bit ruffled.

We were all relieved when that train pulled out.

Mr. Shaeffer was beaming. "Fine job, Emmy," he said and actually patted Emmy on the back, which was unheard of, and Emmy blushed and said thank you.

The man turned out to be a supervisor, one of a pair, and while he was having his meal and complaining about everything, a second supervisor was back in the kitchen, checking whether the floor and the cooler and the stoves were spotlessly clean. This strategy was something new.

When there was a break after the westbound had come and gone, I told Emmy, "I know they say it's our business to please cranks, but it must have been hard to keep that particular crank from getting under your skin."

Emmy shrugged it off. "It was no trouble. He reminded me of my daddy. Pap's just like that—you can't do anything right, no matter what, so you just go on with whatever it is you're about and don't pay him any mind."

Still Friday, July 9th

I'M GOING TO NEW MEXICO!

A few minutes ago, after the westbound pulled out, Queen Bea called Emmy and Cordelia and me aside and told us a telegram had come in from Kansas City.

We've been approved to go out on the line. She asked if we were ready to accept an assignment for the remainder of our six-month contract.

I said, "Oh, yes!" and glanced at Cordelia.

Cordelia said, "You bet!"

We both turned to Emmy.

Emmy, smiling a little uncertainly, nodded and asked where we're going.

Queen Bea named a town that I didn't catch, adding, "It's an excellent place to get more experience."

We're each to pack one clean uniform and send the rest on the local to the central laundry in Newton. They'll be delivered to the Harvey House in New Mexico shortly after we arrive. Queen Bea will have our tickets ready tomorrow. We leave Sunday afternoon.

"Questions?"

We were too excited to ask questions, but after Queen Bea flew off, we thought of one.

"What was the name of that town?" Cordelia wondered. "Is it in the United States, or are we going to Mexico?"

Saturday, July 10th

Franny K. says New Mexico is one of the forty-eight and there are several Harvey Houses in the state. The Alvarado in Albuquerque is really famous. She's dying to go there, but her contract won't be up until October, so she'll be in Emporia for another few months.

"I don't believe Albuquerque is where we're going," Emmy said. "We're not sure exactly *where* we're going."

Franny K. went with us to look at the map outside the newsstand that shows the location of all the Harvey Houses, from Chicago to California. New Mexico is between Texas and Arizona.

"There it is," she said. "Belén. Spanish word, I think."

I wrote to Mother and Daddy with the news that I'm going out West, to a place I've never heard of and do not even know how to pronounce. *Hope you are fine. I miss you all a lot. Tell O'Reilly I'll be home for Christmas.*

Cordelia is already talking about cowboys and horses, and she's happy she packed her jodhpurs and riding boots.

But in the midst of feeling glad that my exciting new life is actually beginning, I got a lump in my throat that wouldn't go away. If I don't even know how to pronounce the name of the town, what else is going to seem foreign and strange?

Five more months! It seems like a very long time.

Sunday, July 11th—on the train

HERE WE ARE, FULL SPEED AHEAD TO A BRAND NEW adventure.

I'm excited to be on my way to someplace different and curious what it will be like, but I'm also a little sorry to be leaving Emporia. Maybe more than a little. One of the things I liked about Emporia is that I saw Mr. White almost every day when he came in for lunch, even though I never had another chance to wait on him. If I happened to be the drink girl that day, he'd say, "Hello, Kitty, how's the future journalist?" and I'd say, "Fine, thank you, Mr. White." I always hoped he'd ask for me again and we'd talk more, but that didn't happen.

This morning Mr. Shaeffer shook our hands and wished us good luck. "I know you'll proudly keep up the Harvey standard," he said and went back to keeping his tiger's eye on every little thing.

The next batch of new Harvey Girls arrived while we were out on the platform with our baggage. Three dazed-looking girls climbed off the train with their suitcases as we climbed on. Queen Bea was there to greet them.

We'll spend the night on the train. For a while, as we rolled across most of Kansas and Oklahoma on the way to the southwest, we played cards until we were sick of it. I started reading a novel by Sinclair Lewis that Cordelia said bored her half to death, and she dealt herself a hand of solitaire. Emmy mostly stared out the window, but when she realized we were crossing the state line into Oklahoma, her cheeks glowed bright pink and her voice went up at least an octave.

"You mean there's not a real line?" she asked. "A fence or something? It's the first time I've been outside of Kansas, except when I went to Kansas City for my interview. I thought sure I'd know when it happened."

Monday, July 12th—Belén, New Mexico

I DIDN'T THINK I'D BE ABLE TO SLEEP, BUT THE RHYTHMIC clatter of the wheels all night was so soothing that I dozed off and slept across most of the Texas panhandle. Emmy says I didn't miss much—there was no official state line to cross there, either. We had a breakfast stop at the Harvey House in Amarillo, and a few hours later we turned our watches back an hour when we made a lunch stop at the Gran Quivira Harvey House in Clovis, New Mexico. According to some old-timer sitting near us, this land used to be a part of Mexico, then became a United States territory, and became the forty-seventh state in 1912. Cordelia was rolling her eyes before the history lesson ended and the old-timer got off at the next stop, Vaughn.

Vaughn is tiny, but the Harvey House is a grand-looking place with a red tile roof and a long row of graceful arches across the front. It looked as though it could be in some foreign place. A girl who climbed aboard picked us out immediately as Harvey Girls. Her name is Maggie. She has wildly curly rust-colored hair, green eyes, and a dusting of freckles like cinnamon on a pudding.

"Been in Vaughn for six months," she said, plunking down in the empty seat next to Emmy. "That was plenty long for me! I've had enough of Vaughn—nothing to see here and nothing to do. Just signed up for six more months, as long as they're someplace else. *Any*place else! I was hoping they'd send me to Las Vegas—the one in New Mexico, not Nevada. They say the hotel there is swell. I'm ready for some excitement!" She rubbed her hands enthusiastically. "Don't know if I'll get that in Belén, but I guess we'll soon find out, won't we! So where are you all from?"

Maggie's eyes widened when Cordelia mentioned Philadelphia. Cordelia has stopped telling people she's from Reading, Pennsylvania, which nobody's heard of. Philadelphia sounds much more glamorous, almost as glamorous as New York City.

Maggie is from Nebraska. "My dad raises pigs. He also has a barbershop in Ogallala. The closest shave and the best bacon west of Omaha!"

Soon she had us all talking and laughing like we'd known her for years—even Emmy, who is usually so quiet. It was quickly settled that Maggie and Emmy would room together.

"Two farmers' daughters," Maggie said. "We make a team, don't we?"

I have my doubts about that. They couldn't be more different.

At another little town, called Mountainair, the conductor came through announcing that Belén was the scheduled dinner stop and counting the number of passengers planning to eat in the lunchroom or the dining room—he'd telegraph ahead and let the manager know how many to expect. West of Mountainair the train slowed and began to climb, crawling up and up past bare rocks and sparse, scrubby trees, making its way through a rugged mountain pass. Coming down the other side, we picked up speed again, descended onto a flat plain, and crossed a strip of green and a river that Maggie said is called the Rio Grande. "That's Spanish for 'Big River.'"

"*Big River*?" Cordelia hooted. "I'd say it's more like a creek."

"Better not let anybody hear you say that," Maggie warned. "They're real proud of it around here."

A mile out of Belén the engineer blew two sharp blasts on the whistle to alert the Harvey House staff, and the conductor called out the next stop.

"My glory!" Maggie said when she saw the amount of baggage Cordelia was getting ready to haul off the train. "That stuff is all yours?"

Cordelia admitted that it was. We all grabbed something and helped her. Emmy carried the shiny black hatbox.

We stood on the platform for a minute, glad to be off the train, glad to be here at last. The train was stopped in front of a white stucco building that looked a lot like the Harvey House in Vaughn—a red tile roof and a row of arches draped with vines. Out stepped the busboy with mallet and gong to greet the dinner customers and lead them inside. A railroad crew loaded coal and water into the tender, while the cooks and the waitresses made sure the customers were served a good meal in exactly thirty minutes. That much would be no different.

A plump woman with a head waitress's long white necktie came out to meet us, beaming a crinkly-eyed smile that made me like her immediately.

"Welcome to Belén," she said, accenting the second syllable. "It's Spanish for 'Bethlehem.' My name is Mrs. McCreary." She looked us over as she's

probably done dozens of times, with hundreds of girls. The pin she was wearing said "16," and she told us she's been here since this Harvey House opened in

1910. She prefers to be called Mrs. McCreary instead of her first name, because she's responsible for us, and it's better for her to have a formal title.

A man with slicked-back hair parted down the middle stood by the entrance, greeting customers getting off the train—the manager, I assumed.

"Do any of you speak Spanish?" Mrs. McCreary asked.

Emmy whispered, "No, ma'am." Maggie boasted that she'd picked up some in Vaughn from the ranch hands, words that probably shouldn't be repeated in polite company. And Cordelia announced breezily, "No Spanish, but I've been working on my German." She'd been working on her German in the Emporia kitchen, flirting with Klaus.

I said no and two years of Latin probably didn't count, but Mrs. McCreary said, "They'll surely help."

We grabbed our bags and followed Mrs. McCreary upstairs as she explained our duties, starting with the morning shift. Only one passenger train a day makes a meal stop here—the westbound we came in on—and we're to wear our regular uniforms. At breakfast and lunch, when we're waiting on railroad men and local people, we're to wear a skirt and a white shirtwaist with an apron. Breakfast is at five, and our shift starts at six.

Mrs. McCreary's room is the corner room at the top of the stairs. "Curfew is ten o'clock," she said. "Be forewarned—the stairs creak, and I'm not a sound sleeper. Any questions?" There were none. "You must be hungry! After the train departs, come down and have some dinner."

Cordelia scowled as Mrs. McCreary disappeared down the hall. "Twenty years old and I still have a ten o'clock curfew! That's absurd. The curfew was midnight when I was at the conservatory, and I objected even to that!"

Now she has swept off to take a bath. For a while I could hear Maggie's laughter bubbling in the next room, but it's grown quiet. I've looked around the small, spare room that will be my home for the next six months—pea-green walls, white curtains, green-and-white crocheted counterpanes on the twin beds. Green is my least favorite color. I like fat pillows, and these look awfully thin. A freight train thundering past rattles the windows.

Suddenly tears are pouring down my face. If I don't stop writing now, they'll be dripping all over my diary, and Cordelia will be back any minute, asking what's wrong.

Later Monday

I WASHED MY FACE, COMBED MY HAIR, AND WENT DOWNstairs as the last of the passengers were boarding the westbound train. The manager of the newsstand was straightening up the postcard rack. He moved behind a case filled with boxes of cigars and souvenirs and began polishing it with a cloth. "Gotta get rid of the fingerprints," he said. "Harvey standard, you know."

His name is Enrique, *Henry* in English, and he spelled it for me. When I mentioned that it feels like a foreign country here—Mexico, maybe—he said, "That's what the Santa Fe Railroad people want you to think." The hotels and Harvey Houses from here to the Pacific Ocean were built to look like the old Spanish mission churches in California.

The population of Belén is only about two thousand. That's hardly even a town, in my opinion. More like a village. I asked if there's a newspaper here, and Enrique pointed to a pile of the local *Belén News* next to a stack of the daily paper, the *Albuquerque Journal*.

"Albuquerque is the only real city around, and it's thirty miles north," he said. "The *Belén News* is weekly. Not much happens here." He gave me a copy, compliments of Harvey House.

Local people began to arrive, the men in coats and neckties and the ladies in hats, all properly dressed to eat in the dining room. The manager with the slicked-back hair met them at the door, shaking hands with the men and greeting the ladies by name with a stiff little bow. Railroaders in blue-and-white striped bib overalls stood aside, holding their billed caps, and waited for places at a section set aside for them at the long marble counter in the lunchroom. There are three serving stations in the center, one of them an icebox with bowls of fresh fruit arranged on top next to pies displayed under glass covers.

A few Negro workers went all the way around to the back, near the doors to the kitchen. In Emporia the cooks always fixed box lunches for the Negroes to take somewhere outside to eat. Whites don't believe in mixing with colored people in Emporia, and I guess they don't in Belén, either. Not that it was different in Leavenworth. There were only a handful of Negroes in my high school, and they never ate in our lunchroom. I don't know *where* they ate, and now I'm wondering about that.

I stepped out onto the station platform and looked around. Everything was hot and dry, baking in the late afternoon sun. Rugged mountains rimmed the distance. The sky was the bluest I've ever seen, not even a wisp of cloud in sight. The iron tracks shimmered in the heat, but the Harvey House is surrounded by cool and inviting green lawns, big shade trees, and flowerbeds blooming with yellow and purple flowers that my mother would love. A man in a straw hat, holding a garden hose, grinned and waved.

A wide street, unpaved and dusty, leads west from the depot, stretching past low buildings no more than two stories high. A few automobiles kicked up choking billows of dust, and a couple of horse-drawn wagons rattled by. Take just a few steps from the Harvey House and it doesn't feel like an old Spanish mission anymore. More like the Wild West in those Tom Mix movies Jimmy Bedwell is so crazy about.

Disappointment settled over me like a scratchy blanket. It looked so dry and desolate that I struggled not to start crying.

Cordelia joined me and flung her arm around my shoulders. Her bath had pepped her up. She'd put on one of the straight flapper dresses she never had a chance to wear in Emporia, tied a purple headband around her blond bob, and painted her lips a bright red that you could spot halfway across a room.

"Ye gods! This is it? I'm not sure what I expected—but certainly not so much *dirt*. How long do you suppose we'll have to stay here?" When I didn't say anything, she said, "There are times when I wonder why I left Reading. This is one of them."

Emmy and Maggie were sitting on a bench in the shade, fanning themselves. Emmy was her usual sober, well-scrubbed self, in one of her homemade dresses, and Maggie was popping out of an outfit that was more than a little too tight, her hair in a frizzy halo. I wished I'd changed my clothes and put on a clean middy blouse, but the girls insisted I looked fine.

"Let's go have dinner," Maggie said. "I'm starving."

Almost all the seats in the workers' section of the lunchroom counter were taken. The railroad men seemed to be mostly done with their dinners, and they were slowly sipping coffee and stealing surreptitious glances at us.

We lined up on four swiveling stools, and the waitress doled out menus. Her name is Gladys, she said, and she's from Missouri. I decided on codfish balls and coleslaw, chocolate cake, and a glass of milk. Gladys left to place our orders. Nobody said a word while she was gone. The only sound was the clink of spoons against coffee cups. The railroaders kept eyeing us.

"Seems like the word's gotten out that four new Harvey Girls just hit town," Gladys stage-whispered as she set down our plates. Gladys is not the prettiest Harvey Girl I've met so far, but she has the brightest smile and a hearty laugh. "I think some of our steady customers are here to look you over."

I wasn't used to being studied so openly. "I hate to be stared at," I murmured to Maggie.

"Don't let it bother you," Maggie said, tossing those red ringlets. "The boys in Vaughn were the same. They don't mean to be rude. Just *appreciative*." She flashed the railroaders a big smile. The men, caught staring, frowned at their coffee cups. "Seems like the welcoming committee is here," she said. "How about some introductions?"

Cordelia *tsk-tsk*ed. "Maggie, what on earth—?"

"This isn't Philadelphia, Cordy," Maggie said, and Cordelia winced—she detests being called Cordy. "You're out West now."

The railroaders chuckled and slid sidelong looks at Maggie and her mischievous grin. Also at her bosom, about to burst out of her tight shirtwaist.

Evidently enjoying the attention, Maggie told them her name. "These gals are my friends. They can introduce themselves, and then you'll excuse us, please, if we eat our dinner."

The men grinned and nodded.

Cordelia shot daggers at Maggie. "My name is Cordelia, not Cordy," she announced. The men gaped at her. I'll bet they'd never seen a flapper up close. "And as you no doubt heard, I am from Philadelphia."

I glanced at Emmy, waiting for her to say something, but Emmy was cutting into a veal chop and ignoring the whole scene. My mind was blank as a stone. I couldn't think of anything clever to say, and I was afraid I'd say something dumb if I tried. I stated my name and where I was from and let it go at that.

Emmy set down her knife and fork and glared at the

railroaders. "I'm Emmy, and I'm also from Kansas. We're nice girls, and we're here to work. Same as you are."

I thought Emmy was very brave to speak up. Sending that letter to Carl must have given her courage. But then, to everyone's consternation, she burst into tears.

The men looked shamefaced, except for a good-looking boy with blazing blue eyes and light brown hair that curled down over his collar. He spoke up. "Ladies, we do apologize sincerely. It's true—we always come down to see the new Harvey Girls, soon as they arrive. One of our local customs. Not because we intend to be rude and insulting, but because we're genuinely curious about the young ladies who suddenly find themselves in our midst."

He went on about how the boys probably hadn't learned their manners as well as their mothers wished, but that they respected us and promised not to say or do anything more to make us uncomfortable.

"By the way, my name is Gus," he said at the end of his speech, and nodded to the other men. One by one they said their names—Tom, Mickey, Stan, a couple of others—then followed him out of the lunchroom. Each one had left a quarter under his saucer, a large, apologetic tip.

Mrs. McCreary, who'd come to see what was transpiring, stood hands on hips, shaking her head and watching them go. "Well, now, that's a first! They may be a mite rough around the edges, but at heart they're hardworking and decent boys. A good bunch."

"The one who spoke up is certainly very good-looking," Cordelia said, now that she'd calmed down.

"I thought he was full of baloney," Emmy said, and that shocked us all, because she never talks that way.

Then Mrs. McCreary lectured us about Harvey Girls not engaging in conversations with customers, even when we're off-duty. We are to be polite. We are to smile. We are to answer questions briefly. But we do not flirt! Mr. Lawrence is very strict about that. And if we want to go out on a date with a railroad man, we have to ask Mr. Lawrence for permission.

"Not like the manager over in Vaughn," Mrs. McCreary added sternly. "Are you listening, Maggie?"

Maggie nodded.

"Good." Mrs. McCreary turned and left.

"Don't mind her," Gladys said. "She sounds tough, but she's a softy. Just get her talking about her little girl, Faye! Her husband died of Spanish flu when poor little Faye was just a few months old."

Emmy asked where the little girl is now, and Gladys said, "With Mrs. McCreary's mother," and then hushed us, because Mrs. McCreary was looking our way.

In the dining room, girls in crisp black-and-white uniforms moved efficiently among the tables, serving the regular customers. I suggested that we go up to our rooms and unpack. The others agreed, but first we stepped outside again. The sun was going down, spreading a wash of orange across the western horizon, the most spectacular sunset I've ever seen. We watched until the sun disappeared, the orange turned to purple, and a million stars filled the sky.

Tuesday, July 13th

MAGGIE IS IN TROUBLE ALREADY. MRS. MCCREARY lined us up this morning and checked our faces for makeup. We all passed the "clean" test, but then she walked behind us and patted each of us on the rear.

Maggie was not wearing a corselet.

"You know the rule!" Mrs. McCreary said.

"But it's too hot for a corselet!" Maggie complained.

"Harvey Girls are ladies, and ladies do not walk around with jiggling bottoms," Mrs. McCreary reminded her. "Now go upstairs and get properly dressed."

Thursday, July 15th

You might think that, being out in the middle of nowhere, the Belén Harvey House would be a quiet place. It isn't. Freight trains rumble through at all hours of the day and night, although only one passenger train—the one we came on—is a meal train. That doesn't mean we aren't busy. The railroaders get their meals at cut-rate, and they keep us hopping. This isn't the only restaurant in town, but everybody says the Harvey House is far and away the best.

The Harvey standard doesn't vary from one place to the next, so the way of doing things in Belén is the same as it is in Emporia, and at every other Harvey House. But in other ways everything here is new and different.

A few dark-haired, dark-eyed girls work in the kitchen—Alicia, Maria, Susana—and they speak Spanish to each other and English to everyone else. They don't have foreign accents, like the German chefs do. They're friendly, but they are local girls and don't live in the upstairs rooms with the rest of us, so there's not much chance to get acquainted.

During a brief lull before the lunch rush, I asked Alicia, the salad girl, why she works in the kitchen, and wouldn't she rather be a waitress where she'd make more money from tips?

Alicia was shredding cabbage for coleslaw and reached for another head. "The Fred Harvey Company doesn't hire us to work as Harvey Girls. White girls only," she said. "They want blue-eyed blonds."

She used to dream of being a Harvey Girl, she said. The gardener—the man in the straw hat watering the flowers—is her uncle, and her father and two older brothers work for the railroad. They've told her over and over that most railroaders are white men who say they don't want to be waited on by "Mexican" girls.

"So we work in the kitchen." She set aside the grater, grabbed a big onion and a big knife, and in no time at all she'd chopped that onion into tiny pieces.

"That doesn't seem fair!" I said. "But are you Mexican or Spanish?"

"Neither one," she said. Her family has lived here for generations, since long before the territory became a state, and that makes her a New Mexican. "I don't dream about being a Harvey Girl anymore," she said. "I want to be a nurse someday." She glanced at the clock above the door to the dining room and attacked another onion.

After the noonday crowd clears out, we take turns eating lunch in the employees' lunchroom, which doubles as a storage room. Strangely, there's an upright piano buried beneath items that aren't called for every day, like a couple of ice-cream makers.

Alicia has her afternoon break at the same time I have mine, and today she asked if I wanted to go with her to buy paraffin. Her mother was making peach jam and needed paraffin for sealing the jars. Her home isn't far, she said. We'd be back in plenty of time to get ready for the dinner train.

We started down Becker Avenue, the road heading west from the depot. It had rained hard during the night, and the dusty street was now mud. Trucks and autos splashed through the puddles. We picked our way past a row of small shops, the Cutoff Café, and two hotels, the Belén Hotel and the Central. Mud sucked at my shoes.

A horse and wagon rolled by, and the driver called out to Alicia and waved. "My *tío*," she said and waved back. "My uncle."

Next it was the Sanitary Milk and Cream truck, delivering blocks of ice from Becker's ice plant to customers up and down the avenue. The driver honked and waved.

"Another *tío*? I asked.

She shook her head. "My cousin's husband."

Everywhere I looked, something was named Becker. Alicia said Mr. John Becker owns several businesses, bought the first automobile in Belén, and founded the first bank.

"Must be awfully rich," I said.

"The whole family is. He came here from Germany. You'll probably wait on him one of these days. Since

Mrs. Becker died, he eats breakfast at the Harvey House almost every morning."

She said he orders two eggs—soft-boiled on Monday, sunny-side-up on Tuesday, poached on Wednesday, scrambled on Thursday, and a cheese omelet on Friday—plus one slice of toast, buttered but not too much, with English marmalade on the side. "I always cook his eggs, because he says I'm the only one who knows how to make them the way he likes them."

He drinks a cup of coffee while he's waiting for his eggs and has a second cup while he reads his newspaper. Saturday, she said, he treats himself to our special little orange pancakes, and he doesn't come for breakfast on Sunday. He brings his family for dinner after church.

Becker Avenue ends at Main Street where it's joined by Dalies Avenue, named for Mrs. Becker's nephew, Paul Dalies, who manages Mr. Becker's bank. Where the roads meet there's a flourmill owned by John Becker, and across from that is Becker's Mercantile, a department store that sells practically anything you can think of. While Alicia looked for paraffin, I wandered through the store. Besides groceries, I noticed all kinds of clothing, shoes, baby things, furniture, and household supplies, and also hardware, lumber, animal feed, and tools of all sizes. Back in a far corner I discovered a selection of wooden coffins. Everything a person might need from birth to death.

Before we left, I bought a straw hat with a wide brim

to keep my face from getting sunburned, and a notebook and pencil that fit in my pocket so I can jot things down as I observe them and won't forget them later.

We turned down a mud-caked road into a neighborhood of small houses. There are no lawns, just patches of weeds, but lots of flower gardens. The houses don't resemble any brick or stone or clapboard house I've seen in Kansas.

Alicia said they're built of adobe, bricks made of clay and straw, and the thick walls stay cool in summer, warm in winter. "My *abuelo*—my grandpa—built our house."

Two little boys sat on the front step eating peaches, the juice running down their chins. They regarded me curiously with big brown eyes. "Harvey Girl?" the older one asked, and Alicia laughed and answered, "*Sí*. Her name is Kitty."

It *was* cool inside the house, except in the kitchen, where her mother was stirring a pot of simmering peach jam. Her grandmother was pulling glass jars out of a kettle of boiling water and lining them up on dish-towels. They switched from Spanish to English when Alicia introduced me, and asked where I was from and how many brothers and sisters I had.

On the way back, we walked up Main Street to look at the posters outside the Central Theater. *The Black Pirate* is playing, starring Douglas Fairbanks. I've already seen it with Maudie, but I told Alicia I wouldn't mind seeing it again.

We turned toward the railroad tracks and passed a drugstore, a pool hall, and a dingy little café. "Almost everything you'd find in a city, just not so much noise and traffic. Much nicer, don't you think?" Alicia looked at me, smiling.

"Oh, yes, much nicer," I said. She was so friendly, so obviously proud of her town and wanting me to like it, that I had to fib.

I'm getting used to fibbing: *No, I'm not homesick,* and now, *Yes, this dusty little village in the middle of nowhere is much nicer than a bustling city with paved streets and tall buildings and streetcars.*

There was barely time to knock the mud off my shoes—the next time I'm at Becker's Mercantile I must remember to buy some black Shinola—and change into my dinner uniform. The five o'clock meal train was already barreling toward Belén.

Saturday, July 17th

INDIANS! I'VE SEEN MY FIRST INDIANS! THEY COME HERE on Saturdays from Isleta Pueblo, a few miles north of here between Belén and Albuquerque, to sell their pottery and jewelry. Gladys has a silver-and-turquoise ring that a customer bought from one of the Indian men and left her as a tip, obviously enchanted by Gladys's dazzling smile and infectious laugh. She gets bigger tips with that smile than anybody else does.

At the newsstand I bought a postcard of an Indian woman in her native dress, an embroidered skirt and thick leggings. She's sitting in front of a wall, surrounded by pots, and decorating one of them with traditional designs. Enrique says many Isleta Indians work at the Alvarado in Albuquerque. I'll send the card to Maudie and tell her to save her money and come out here, and I will be her tour guide.

How did I ever get the idea that because there's only one meal train a day stopping here, it was going to be easy? We're just as busy as we were in Emporia, but it's a different kind of busy—railroad men and local people, coming in all day long. We're still not allowed to sit down when we're not serving customers—not that there's ever a chance to break that rule. Belén might be a one-horse town, but everybody loves a good time. Tonight a crowd of young people, most of them about my age and dressed up for a night out with their dates, gathered at the lunch counter and ordered pie á la mode and coffee, adding so much cream that the pitchers were soon empty and we hurried to refill them. Meanwhile, in the dining

room, two families were having birthday parties, and a baseball team from the nearby village of Peralta was celebrating a victory. Mr. Lawrence carried in tray after tray loaded with platters of steaks. When it was all over, somebody suggested getting permission to take in the late show at the Central, but I was too tired, even for Douglas Fairbanks. Almost too tired to write in my diary, until I remembered Mr. White and his advice to me: *Keep notes. Write everything down.*

Sunday, July 18th

WHENEVER I SEE ALICIA IN THE KITCHEN, SHE GREETS me in Spanish and then tells me what I'm supposed to say in reply. She pronounces the words carefully and says my accent is good, but I don't know if I should believe her.

So I'm beginning a new list:

SPANISH WORDS AND PHRASES

BUENOS DÍAS: good morning
BUENAS TARDES: good afternoon
BUENAS NOCHES: good night
POR FAVOR: please

GRACIAS: thank you
DE NADA: you're welcome
¿CÓMO ESTÁ USTED?: how are you?
MUY BIEN, GRACIAS: very well, thank you
TÍO: uncle
ABUELO: grandfather; *ABUELITA:* little grandmother
RÍO GRANDE: "Big River." It's not wide or deep, but it is long, beginning up in Colorado and flowing through New Mexico and Texas all the way to the Gulf of Mexico. *Do not* say "Rio Grande River."
MANZANO (as in name of mountains): apple
HUEVO: egg (to come: words for fried, boiled, etc.)
ALBÓNDIGAS: little meatballs

One of our specialties is soup with these little meatballs. Alicia says the chef at La Castañeda (the hotel in Las Vegas, New Mexico; the mark over the *n* is called a *tilde*) takes credit for putting it on the Harvey House menu, although anybody's *abuelita* in Belén could show the cooks how to make it.

Alicia has promised to teach me more "kitchen Spanish."

Tuesday, July 20th

Cordelia is in a foul mood. It's been twelve days since she mailed the engagement ring back to Walter from the Emporia post office and we celebrated her "disengagement." She hadn't heard from him until today, when the telegraph operator over at the depot brought her a telegram. Cordelia glanced at the yellow Western Union envelope, folded it up, and stuck it in her apron pocket.

"Aren't you going to open it?" I asked, and Cordelia gave that little shrug that means *I couldn't care less.*

"It's from Walter. It's not like I don't already know what he has to say. I'll look at it later."

If someone sent me a telegram, I'd take thirty seconds to duck behind the coffee urn and read it on the spot. But Cordelia, cool as a cucumber, went right on serving lunch to customers. It wasn't until we were through with the lunch service and had gone up to our room that she finally opened the yellow envelope. I hovered around, pretending not to be the least bit interested—*Ho hum, it's no concern of mine*—while she kicked off her shoes and rolled down her stockings.

She removed the telegram, smoothed it out with excruciating slowness, glanced at it, and passed it over to me.

DEAREST CORDELIA

HEARTBROKEN YOU RETURNED RING STOP
PLEASE RECONSIDER AND COME HOME
SOONEST STOP

ALL MY LOVE WALTER

"It doesn't sound as though he even read my letter. And if he did, he doesn't take me seriously." She wadded up the telegram, tossed it toward the wastebasket, and missed.

I suggested that maybe we should write another letter, but Cordelia shook her head. "Better to ignore him."

I hope the letter I wrote to Carl for Emmy will work out, but it's been a while since Emmy mentioned him. I don't want to bring up the subject and make her feel bad. It's not always easy to figure out how Emmy feels. Not like Maggie, for instance, who tells everybody her state of mind whether they want to know or not.

We were in the dining room, the dinner train due in a few minutes, when Mrs. McCreary came looking for Cordelia and told her she had a long-distance telephone call from Reading, Pennsylvania. The telephone is in the manager's office. Mrs. McCreary laid a sympathetic hand on Cordelia's shoulder. She probably thought it was something serious, illness or even death, but I figured it must be poor, rejected Walter calling about his broken heart.

Cordelia threw me a worried look, and I signaled that I'd finish setting up her tables. This is my first week in the dining room, and I double-checked to make sure everything was perfect, silverware "shined and lined"—set exactly half an inch from the edge of the table—and starched napkins standing stiffly at attention. A few minutes later Cordelia was back, her mouth pinched tight.

"Mummy," she said shortly. I was under the impression that nothing ever made Cordelia cry, but she seemed close to it now, she was so mad. "Bawled me out for treating Walter so badly." It seems Mrs. Hart has the wedding all planned and threatened to disown Cordelia if she doesn't come home immediately. "Mummy says she'll cut me off without a cent."

Although we've never discussed it, I guessed she'd been getting an allowance from her mother all along. "What did you say?" I asked.

"I said we had a bad connection, and then I hung up." Cordelia tried to sound flippant, but it didn't quite come off. "Kitty, I'm not going back, and that's that. If I have to, I'll stay here until I die."

A mile out of town, the westbound train hooted. I squeezed her hand and held it for a second, and then we hurried to our stations and prepared to greet the customers about to pour through the door.

Thursday, July 22nd

I've tried to convince Cordelia to explore the town with me, but she says she's not interested. I think she's bothered by the situation with her mother and Walter more than she lets on. I haven't asked questions, even though I'm dying to.

Emmy is much more curious about Belén. She's also more adventuresome than I expected. Opal and Pearl, two sisters from Illinois who were schoolteachers before they became Harvey Girls, told us about Belén Lake, only a five-minute walk from the Harvey House. The sisters have been dating two ranchers from Mountainair, and they say that most of the courting takes place at that lake when the boys come over for a visit.

Yesterday Emmy and I went to investigate the lake. It's more like a big pond. The water in it comes from irrigation ditches in Mr. Becker's alfalfa fields. It was such a hot day that it would have felt good to take a dip, but I didn't think to pack a bathing suit when I left home. Emmy says she doesn't know how to swim, and the idea of appearing in public in a skimpy costume makes her blush.

Today we explored in the opposite direction, to the rail yard—where the cars are uncoupled and recoupled, depending on their destination—and the roundhouse, where the locomotives are serviced and repaired. Maggie came, too. She's always looking for a chance to meet railroaders.

On the far side of the depot is a long, low building with a sign on the roof: "AT&SF Reading Room." A few men were lounging on the shady porch that faces the tracks, and they waved and called out as we walked by. Maggie, naturally, waved and hollered back. I'm surprised she didn't go over and start a conversation. Emmy looked the other way. As usual, I didn't know quite what to do.

As we neared the roundhouse, a railroader I recognized as one of our regular customers came out to meet us, and I could see from the way he stood with his feet apart and his arms folded over his chest that we wouldn't be going any farther.

"What are you girls doing here?" he asked. "This is no place for ladies."

"We were hoping for a tour," Maggie said, flashing a bright smile. Maggie knows how to flirt better than anybody, although Cordelia is more subtle. "We're just so curious about how you boys spend your time. For instance, why do you call it a roundhouse when it's not round?"

The railroader rubbed his stubbly chin. "Well, miss, that's just tradition, because in the old days they were round. Railroaders love tradition."

He explained how it works: A locomotive is driven onto a huge turntable, which moves it to one of the empty bays, thirty of them arranged in a semicircle. When the job is finished, the engine is hauled back out onto the turntable and moved so that it's facing in the direction it's supposed to go.

He made it clear we were also supposed to turn around and go back the way we came. There would be no tour of the roundhouse.

A freight train rumbled by as we were walking. Maggie made us stop and count the cars as it passed. "Brings good luck," she said when sixty cars had disappeared down the track. "But it's good only for freights. If you count the cars of a passenger train, you'll hear news of a death."

Emmy was skeptical. "You don't believe that, do you?"

Maggie swore she did. There are a lot of superstitions among railroaders, she said. For instance, if you want to get rid of a fella, you lay his sock on the track, and when a train runs over it, your fella will leave. "I tried it in Vaughn, and it worked," Maggie said.

Emmy said she wasn't looking to get rid of anybody, just the opposite, and besides, if you do manage to get hold of a boy's sock, how do you make him stick around? This was the first I'd heard Emmy make even an indirect reference to Carl in some time.

"You know what I think?" Maggie asked. "I think you ought to forget about Carl. You write to him, what, three, maybe four times a week?"

"Twice a week," Emmy admitted. "Sometimes just once."

"And do you ever hear back?"

"I've had a couple of letters. Short ones."

"You're too good for him, Emmy!" Maggie declared. Exactly what I'd been thinking. "There's plenty of nice boys right here in Belén, and I've seen how they look at you. You'd have half a dozen of them lined up to talk to you, if you'd just give them half a chance."

Emmy walked along between us, staring down at the ground, not saying anything. I wished Maggie hadn't started this.

"We've been sweethearts since we were twelve," Emmy said finally. "He's a habit—like chewing gum. I used to chew gum all the time. It was the hardest thing for me to quit when I came to work as a Harvey Girl." She smiled wanly. "But you're right. I'm not going to write again until I hear from him."

"Well, hooray!" Maggie said.

Will Emmy keep her resolve? Stay tuned to this station for further news.

Friday, July 23rd

I asked Mrs. McCreary about the Reading Room. She says the east-west railroad line and the north-south line cross in Belén. Over a hundred trains may go through in twenty-four hours. Some stop here and change crews. A lot of railroaders live in Belén, but many don't, and the Reading Room with shelves of books and magazines is a place for them to rest and wash up. About once a month the company sponsors an educational lecture or a musical program for the whole community.

"Last spring a professor from the university in Albuquerque came and talked about local history, and half the town showed up to hear him," Mrs. McCreary said.

I asked if I could go there to write in my diary—it's hard, not having a desk in our room—but she said no. And when I asked if I could borrow books if I promised to return them to the proper place on the shelf, she said no to that, too: "The men need a place of their own."

When I said I thought we girls also need a place of our own, she looked at me as though that comment did not deserve a reply.

NOTES ON RAILROADING

Big Mike: *nickname for type of freight locomotive, based on number of wheels and pistons. Strange and interesting fact: "Mike" is short for "Mikado," engines originally built for the Japanese railway.*

Crew: *five or six men per train, whether passenger or freight.*

Conductor: *man in charge, keeps track of everything, makes sure cars go where they're supposed to. (Mrs. McCreary's husband was a conductor before he died of influenza.)*

Engineer: *watches for signals, keeps his hand on the throttle; speeds up, slows down, or stops, depending on signals.*

Fireman: *makes sure fire is burning properly and there's enough water in boiler. Coal used to be shoveled by hand; hard, dirty job; now mechanical stokers feed coal.*

Brakeman: *rides in locomotive with engineer and fireman; 2nd brakeman in cupola on top of caboose. Throws switches sending train onto another track; couples and uncouples cars that we hear crashing and banging when we're trying to sleep.*

Flagman: *signals engineer with flag or lantern to slow, stop, or proceed.*

Sunday, July 25th

Six weeks as a Harvey Girl now completed. I'm glad I made the decision and *very* glad I'm not back in Leavenworth selling shoes.

The kitchen stays open all night for railroaders who come by wanting coffee and something to eat, and there's always a cook and a kitchen helper to take care of them. We're allowed to go down to the employees' lunchroom after hours and have a piece of pie or cake.

Last night Max, the baker, treated us to cinnamon buns. Cordelia said they compare favorably to the sticky buns she used to buy at the Reading Terminal Market in Philadelphia when she was a student at the conservatory. We listened, fascinated, to stories about her days in Philly, attending concerts when Leopold Stokowski conducted the orchestra and taking the train down to the Jersey shore on weekends in the summer.

"If I were there right now," Cordelia said, "I'd be sunbathing on the sand and diving into the ocean to cool off. In the evening I'd be riding up and down the Atlantic City boardwalk in a rolling chair, and eating saltwater taffy after I watched it being pulled on big machines."

To us Midwesterners, Atlantic City sounded like another world.

The cooks listened, too, but didn't say much. Viktor is from Vienna, and Max is from some little town in Bavaria, and their German accents are so thick you could cut them with a knife. Both are about thirty years old—the age at which men stop being boys, according to Cordelia—and they live at the Central Hotel. They came to the U.S. after the World War to work for the Harvey Company. They put in hard, long hours, just like we do, and the rumor is that they're paid really, really well. There's not much in Belén to spend money on, so they save up their leave for trips to Chicago or Los Angeles or New York.

Cordelia flirts madly with Viktor, although he's not good-looking. I don't think this flirtation will go anywhere. She flirted just as madly with Klaus when we were in Emporia. It's impossible to tell what Viktor is thinking. Cordelia speaks German with him, or at least pretends to. She says her grammar is terrible, but she knows a lot of German words and strings them together and hopes they make some kind of sense. Max laughs at her, and Viktor gives her bemused looks.

She studied German at boarding school. "A lot of my relatives speak German," she said, and it surprised me when she said that she has a lot of relatives, because her mother and Lorenzo are the only ones she talks about. She's never mentioned her father. I don't know where her father lives, or if he's remarried, or even if he's still alive.

I wonder if he's a bootlegger, dealing in illegal booze. It's not the kind of thing I can ask her.

Wednesday, July 28th

TOMORROW IS MY SEVENTEENTH BIRTHDAY. SO FAR nobody has found out that I'm still too young to be a Harvey Girl, but at least I'm a year closer.

Every week I get a letter from Daddy, who always writes that everything is fine, and it's as though I'm just visiting Aunt May and Uncle Hal and my cousins up in Atchison and will be back home in a few days. Today a much longer letter arrived, wishing me a happy birthday and enclosing a check: a dollar for every year. Seventeen dollars! During my afternoon break I went to Mr. Becker's bank and opened an account. I also took a box of coins, six dollars and thirty cents in tips that I've been squirreling away, and deposited most of that, too. Soon I'll be paid a regular wage, fifty dollars a month.

If I were back home, Maudie and I would be cooking up a birthday celebration, maybe having a picnic down by the river or seeing a picture show. Mother used to invite Maudie and some of my friends for ice cream and cake on the Saturday afternoon closest to the twenty-ninth.

Last year Gramma Blair gave a tea in honor of my sixteenth birthday and invited a bunch of old ladies in hats and gloves. It must have been ninety-five in the shade. I was sweltering in my first pair of silk stockings, and my new dotted swiss shirtwaist was sticking to my back. Maudie had curled my hair in rags so I could wear it in an updo for the first time, but it had already begun to droop.

Gramma's hired girl, Josephine, passed around silver platters of tiny sandwiches, cucumber slices and bits of watercress on white bread with the crusts removed and cut in triangles. Then she carried in a sponge cake slathered with white icing, like the ones she's made me every year for as long as I can remember, with a little bunch of flowers in a jar stuck in the hole in the center of the cake. The ladies *ooh*ed and clapped, and I went around and let them kiss my cheek and tell me what a fine young lady I had become and how proud my grandmother was of me.

Wouldn't those dear old lavender-scented ladies drop their jaws if they could see me now!

Thursday, July 29th—My birthday!

In the mail today: a birthday card from Maudie, who writes that her job at the funeral parlor is okay, but she'd rather be someplace else; a funny card from Jimmy, who signed it "XOX"; a card from Howie enclosing a five-dollar bill; a pair of sterling silver napkin rings from Gramma Blair with a note saying they're for my hope chest; and a package from Mother with a long cotton nightie, three pairs of black rayon stockings, six pairs of plain white drawers, and a box of hankies.

I don't even want to show my new undies to Cordelia, who trots around in peach-colored silk step-ins and sleeps in black satin pajamas.

I'll write a thank-you note to Gramma Blair, not mentioning that I don't have a hope chest and have no use for silver napkin rings. And I'll send a postcard to Howie, telling him what I intend to do with the five dollars: buy a camera.

Whenever one of the Belén Harvey Girls has a birthday, Max, the baker, makes her a cake. Max asked what my favorite is, and I told him about Josephine's sponge cakes and how I used to watch her pour the batter into a special pan with a tube in the center.

"You're in luck," he said. "I've got the right kind of pan."

During the slow part of the afternoon, before we'd begun setting up for the dinner train, Mrs. McCreary laid out plates and forks. The railroaders who came around to look over the new crop of Harvey Girls when we first arrived somehow got wind that one of us was having a birthday. They showed up just as Max set the cake on the lunchroom counter and Mrs. McCreary was lighting the candles.

"Are we in time for the party?" asked the good-looking blue-eyed boy, Gus, who'd apologized for all of them that first day. He wasn't in his work clothes but wore a white shirt, crisp as the linen tablecloths. His hair was wet, as if he'd just washed it, and neatly combed.

"Just in time!" Gladys sang from behind the counter, so I suppose she's the one who told them it was my birthday.

"Make a wish!" Cordelia commanded.

I squeezed my eyes shut. What to wish for? *To be a Harvey Girl at the Grand Canyon? To be a journalist?* I wished for both and blew out all nineteen candles, telling myself the two extras were for luck. Max sliced the cake.

"Are the girls in the kitchen having any?" I asked. It bothered me that Alicia and the other kitchen girls weren't included. Max said he'd make sure they got some. He'd baked two cakes, so there'd be enough for everybody.

Then—and this was a surprise—Gus stood up and recited a poem:

Oh, the pretty Harvey Girl beside my chair,
A fairer maiden I shall never see,
[Gus gestured toward me dramatically]
She was winsome, she was neat,
She was gloriously sweet,
And she certainly was very good to me.

He bowed deeply, everybody laughed and clapped, and I must have turned five different shades of red.

Enrique, the newsstand manager, came around and wished me happy birthday, and then Mr. Lawrence said I didn't have to stay to set up, as long as I was back and in my dinner uniform before the five o'clock train was due.

I thanked him and ducked out of the lunchroom, intending to go up to my room. I didn't have anything in mind, except maybe writing about it all in my diary.

Gus followed me to the foot of the stairs. "When you've changed your clothes," he said, "we could take a walk."

I stared at him. *A walk? He wants me to go for a walk?* Until he recited that poem today, I wasn't sure he'd ever really noticed me, but there he was, gazing up at me, smiling.

I smiled back. "I'll be right down," I said.

Friday, July 30th

I HARDLY KNOW WHERE TO BEGIN. IT'S LIKE I'VE BEEN ON one of those carnival rides where you get turned upside down and swirled around, and even when you finally stagger off, not knowing which end is up, you don't regret it for a single minute. That's how I feel.

Gus and I didn't walk far, just around to the back of the Harvey House where the cooks and kitchen helpers go to smoke. We sat down on a wooden bench in the shade of some old cottonwood trees, and Gus stretched his long legs out in front of him. He was wearing boots polished to a high shine. I felt self-conscious, not knowing what to say, but I mentioned the cottonwoods back home, along the Missouri.

"They grow where they can get their roots down to water," Gus said. He explained that the Belén Harvey House was designed by an architect in Chicago who didn't know that the water table near the Rio Grande is very high. Nobody in Belén has a cellar—except the Harvey House. "Guess they don't use it much," Gus said, laughing. "Can't store a whole lot in a wet cellar."

His last name is Becker, and I thought it was interesting that Gus has a name that's so common here. We were looking at the east end of Becker Avenue with the Becker Mercantile at the west end. When I mentioned the coincidence, he told me that he is indeed a relation of the Becker family. "Maybe not distant enough for old John Becker. You might even say I'm a black sheep." Arguments with his father had led Gus to leave home and come to Belén to work for his uncle. When that didn't pan out, he took a job with the railroad as an engine wiper. His job is to clean the locomotives when they come into the roundhouse for service. "I know Big Mike as well as I know my own hand."

I said I'd add "engine wiper" to the list of crew in my notebook, and Gus wanted to know why I was keeping such a list in a notebook.

I explained that I plan to be a journalist someday, but my father didn't have the money to send both me and my brother to college. So I'd applied on a whim to be a Harvey Girl and was surprised when I was hired, and now here I am. I told him about Daddy's haberdashery and Howie who's going to college instead of me. I talked more than usual. Maybe it was the way he looked at me, as though every word I said were interesting and important.

"I counted nineteen candles on your cake," Gus said. "Are you really nineteen?"

"Eighteen," I said. I didn't want to lie to him, but I didn't want to admit the truth, so I settled for a smaller lie.

"Me, too," said Gus. He has crinkles around his eyes when he smiles.

I asked about the poem he'd recited, and he told me a poet named S. E. Kiser had written it. Gus said he sometimes writes poetry. "I'm not much good at it, though. I'm better at memorizing what somebody else has written. It's something I've been doing since I was a little kid."

Gus began to recite:

A bunch of the boys were whooping it up in the Malamute saloon;
The kid that handles the music-box was hitting a jag-time tune;
Back of the bar, in a solo game, sat Dangerous Dan McGrew,
And watching his luck was his light-o'-love, the lady that's known as Lou.

"That's by Robert Service. It's his best-known poem, 'The Shooting of Dan McGrew.' I know the whole thing by heart."

I don't know how long we talked, but it must have been too long, because I heard Cordelia calling my name. I jumped up and hollered back.

"Do you know what time it is?" she cried. The dinner train was due any minute, I wasn't ready, and Mr. Lawrence was mad as hops.

"Happy birthday, Kitty!" Gus called as I hurried off.

I raced up the stairs and threw on my dinner uniform, hoping I had the apron straps fastened the right way, and raced back down just as we heard the three-minute signal from the five o'clock train. My friends had set up everything for me, but I'd broken two BIG rules: I had gone out with a railroad man without the manager's permission—Mr. Lawrence had given me an extra hour or so off, but that didn't include approval to spend that free hour with a railroader—and I was late. I was shaking when the passengers crowded in pell-mell, as they always did, but I made it through.

They haven't said anything yet, but I know I'm going to catch thunder from Mr. Lawrence and probably Mrs. McCreary, too. That hour with Gus Becker could cost me my job.

Later, Friday night

I'm in Dutch, but at least I haven't been fired—just a stern lecture this afternoon from Mr. Lawrence about never, never, *never* going on a date without his permission. I tried to explain that I hadn't gone anywhere on an actual date, we'd just stepped outside for a little while, I hadn't even left the property with Gus, and all we did was *talk*.

But Mr. Lawrence snapped his fingers in front of my eyes and said loudly in my face, not quite shouting, "Listen to me when I speak to you, Miss Evans! Do not argue! You will obey the rules, each and every one of them, or you will be dismissed! Do I make myself clear?"

"Yes, Mr. Lawrence," I whispered. I'm not used to people getting mad and yelling at me, and it was all I could do to keep from bursting into tears.

Then I had a talking-to from Mrs. McCreary, who said she was disappointed that I showed such little sense of responsibility for a girl my age. I half-expected her to say then that she'd found out I'm not really nineteen, but she didn't. I apologized over and over and promised I'd never do anything like that again.

She'd let me slide this time, she said, because it was my birthday. Then she gave me a little pat on the shoulder and said she was sure I'll work out just fine, that I'll be an excellent Harvey Girl. I'd just started to breathe normally again, when at the last moment she turned and gave me a worried look.

"Everybody knows the Beckers, of course—solid German immigrants, excellent businessmen, salt of the earth." She paused. "Gus is a bit different, though. Never fit in with the rest of the Beckers—doesn't seem to have any interest in the family businesses. Kind of a wild card with some ideas of his own. Just be mindful, that's all, Kitty."

She walked away, leaving me with a head full of questions.

Saturday, July 31st

I TOOK THE FIVE DOLLARS HOWIE SENT ME AND BOUGHT a Kodak Brownie box camera and a few rolls of film at Becker's Mercantile. The clerk was Miss Lucie Becker, daughter of Mr. John. She showed me how to use the camera. You just hold it at your waist, look down into the viewfinder to see what you're getting, and push a button. It's very simple. When I finish a roll of snapshots, I'm to take the film to Miss Lucie, and she will send it out to have it developed and printed. She suggested that I buy an album and some photo corners to mount the pictures, and I did that, too.

I can hardly wait to get started. I consider this an important step in my career as a journalist, and I'm sure Mr. White would approve. I showed off my new camera to the other girls, and we went right out to the garden and took pictures of each other, posing in our Harvey Girl uniforms.

I intend to carry the camera with me and take pictures of scenes around Belén. I've also offered to take snapshots of each of my friends and have prints made so they can send them home to their families. But when I told Cordelia I'd be happy to take a picture of her to send to Walter, she looked at me, horrified.

"Just kidding!" I said.

"Not the least bit funny, Kitty," she said. "Please don't mention his name to me again."

Monday, August 2nd

Mrs. McCreary sent me to wait on the white-haired gentleman who comes here every morning except Sunday and sits at the same table, eats two eggs cooked a different way each day, and reads his newspaper. He left a quarter tip, which I gave to Alicia. She tried to give it back to me, but I made her keep it. "You cook the *huevos* exactly the way Mr. Becker wants them, and you deserve it."

"Gracias," she said.

"De nada," I replied.

"He looks lonely," I said to Mrs. McCreary after he'd gone.

"Yes, I suppose he is," she said, and told me the

story. His wife, Anna, died a few years ago. She was a nice German lady; John had traveled to a German settlement in Wisconsin and brought her here to Belén as a bride. Her sister, Johanna Vielstich, came with her and married John's brother Fred. A slew of Vielstich relatives all moved to Belén. The whole family learned English and Spanish and worked in the Mercantile.

Anna could sell ice cubes to Eskimos, Mrs. McCreary said. Anna once talked Mrs. McCreary into buying a winter coat for her little girl that was much too big for her, convincing her that the child would grow into it. "She did, eventually, but Faye always hated that coat."

Gladys told another story. "Rumor's going around that there might soon be a new Mrs. Becker. Ina, his housekeeper. That's what the gossips say. They also say that Lucie and her brother, Hans, and the rest of the family aren't too pleased."

I might have to start another section in my notebook for Local Gossip. That would certainly include Gus Becker.

Tuesday, August 3rd

ALICIA HAS GIVEN ME A LIST OF SPANISH WORDS TO STUDY:

KITCHEN SPANISH: LESSON 2

LA COCINA: kitchen

EL COCINERO: cook

LA ESTUFA: stove

EL HORNO: oven

LA OLLA: saucepan

LA CAMARERA: waitress

LA MESA: table

EL CERDO: pork

EL CORDERO: lamb

EL POLLO: chicken

EL PESCADO: fish

ASADO: roasted

ESCALFADO: poached

FRITO: fried

HERVIDO: boiled

LAS CHULETAS: chops

EL CHORIZO: sausage

EL TOCINO: bacon

EL JAMÓN: ham

EL PAVO: turkey

EL VASO: glass

LA SERVILLETA: napkin

EL CUCHILLO: knife

EL TENEDOR: fork

LA CUCHARA: spoon

EL PLATO: plate

EL PIMENTERO: pepper shaker

EL SALERO: saltshaker

LA TRUCHA: trout

EL SALMÓN: salmon

LA LECHUGA: lettuce

EL MAÍZ: corn

LOS FRIJOLES: beans

LA ZANAHORIA: carrot

LA PAPA: potato

LA CEBOLLA: onion

LA COL: cabbage

LA ESPINACA: spinach

EL TOMATE: tomato

Friday, August 6th

GUS HAS BEEN HERE TWICE SINCE MY BIRTHDAY, WHICH was a week ago. Both times he grinned and said hello, but Mrs. McCreary assigned me to the station at the other end of the counter, away from the railroaders. I think she did it on purpose. I just smiled and tried to pay attention to my customers on this end. I could feel my face heat up, and I'm glad I didn't have to wait on him and fumble my way through whatever he ordered. I tried not to look in his direction, but to concentrate on my work and not make any mistakes.

He came here again this morning, and this time my station was at the end of the lunchroom counter where the railroaders sit. I had to take his order, serve his breakfast, bring him a second order of toast, more butter, more jam—all the while pretending that he had not recited a poem on my birthday and we had not sat in the shade of a cottonwood and talked so long that I nearly ended up in serious trouble. As though none of that ever happened!

My fingers had turned into ten clumsy thumbs.

"Guess you've heard about the fiesta next weekend," he said when I wrote up his bill and gave it to him, facedown on a saucer.

I said I'd heard the salad girls talking about it in the kitchen: the Feast of Our Lady of Belén.

"You should go," Gus said. "You'll have a good time."

"Oh, I plan to."

"Good." He reached for his wallet to pay. "Save me a dance, will you, Kitty?" he said, loud enough for everyone to hear.

"Sure thing," I said, my face burning, and moved on

to the next customer. It was the railroader who'd turned us away from the roundhouse. "Good morning! What can I get you?"

"Black coffee and a cinnamon bun. And save me a dance, too, if you'd be so kind," he added, a twinkle in his eye.

I wonder if Gus will ask me to go for a walk with him again. I want to hear the rest of that poem about Dangerous Dan McGrew. At least that's my excuse.

Sunday, August 8th

HANS BECKER (MR. JOHN BECKER'S SON) AND HIS wife, Stella, celebrated their twenty-fifth wedding anniversary with a big dinner yesterday evening. During the afternoon Max finished decorating a three-tiered cake with a pair of tiny Kewpie dolls on top, and as soon as the five o'clock dinner train passengers were back on board, we began setting up the tables. Hans came by to look at the cake and make final arrangements. I overheard him telling Mr. Lawrence that the musician he had hired to serenade his wife had canceled at the last minute, and asked if the manager could suggest a substitute.

"Stella will be so disappointed if we don't have music," he said.

Mr. Lawrence was shaking his head and saying no, he didn't know of anybody offhand, when suddenly, in the middle of a sentence, he had a bright idea. "Come to think of it," he said, "one of our girls studied at a music conservatory back East."

Cordelia heard him. She stopped pleating starched linen napkins into fan shapes, and Mr. Lawrence introduced her to Mr. Hans Becker. Mr. Lawrence mentioned that there was a piano in the employees' lunchroom, and it could easily be moved into the dining room, if Miss Hart would consent to play a few songs.

I strained to hear the conversation. No telling what Cordelia would say.

What she said was, "Is that piano in tune?"

Kitchen boys were called to move the ice-cream makers and such off the piano, and Cordelia rippled through a couple of scales and tried a few chords. "The E-flat is missing," she said. "Otherwise, it's not too bad."

Cordelia and Hans Becker began discussing what kind of music Stella Becker would enjoy. A few minutes later Mr. Lawrence announced that Cordelia was being reassigned, and the rest of us would cover her station for the evening. Emmy and I finished folding the napkins while Cordelia vanished upstairs to change clothes and the kitchen boys rolled the piano into the dining room.

Minutes before the Beckers and their guests were expected, Cordelia strolled in. I hardly recognized her. She wore a slinky black gown, sleeveless and cut down to *here*; a little black cloche that covered her blond hair; and a blue feather boa slung over her shoulders. She'd made herself up with scarlet cupid's-bow lips and blue eye shadow, and she carried an ivory cigarette holder between her fingers, just like in the movies, except the cigarette wasn't lit.

All of us gawked while Cordelia spun the piano stool to the proper height, sat down, and began to play, fingers skimming over the keys. The music was smooth as silk. "It's been months since I've touched a piano," she said. Somehow she kept the cigarette holder clamped between her teeth.

Mr. Lawrence barreled out of the kitchen and stopped short, his eyes popping out of his head.

"Hi, Joe," Cordelia murmured in a sultry voice. "What would you like to hear?"

Nobody calls Mr. Lawrence "Joe." That alone was astonishing.

"Miss Hart!" he croaked. "This is outrageous! No Harvey Girl—"

"Just for tonight, Joe, I'm not a Harvey Girl," she purred and kept on playing, switching to a jazzy piece that Howie used to listen to on my parents' Victrola. "For the next couple of hours I'm Cordelia, an entertainer. When the party's over, I'll go back to being the proper waitress in the proper uniform." She flashed the manager a dazzling smile. "Just like Cinderella returning to sit among the ashes."

Mr. Lawrence's mouth opened and closed a couple of times, like a fish gasping for air. "At least put away that cigarette," he pleaded, nervously clasping and unclasping his hands. "Smoking is not allowed in any of the Harvey Eating Houses."

"I don't actually smoke, you know. Can't stand the taste, but I do like the look of it." Cordelia laid her cigarette holder on the music rack and concentrated on playing. The kitchen doors opened a crack, and the cooks peered in. The salad girls squeezed between them for a better view. Cordelia swung into something up-tempo, stomping out the beat with her high-heeled shoe.

"That's Scott Joplin!" cried Frank, the roast cook in charge of meat and fish. "'Maple Leaf Rag'!" The cooks began clapping.

A busboy who'd been stationed at the entrance rushed in to announce that the first of the Beckers' guests were arriving in their automobiles. Mrs. McCreary, who'd been arranging bouquets of flowers, signaled for us to go to our stations. Cordelia eased into something soft and sentimental.

Hans Becker is tall and thin like his father, always

dressed in a suit with a vest, but Stella is a butterball with two chins and a big bosom, and she was stuffed into a lavender satin dress with too many ruffles. Hans led her to the chair next to his at the head table. As soon as the guests were seated—there were about thirty—we began our service. We'd been instructed that the guests must not be rushed. They weren't about to catch a train, and they were to enjoy the luxury of an unhurried meal, beginning with the pineapple-and-strawberry fruit cup and continuing through each course to the anniversary cake at the end.

Everybody was curious about the talented pianist. Nobody recognized Cordelia as one of the Harvey Girls. Meanwhile, Cordelia just kept on playing. There seemed to be an endless supply of popular songs in her head, and she knew exactly which ones to play as the meal progressed.

The Harvey House dining room always remains open to the public, even when there is a big party like this one, and other customers who came in from time to time were seated at one of the unreserved tables or in the lunchroom. Nobody was in a hurry to leave. They all wanted to stick around and listen.

When Max, in his fresh baker's whites, presented the cake, Cordelia began to sing.

I love you truly, truly, dear. . . . Life with its sorrows . . . life with its tears. . . .

"That was sung at our wedding!" Stella cried tearfully. She leaned over and kissed her husband soundly and then rushed to hug Cordelia, who didn't miss a note.

In our room, when it was all over, Cordelia was triumphant. She'd taken off the slinky dress and cloche and was skipping around in her step-ins with the boa draped around her neck. "So you see, Kitty?" she crowed. "I can certainly get a job in a ritzy Hollywood cocktail lounge someday, don't you think?"

I was sure she could. "But how do you know all those songs? You didn't need sheet music for any of them!"

"If I hear it once, I can play it." She waved the twenty-five dollars Hans Becker had slipped her in an envelope after the dinner—half a month's wages. "Here's our train fare to Albuquerque! The first time we have a whole day off, we're on our way! What do you have to say to *that,* Miss Evans?"

"Ready when you are, Miss Hart!" I cried.

Tuesday, August 10th

THE PIANO PLAYER WITH THE BLUE FEATHER BOA IS THE talk of Belén. She has become a person of mystery. Customers keep asking Mr. Lawrence who she is and saying they want to hire her to play for their parties—especially if she wears that black dress. Hans Becker promised to keep it a secret that the pianist is a Harvey Girl, and Mr. Lawrence has made it plain to the waitresses and the kitchen staff that we're to keep mum. He's afraid he's broken an important rule in the Harvey Way and may have damaged his career. The piano has been moved back into the employees' lunchroom.

Mrs. McCreary hasn't said much about it, except to remark that it would have been more proper for Cordelia to wear a corselet. Cordelia is slim as a reed and doesn't jiggle. Mrs. McCreary says it's a matter of principle: a lady always wears a corselet.

Thursday, August 12th

ALICIA HAS BEEN TALKING FOR DAYS ABOUT THE BIG celebration this coming weekend, the fiesta in honor of Our Lady of Belén. August 15th is the Virgin Mary's special feast day, and a fiesta has been held here every year for more than a century. Alicia says it's the biggest social event of the year—bigger than Christmas—and everybody turns out for it. Visitors have started flocking in, filling up the two hotels.

It starts Saturday with a parade in the morning and a dance that evening. Following Sunday's mass at the Church of Our Lady of Belén, there will be a religious procession. The mission churches in tiny villages around Belén—like Jarales, a few miles to the south, and Los Chávez, to the north—and many businesses here in town enter floats in the parade and compete for prizes. There will be contests and entertainment on both days, and the fiesta ends with a dinner served in big open-sided tents called *carpas* that are being set up in the field near Becker's store.

Alicia's mother and the ladies of the church have planned what they'll serve at the fiesta. This is her description of some of the dishes they'll prepare. It's the same every year.

NEW MEXICAN SPECIALTIES

> CHILE, a long, skinny pepper, is the key to everything. The green *chile* is ready to be picked, and farmers will be selling baskets of it at the fiesta, to be taken home and roasted and peeled. In another month the green *chile* in the field will turn a rich red, and it will be picked and strung onto *ristras* and dried. Both fresh green *chile* and dried red *chile* from last year's harvest are made into sauces that are served on almost every dish. *Chile* is spicy, ranging from mild to hot, but once you get

used to it, Alicia says, you love it and want it on everything. The first question the waitress always asks in a local restaurant is "Red or green?"—meaning "Which kind of sauce do you want?"

TORTILLA: round, flat bread, made with cornmeal or flour

FRIJOLES: pinto beans, spotted dried beans soaked for hours and then cooked slowly for a long time; *frijoles refritos:* leftover beans, mashed and fried—"refried beans"

HUEVOS RANCHEROS ("ranch-style eggs"): corn tortilla with pinto beans and fried eggs, smothered in red or green *chile*

CHILE RELLENO: green chile stuffed with cheese, dipped in batter and fried

ENCHILADA: corn tortilla, flat or rolled around cheese, beef, or chicken, covered with red or green *chile*, grated cheese, chopped onion

BURRITO ("little donkey"): beef or beans, wrapped in a flour tortilla; eaten plain or smothered with red or green *chile*

TAMALES (plural; singular, *tamal*): shredded pork cooked in red *chile* sauce, spread on corn dough *(masa)*, then wrapped in a cornhusk and steamed (Alicia's reminder: "remove the cornhusk before eating")

POSOLE: stew made with hominy, pork, and *chile*

Alicia says the list goes on and on. To be continued, when she thinks of something else.

Saturday, August 14th

THE WHOLE TOWN IS SHUT DOWN, BUSINESSES ARE closed, and everyone is at the fiesta.

The dinner train still stops, hungry railroaders still come in to be fed. The Harvey House is operating with a skeleton crew. The salad girls worked it out with the cooks to take over each other's jobs for the weekend. Mrs. McCreary arranged the waitresses' schedule to give us all time off. We're to go to the fiesta in shifts: Emmy and Cordelia for the first hour in the morning, and as soon as they come back and report to the dining room in uniform, Maggie and I can leave for an hour. In the afternoon we'll have another chance, as long as everything is ready for the dinner train. Mr. Lawrence has given all of the Harvey Girls permission to attend the dance in the evening.

All through my morning shift I thought about Gus. I watched to see if he'd come in for breakfast, as he did last week, and I was disappointed when he didn't. He'd mentioned the fiesta—told me I should plan to go—and

I hoped I'd see him there. I was anxious for Cordelia and Emmy to get back. I didn't want to miss any of it.

"Very picturesque," Cordelia reported as she changed into her uniform and I changed out of mine. "Be sure to take your camera."

I would rather have been going to the fiesta with Emmy, always so quiet and reserved that she never attracts attention, or with Cordelia, who doesn't *try* to attract attention—it's just that, with her bobbed hair and modish dresses, she always *does*. Cordelia doesn't seem to care whether boys look at her or not. The same cannot be said for Maggie, who does her best to catch their eye. I hoped she wouldn't do anything *ostentatious* while we were there together.

The streets were crowded with people dressed in their fiesta best—men in white shirts, women in colorful skirts with ruffled blouses and silver jewelry. The parade was still in progress when we arrived. High school bands played. Cars and trucks had been washed and polished and decorated with red crepe-paper roses. The horses pulling wagons and donkeys with carts were spiffed up with paper roses on their halters. Alicia had helped make dozens of those roses.

Floats on truck beds or wagons moved majestically along Main Street. A float from the village of Los Chávez inched toward the reviewing stand set up near the flourmill, while a chorus of little girls dressed as angels sang songs about the Virgin Mary. Behind it came a float with older girls in uniform, perched on bales of hay and tossing out treats to little boys who scrambled to grab them. In an open car with a sign on the side, "Padrinos de la Fiesta," a couple perched on the top of the backseat called, "*¡Viva la fiesta!*" and waved to the people they knew, which seemed to be just about everybody.

I snapped picture after picture and made cryptic notes to jog my memory.

Food booths were set up under awnings along Becker and Dalies Avenues. A decorated cake was being raffled off and several smaller cakes were offered for sale. Bottles of Coca-Cola cooled in washtubs full of ice. Men took turns churning ice-cream freezers, and kids ran around with cones of chocolate and vanilla dripping on their clothes.

We wandered past the food booths and tables of hand-carved images of saints, wooden crosses with bits of straw glued on them in delicate patterns, and cellulose dolls dressed in the blue robes of the Virgin. Indians from Isleta Pueblo had spread blankets on the ground to display their silver and turquoise jewelry. Maggie stopped for the longest time, trying on earrings, studying her reflection in a hand mirror an old Indian woman held for her, asking my opinion, and in the end not buying anything. "I just like to look," she said as we walked on, leaving the Indian woman to straighten out her display.

A professional photographer had set up his camera and tripod in front of a canvas painted to look like Greek columns. He was posing a couple of fidgety children with their mother in a high-backed wicker chair with a few tall ferns arranged around it. An elderly couple with a yappy little dog studied samples of the photographer's work and waited their turn.

I took a snapshot of Alicia's brother Eddy and his pet burro, wearing a wreath of paper roses. Her mother and grandmother called out, *"Buenos días,* Kitty! *¡Viva la fiesta!"* and I took a picture of them, too. They were frying squares of dough in oil and selling the puffed-up *sopaipillas* (add to list!), served with honey, to raise money for their church sodality. We bought a couple and carried them to a long table set up under a *carpa.* Customers were eating enchiladas and tamales.

We found Alicia in charge of wiping off the oilcloth table covers. When she finishes that chore, she'll rush home and change into her costume, and then hurry back to perform folk dances with a group of her friends. Tonight they'll move out the tables, and a dance band will set up on a raised platform. Alicia asked if we'd be coming back.

Maggie answered for both of us. "Mrs. McCreary gave us a midnight curfew! How often does that happen?"

Last week Maggie made a map of the wooden stairs

leading to the second floor. Mrs. McCreary's room is located at the top of the stairs, where she can hear every creak if someone tries to sneak in after curfew. Maggie believes it's possible to avoid detection if you're careful and count the stairs—number eight and number eleven are especially bad—and remember to step on either the wall side or the railing side, and skip four and nine altogether. Of all the girls, Maggie is the one most likely to try to get away with it.

We left the tent, and Maggie spent a dime at a punchboard, hoping to win a pack of cigarettes. "I'd love to lose weight," she said. "They tell you in their advertisements: 'Reach for a Lucky Instead of a Sweet.' It should be 'Reach for a Lucky instead of a *sopaipilla*.'" She punched out three slips of paper but didn't win. "I'd rather have a *sopaipilla* anyway," she said, laughing. "They were delicious."

I reminded Maggie that we were supposed to be back to help out with the lunch crowd, if there was one. On the way we passed by the photographer's booth a second time. The mother and her children were gone. So were the elderly couple and their dog. Seated on the wicker chair and staring at the camera was Gus Becker, dressed up in a leather vest and a string tie. Behind him, with her hand resting possessively on his shoulder, stood a smiling girl in a large flowered hat. I'd never seen her before. I'm sure I'd have recognized her if she'd ever come to eat at the Harvey House.

Maggie apparently didn't notice him, and I was glad about that. I grabbed her arm and steered her in the opposite direction. "We'd better hurry," I said, pulling her along. "We don't want to be late."

On the way back, Maggie chattered about what she was going to wear to the dance later on, but my mind was somewhere else: *Who was the girl with Gus? Is she his girl?*

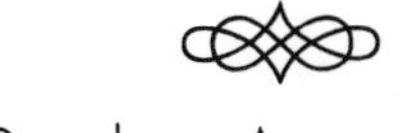

Sunday, August 15th

IT SHOULDN'T HAVE BOTHERED ME, BUT SEEING GUS having his picture taken with whomever she was took a lot of the fun out of the fiesta. I knew it was all in my imagination that he was interested in me. Like Phil Rayburn being my soul mate, just because we both plan to be journalists. And what do I have in common with Gus Becker, anyway?

So I had no wish to go back to the fiesta yesterday evening. The other girls looked at me like I was crazy, and finally, after we'd served the passengers on the five o'clock train and the customers who came later for dinner, I changed my mind and said I'd go. Cordelia and Maggie were excited, wanting to get there as fast as possible. I was glad to hang back and walk with Emmy. It's possible to spend long stretches of time with Emmy without either one of us saying a word.

"You've probably been wondering about Carl," she said after a while. "Well, I stopped writing to him, just like I said I would. I figure he'll catch on pretty soon, and he'll either write to me like he promised, or he won't. So far he hasn't, and so far it hasn't mattered to me. Not so much."

Then she asked me about Gus, and if I've seen him again. It was as though she'd read my mind.

I shrugged in what I intended to be an I-don't-give-a-darn manner. "I've seen him around, if that's what you mean. He was at the fiesta this morning, but he didn't see me." I neglected to mention the girl in the flowered hat, and I was glad Emmy didn't ask any more questions.

It was late evening; the sun was down, the sky a deepening purple, stars just starting to come out. Electric lights had been strung up along the main streets. People were strolling, enjoying the evening, most of them heading toward the big tent and the sound of music.

Cordelia and Maggie had saved us seats. Musicians were playing on a low platform in the middle of the tent—fiddle, guitar, clarinet, saxophone, accordion, mandolin, drums—and the dance floor was already crowded.

Suddenly the music stopped. The fiddler swept off his hat and began to make his way among the dancers. "Get out your dimes, boys!" he announced, and the men dug in their pockets and tossed a dime or two into the hat. When the fiddler decided he'd collected enough, the music started up again, and the couples resumed dancing.

Cordelia, in a yellow silk dress, long ropes of fake pearls, a band around her hair with a feather in it, cupid's-bow lips, and eye shadow, was the center of attention. It wasn't just the boys who were staring—the local girls were, too, suspicious and envious and somewhat disapproving. You just don't see flappers in Belén, and Cordelia really stands out. I wished I wasn't wearing my boring old middy blouse, but even if I owned flapper clothes, I probably wouldn't wear them here. If I lived in Philadelphia, or even Kansas City, I'd dress like a flapper. But not in Belén.

It didn't take but a minute for some bold fella to step up and ask her for a dance. Cordelia smiled and said she was with friends. The boys figured out fast that if they were going to have a turn with the beautiful flapper, they'd have to make sure her friends were dancing, too.

Cordelia could dance to anything, and she made even clumsy dancers look good. Maggie, spilling out of her tight dress, was game to *try* to dance to anything, and railroaders who recognized her from the Harvey House were happy to take her out on the floor for a foxtrot or a waltz. A stocky older man, probably at least twenty-five, asked Emmy to dance. She was a couple of inches taller than him, but he steered her around like a man who's used to being in charge. His being shorter didn't seem to bother her. When the music stopped, he sat down with her, and the two of them were soon in deep conversation.

I danced a few times with railroaders, including the one who'd turned us away from the roundhouse and later asked me to save him a dance. His name is Clarence, and he stepped all over my feet.

Then Gus was standing in front of me, a crooked grin on his face. "Dance with me, Kitty?"

Gus was a good dancer, nothing fancy, but smooth and easy to follow. I stopped being nervous.

"I've been looking for you all day," he said. "Thought I caught a glimpse of you once or twice, but then you always took off in another direction."

"That's funny, I didn't see you at all," I lied.

We left the tent, and Gus bought us each a soda. When we wandered back, Gus pointed to the musicians' platform. There was Cordelia. She'd borrowed a guitar and was playing along with a song that everybody seemed to know—the crowd was singing along in Spanish. When they reached the chorus, she belted it out, along with the audience:

¡Ay, ay, ay, ay,
Canta y no llores!

It was still early, but Gus asked if he could walk me back to the Harvey House. My friends and I hadn't discussed what we'd do if somebody wanted to walk one of us home. Cordelia was obviously having a great time. Emmy and her friend were still talking, paying no attention to the music. And Maggie had disappeared.

I went to tell Emmy that Gus was walking me home. She nodded and turned back to her new admirer.

"That's Nick Mayfield," Gus said. "I think he has his eye on your friend Emmy."

He took my hand and held it as we walked slowly up Becker Avenue. A sliver of moon hung in a sky full of stars. I used to dream of holding hands with Phil Rayburn, but it had never happened. Now I was actually walking along with Gus's fingers laced through mine, and I worried that my hand would start sweating, like my hands always do when I'm nervous.

I kept thinking about the girl who'd been standing beside him, touching his shoulder, smiling at the photographer. "I saw you having your picture taken this morning," I said. "You and a girl." The words were out of my mouth before I was ready to let them go, and then it was too late to call them back.

I could see Gus's gleaming smile, even in the dark. "That's 'the lady that's known as Lou.' Remember? From the poem, 'The Shooting of Dan McGrew.'"

Her name isn't really Lou, he told me; it's Sally Perkins. She and Gus and her brother, Tom, have been rehearsing a little performance of the poem, and she acts out the part of Lou. They plan to put on a show at the Central Theater over Labor Day.

That didn't explain why they were having their picture taken. But if I'd said any more, it would've seemed as if I was jealous, which I'm not. Just curious.

We'd almost reached the Harvey House when Gus had a bright idea. Why not go over to Belén Lake, only a couple of blocks away?

There was still plenty of time before the midnight curfew. It was a beautiful night, perfect for a stroll around the lake. Moonlight flickered over the surface, smooth as a mirror. A couple of rowboats were pulled up on the muddy bank.

"Come on, Kitty—let's go for a boat ride!"

It's the kind of thing Cordelia would do without hesitating. Maggie, too. Not Kitty Evans. *A boat ride? Who do the boats belong to? Would it be all right to borrow one? What if, what if . . .*

I thought it over for about fifteen seconds, and then I said, "Yes, let's!"

Gus pushed the boat into the water, helped me climb in, and jumped in after me. He shoved the boat away from the bank with the oars and began to row with smooth, easy strokes. I sat opposite Gus, thinking it had to be the most romantic thing that had ever happened to me. I trailed my fingers in the water. Slowly circling Belén Lake, we talked—the kind of conversation you have when you're still getting to know each other. I told him about O'Reilly, and Gus said he'd decided to leave his dog, Trapper, behind when he left home, because he had no idea where he might end up living. Then I told him about my brother.

"Soon, I guess, Howie will be going back to college. My father expects him to take over the business, but he dreams of becoming an actor," I told Gus. "You have a lot in common with him—he likes to recite Shakespeare. 'Cowards die many times before their deaths; the valiant never taste of death but once.' That's from *Julius Caesar.*"

We circled the lake again, not saying much. The oars creaked in the oarlocks. Way off in the distance I could hear the music from the fiesta. Nearby, crickets were chirping. Mosquitoes sang. I swatted the back of my neck.

Gus stopped rowing and laid the oars in the boat. The boat drifted. "I have a crazy dream, too, but it's not of being an actor."

"Tell me your dream."

"If I tell you now, you have to promise not to laugh."

I promised.

"An aviator," he said. "I don't want to run a train, I want to fly an airplane."

That did sound awfully farfetched, but I'd promised not to laugh, and I didn't.

He'd once spent a summer on a farm in Colorado. A barnstormer flew low over the town and dropped leaflets advertising "Daredevil Lindbergh" doing aerial stunts at the county fair. The whole town gathered in an empty field near the fairgrounds one Saturday afternoon to watch. The plane swooped in, circling over the crowd, and a young fella did the craziest thing—he climbed out of the plane and stood on the wing while the plane did loop-the-loops. It's called wing-walking. The plane circled higher, and the daredevil jumped out with a parachute, freefalling until he was almost at the ground. The crowd was screaming, thinking it was all over for him, when the parachute opened. After the plane landed, he offered to take passengers for a flight. It cost five dollars.

"Did you go up?"

"I did. I took the money I'd saved that summer and spent it on airplane rides—two of them! It was tremendously exciting. You can't imagine what it's like, Kitty, being up there, looking down. I'll never forget it."

The pilot's name was Charles Lindbergh. Gus said he's read about him in the St. Louis newspaper at the Reading Room. Lindbergh is a mail pilot, and he's planning to fly solo across the Atlantic Ocean next spring, from New York to Paris. There's a twenty-five-thousand-dollar prize for the first man to make that flight.

"Someday that's how we're going to travel—not bound to the earth by iron rails and an iron horse, but through the sky! And I want to be part of it."

Gus leaned toward me and reached for my hand. "You're not laughing, but you think I'm crazy, don't you, Kitty?"

"Yes," I said. "But an interesting kind of crazy."

I'd lost track of time, and when I finally came to my senses, I realized that it was probably close to midnight, or maybe even past it and I'd missed my curfew. I tried not to get upset. I couldn't see my wristwatch in the dark, but Gus could read his railroad watch. He didn't want to tell me what time it was. We were on the far end of the lake, and Gus began rowing like mad while I fretted. When we'd almost reached the bank where we'd found the boat, I made the mistake of standing up. It was a stupid thing to do. The boat rocked, I lost my balance, and in I went, flopping into the water like a big ungainly fish.

It wasn't deep—really not even deep enough to swim in—but deep enough for me to get thoroughly soaked. Gus jumped in to grab me and pulled me out, sputtering and choking.

"Kitty, are you all right?"

Of course I was all right, just horribly embarrassed, but my eyeglasses had come off, and for the next few minutes we both groped around in the murky water, searching for them. Gus somehow found them and wiped off the lenses with his shirttail. It was a warm evening, but I was shivering. Gus pulled off his leather vest and put it over my shoulders. I tried to wring out the bottom of my skirt. My shoes squelched with every step. The wristwatch that I won as first prize in the essay contest is probably ruined. I was practically in tears when we reached the Harvey House.

"One of these days," said Gus, "I'm going to kiss you. But this is not the time." He touched my cheek. "Good night, Kitty."

I watched him disappear into the darkness. Then I took off my soggy shoes and tried to avoid the steps that squeak. It didn't matter, because Mrs. McCreary was waiting at the top of the stairs, and she wasn't smiling.

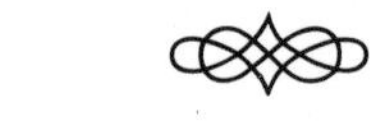

Tuesday, August 17th

Break the curfew three times and you're fired. That's the rule. Cordelia thinks it's hilariously funny that of the four of us, I'm the one who's already got a strike against me.

I'm still worried that Mrs. McCreary or Mr. Lawrence will find out that I'm only seventeen, and now I've been caught coming in after curfew. Dripping wet!

Cordelia was sitting on her bed, filing her nails, when I came in soaked to the skin and shivering. She stared at me, her mouth open. I must have looked a sight.

"Where have you been?" she demanded. "I've been worried about you!"

So I had to tell her about Gus, and then Maggie and Emmy came over from their room next door to hear my story. I made them promise to wait while I took a hot bath and washed my hair, and then we sat up rehashing everything that had happened during the evening.

Emmy, blushing red as a beet, told us about the nice man she'd met, Nick Mayfield. He's twenty-six and works on John Becker's sheep ranch near Jarales. He bought her a soda and they sat talking until he walked her home.

Maggie complained that all of her dance partners had been hayseeds and dimwits, not much smarter than John Becker's sheep. But Cordelia'd kept everybody pepped up until the Queen of the Fiesta arrived with her escort and a court of six young ladies and replaced Cordelia as the center of attention.

Then I told them about Gus, and the boat, and the dunking in Belén Lake.

Now my friends will be watching to see what happens the next time Gus stops in the lunchroom. Maggie says if he sits at her station, she's going to step aside and let me wait on him, but I'll be awfully self-conscious if she does, even though I'm dying to see him again.

Tuesday, August 24th

Opal and Pearl, the former schoolteachers from Illinois, are in shock. The sisters have a radio in their room and heard the news last night in a broadcast from Chicago: Rudolph Valentino is dead.

This morning Enrique had the papers with Valentino's photograph and the headline prominently displayed. Motion picture fans everywhere are mourning the sudden death of their favorite male star. According to the *Albuquerque Journal*, when his death was announced yesterday in New York, his fans were hysterical. The article called him "The Great Lover."

Pearl is inconsolable. "He was magnificent! Just so handsome!" she cried. "We heard that he stayed at the Alvarado in Albuquerque last February. I would have given anything to see him!"

"Oh, this is just so sad," Opal sobbed. "We've seen every movie he ever made. *The Sheik* was our favorite. We saw it four times when it came out, and his next movie, *The Son of the Sheik,* is supposed to be released in a couple of weeks. Imagine, he was only thirty-one! Just think of all the wonderful movies he never made."

Cordelia and I looked at each other. Opal and Pearl are normally on an even keel no matter what, but they were carrying on as though they'd lost their best friend. I've never seen a Rudolph Valentino movie—my mother always said I was too young for his films—and now I wonder what I've been missing. Maggie tried to comfort the sisters, and big-hearted Emmy went out into the garden and picked a few flowers, found a vase in the employees' lunchroom, and set the bouquet in front of the newspaper rack with the tragic headline: RUDOLPH VALENTINO DEAD.

Friday, August 27th

LABOR DAY IS A WEEK FROM MONDAY, AND THE TALK AT the lunch counter is that the railroaders are planning a celebration. After Belén's traditional parade, Gus, Sally Perkins, and Sally's brother, Tom, will perform "The Shooting of Dan McGrew."

This afternoon I went over to Becker's Mercantile to buy a new pair of semi-dressy shoes to replace the ones I ruined when I fell out of the rowboat, and also to see if there was someone to fix my waterlogged wristwatch. I've been to the store a time or two since I went with Alicia for paraffin for her mother's jam jars, but only to buy a few little things like tooth powder and a bottle of ink. I've thought of buying a bathing costume, but summer is almost over.

I had enough nickels and dimes, and a couple of quarters saved from my tips, so that I didn't have to withdraw money from the bank. Cordelia volunteered to go with me. She was thinking of buying a guitar, because she had so much fun playing one at the fiesta dance. Gladys said Becker's probably sells guitars. If she can't find any she likes, Cordelia says she'll wait until we go up to Albuquerque and look for one there.

We walked over to Becker's after the lunch service was done. Cordelia went in search of a guitar while I shopped for shoes. I didn't do a very good job of hiding my surprise when the girl selling shoes turned out to be Miss Sally Perkins. I recognized her right away. She's a pretty girl with thick, wavy dark hair and hazel eyes. The kind of looks a boy would be likely to fall for.

"May I help you?" she asked, and I gave her a nice smile and told her what I was interested in. She measured my foot and went in back to bring out some shoes for me to try on. "These are just a few that we carry in your size," she said. "If they feel right but you'd prefer a different style, I'm sure we can find something that will please you."

I knew that nothing was going to feel right, and nothing was going to please me. It was not her fault. She tried to be friendly as well as helpful and asked me if

I happened to be one of the new Harvey Girls. I said I was. She told me that her brother often eats his lunch at the Harvey House.

"He's a railroader," she said. "His name is Tom Perkins. I bet you've met him."

I already knew that—Tom is one of the quiet boys who never has much to say—but I didn't let on. She slipped the shoes on my feet and suggested I walk around to see how they felt. The shoes pinched a little, and I said so.

I was still trying on shoes, fighting completely unreasonable feelings of jealousy, when Cordelia found us and plunked down beside me. "They have guitars, but none I really like. We'll just have to make that trip up to Albuquerque. Find any shoes? Those look good, Kitty!"

Sally smiled at Cordelia. "I remember *you!*" she said. She'd seen Cordelia at the dance on Saturday night, and she loved the way Cordelia went right up on the stage, borrowed a guitar, and started playing while she showed everyone steps for the Charleston. "I'd never have the nerve to do that!" Sally said.

Cordelia and Sally immediately fell into conversation. Cordelia confided that her goal was to go to California and launch a career as a musician, and Sally said that she dreamed of being on stage someday, not just at the Central Theater where she'd be on Labor Day with her brother and their friend Gus Becker.

"You're a Harvey Girl, too, aren't you? You probably know Tom and Gus!"

Cordelia threw me a quick look and said smoothly, "Oh, I know them! They're regular customers. Some of our best!"

"Tom and I live with our Auntie Gertrude—she's our great-aunt who raised us—and Gus boards there, so we're all real close. You'll come to see us perform, won't you? And bring the other Harvey Girls, too? We want a big audience."

"Of course we will!" Cordelia promised, much too enthusiastically. "We wouldn't miss it, would we, Kitty?"

They both seemed to have forgotten all about my shoes. "Thank you for your help," I said. "I haven't found quite what I'm looking for." I turned to Cordelia and reminded her that it was almost time to set up for dinner and we'd better start back.

Sally spoke up. "You mentioned having a watch to repair, Miss." She explained that the watchmaker wasn't in at the moment, but she would be happy to take the watch and fill out the order if I'd step over to the jewelry department.

But I just wanted to escape. "Next time," I said, and grabbed Cordelia's arm.

"I don't know what you were in such a hurry about," Cordelia complained as I dragged her out of the store. "We have plenty of time for a soda."

We stopped at the drugstore and ordered lime phosphates. Cordelia waited expectantly for me to tell her what was ailing me. She knew about Gus and of course about me falling out of the rowboat, but I hadn't mentioned seeing him and Sally getting their picture taken at the photographer's booth. So then I had to explain it to Cordelia.

She pointed out that I don't know a thing about what is going on between Sally and Gus, except that: A, her brother is Gus's friend and they all live with Auntie Gertrude; B, they are putting on some kind of play on Labor Day; and C, they had their picture taken together, which could have been for a poster for the play or just because they're friends, and so what if Sally had her hand on Gus's shoulder?

"You're making yourself miserable over nothing. Gus took you, not Sally, for a boat ride on Belén Lake."

There was one more part of the story I hadn't told Cordelia: that Gus had said he wanted to kiss me. I decided to tell her that part of the story, too.

Cordelia let out a whoop, startling the soda jerk behind the counter. "There!" she cried. "I knew it! Gus is going to kiss you, and you'll see that everything is going to be just fine!"

Sunday, August 29th

Nick Mayfield turned up yesterday and invited Emmy to go for a picnic down by the river this afternoon. Mr. Lawrence gave permission. He's more likely to approve a Harvey Girl going out with a rancher than with a railroader. No one knows exactly why, but people do have strange prejudices.

As soon as we'd finished the lunch service, we ran up to our rooms to make sure Emmy was all set for her date with Nick. Were they going to swim? Did she have a bathing costume? Maybe she could borrow one from Gladys. Cordelia has one, but she isn't as tall or as husky as Emmy. But Emmy said she had no intention of going swimming anyway, so it didn't matter. Pearl loaned her a skirt and Opal offered a shirtwaist and a straw hat.

Emmy looked very nice in her borrowed clothes, but she was nervous and asked us to go downstairs with her to wait for Nick. We were curious and glad to oblige. When we heard the roar of a motor, we went outside to investigate. He'd come on a motorcycle! None of us had seen a motorcycle up close before, let alone ridden on one, and Nick was happy to show off the Indian—a famous make of motorcycle, he said. He answered all our questions, plus a few we hadn't thought to ask, telling us all about the speed and horsepower. Practical for the rough, unpaved New Mexico roads, he said.

"But where am I supposed to sit?" Emmy asked and laughed a little uneasily. I was wondering the same thing.

"Behind me," Nick said.

But how was Emmy supposed to ride a motorcycle when she was wearing a skirt? Cordelia said golfing knickers were the thing and she'd be happy to lend hers, although there was the size problem for those, too, but Emmy said she disapproves of knickers anyway. Too unladylike. And what about the straw hat? Wasn't it sure to blow off? And what was she supposed to hang on to?

He'd sit on her skirt to keep it from blowing, Nick said, he had a scarf for her to tie her hat down, and she was to wrap her arms around his waist and hang on. Emmy looked dubious, but she climbed on and leaned against Nick's back.

Just before they roared off, Emmy turned and waved, and I snapped a picture.

Monday, August 30th

EMMY COULDN'T WAIT TO TELL US ABOUT HER DATE WITH Nick Mayfield, starting with the thrilling ride on the back of the Indian.

They went down the bumpy, rutted road through the village of Jarales, past the ranch where Nick looks after John Becker's sheep, and onto a rough track that eventually led to a clearing on the banks of the Rio Grande. Along the way the scarf came undone and Emmy's borrowed straw hat flew off, but Nick turned around and doubled back until they found it.

Meanwhile, three other couples had arrived in someone's truck. The fellas pounded in a couple of stakes for pitching horseshoes. Another fella brought a fishing pole and announced that he'd catch their dinner. Everyone hooted—"Charlie never catches anything!" Two jumped into the water. The other girls peeled off their stockings, hiked up their skirts, and waded in. Emmy said she'd rather just sit on the bank and watch.

Nick opened them each a bottle of soda pop from a washtub filled with ice. Late in the afternoon they built a fire and roasted ears of corn and cooked wienies on peeled sticks. As predicted, there were no fish to deal with. When it got dark, Nick played his harmonica, and they sang until it was time to get the girls back. On the way, the truck had a blowout and Nick stopped to help them change the tire.

Emmy made it in time, but just barely. We were all waiting for her.

Sunday, September 5th

Nick wants Emmy to go with him to the Labor Day celebration tomorrow, and Emmy is in a tizzy. She likes Nick, but she's feeling guilty because she's not being true to Carl. We've tried to convince her that it's not as though she's having a passionate affair with Nick, and she should simply go and have a good time.

I keep thinking about Gus. *Gus Becker, aviator.*

So far he hasn't invited me to go out with him—he just shows up in the lunchroom. Sometimes he waits for me afterward in the back garden, and we talk for a few minutes before he squeezes my hand and heads back to the roundhouse. He reminded me that tomorrow he and Sally and Tom will be performing "The Shooting of Dan McGrew."

Of course I'm going. I don't need reminding.

Cordelia promised to come along for moral support.

Maggie is coming too, but Cordelia complains to me that Maggie gets under her skin. Maggie thinks Cordelia is crazy for not accepting Walter's proposal and the big diamond ring.

"I would give my eye teeth for a ring like that!" Maggie has told her once too often. "Being a Harvey Girl can be a lot of fun, but who wants to work this hard for years and years?" Maggie's goal is to see the Grand Canyon, and after she's done that and maybe even worked there or at one of the big hotels for a while, then she hopes to find some rich man to marry. She's very clear about that.

"You're welcome to Walter," Cordelia replied, and Maggie looked at her to see if she was kidding. I'm pretty sure she wasn't.

Alicia is teaching me words she thinks I ought to learn. If we happen to eat lunch at the same time, she drills me in how to pronounce them: *La cocina* (co-SEE-na), kitchen. *El cocinero* (co-see-NEH-ro), cook. *La estufa* (eh-STOO-fa), stove. *Pollo asado* (POY-oh a-SAH-do), roast chicken.

She also continues my lessons in local history. During the fiesta a couple of weeks ago you might have thought you lived in a village in Mexico. But on Labor Day weekend it seems that everything German takes over.

Alicia says that when Anna Becker was alive, they set up a wooden dance floor under a tent on this holiday.

Now John's daughter, Lucie, is carrying on her mother's tradition. There will be polkas and waltzes, with a German band and singing, and supposedly a yodeling contest—now *that* is a novelty.

Viktor, our usually dour chef, is smiling. He promises there will be Wiener schnitzel and spaetzle, German potato salad and red cabbage, bratwurst and sauerkraut, potato pancakes and pretzels. Max is baking Black Forest cake and apple strudel, to be offered for sale by the Ladies' Aid Society of the Lutheran church. Not an enchilada to be had.

When I asked Gus why they were performing "The Shooting of Dan McGrew" on Labor Day, he shrugged and said he and Tom and Sally just wanted to do something that would entertain the crowd after all the long, boring speeches.

Monday, September 6th, Labor Day

WELL, IT *WAS* ENTERTAINING, I'LL SAY THAT. A BIG audience crowded into the theater, most of them railroaders turning out to cheer for their friends. Cordelia, Maggie, and I found seats near the front.

Sally made her entrance from the wings, in a long,

frilly dress and looking extremely pretty, although I did think she'd put on too much rouge. She settled onto a stool at a tall table that was supposed to represent a bar. Tom, well-dressed in a white shirt and neatly pressed trousers, was already at the bar with a glass and a brown bottle. He was Dangerous Dan McGrew.

In sauntered Gus, wearing his leather vest and a cowboy hat, along with a couple of railroaders that I recognized from the lunchroom. They were carrying glasses of lemonade and leaned on the top of an upright piano. Gus began to recite the poem:

A bunch of the boys were whooping it up in the
Malamute saloon.

The "boys" pantomimed drinking their lemonade. In stumbled another "boy," also a railroader, this one dressed in dirty clothes: the Villain. He spun the piano stool around a few times for dramatic effect before he sat down and pretended to play. Offstage someone had cranked up a Victrola, and music was pouring out—that was supposed to be the Villain playing. Gus's dramatic rendering went on, verse after verse.

Then I ducked my head, and the lights went out,
and two guns blazed in the dark,
And a woman screamed, and the lights went up,
and two men lay stiff and stark.

On cue, the lights went out, two guns went off—*Bang! Bang!*—making everybody jump, and Sally screamed convincingly. When the lights came up, both Dangerous Dan and the Villain lay sprawled on the floor of the Malamute Saloon.

Pitched on his head, and pumped full of lead, was
Dangerous Dan McGrew.

The "lady that's known as Lou" was clutching the dead Villain in one hand, holding up Dan's bag of gold in the other, and smiling triumphantly.

The End. Applause.

Bows from the Villain and Dangerous Dan (now brought back to life), grins from the Narrator, and pretty smiles and curtseys from Lou. The Narrator was holding Lou by the hand as they exited. That sight put me off, much as I tried not to let it bother me.

Maggie wanted to stay and see what mischief she could stir up, but I was feeling glum and ready to leave. Cordelia went with me.

On our way back to the Harvey House, Cordelia said, "Know what? I've had enough of small town life for a while, and so have you. We're big-city gals, and we need a break. Next week we're going to take the local up to Albuquerque and visit the Alvarado. Are you game?"

Absolutely, I am game! By the time we'd reached our room, we had a plan. Next Tuesday is the day.

Thursday, September 9th

Daddy's usual Sunday letter brings the news from Leavenworth. He and Mother and Gramma Blair took a car trip to St. Louis last week to visit Gramma's relatives and endured all kinds of car trouble along the way. Howie was in charge of the store while they were gone and did very well. Now they're having an End-of-Summer Sale. O'Reilly had a problem with ticks this summer, but all is well with him now. Betty Jane sprained her ankle playing softball and Mother said she should've known better because she's not getting any younger. The neighbors are having their house painted, and Mother doesn't like the colors they chose and said it makes the neighborhood look cheap.

I'd written them about the fiesta—the food and so forth, not mentioning the incident with Gus and the boat—but I think Mother has some suspicions. She added a P.S. to Daddy's letter:

I'm surprised that you're there with all those Spanish people, and Indians, too, and the railroad men have never had much of a good reputation. I assume that you are well chaperoned and that you are not being overly sociable with the boys you meet.

She doesn't need to worry about me being overly sociable. Unfortunately!

Monday, September 13th

TOMORROW WE GO TO ALBUQUERQUE—CORDELIA, Emmy, and I.

Mrs. McCreary and Mr. Lawrence agreed that after two months here and a stellar record—that's their word, "stellar"—we deserve to have a whole day off to do as we please.

Maggie was dying to go, too, but she's got a couple of blots on her record. She's developed a crush on one of the kitchen helpers, Pedro, and has been meeting him after hours in the garden behind the Harvey House, earning her another curfew violation. And this crush of hers could mean trouble of a different kind, too: Alicia told me that one of the other salad girls, Susana, has been going out with Pedro for two years and thought they were a steady couple, maybe even headed for the altar, until Maggie came to town. Now Susana is looking for a way to fix Maggie but good and win Pedro back.

I don't know if Maggie has the slightest idea of the trouble she's causing every time she sashays into the kitchen and beams her radiant smile on Pedro, who turns bright red.

Cordelia is relieved that Maggie won't be going to Albuquerque.

We plan to catch the early morning local, see what there is to see, treat ourselves to a nice lunch, maybe walk around the town if there's time—Cordelia wants to inquire about guitars—and take the late train back. Except for the days we traveled from Emporia to Belén, it's the first whole day off we'll have had since we started our lives as Harvey Girls. What a treat!

Tuesday, September 14th

THE LOCAL TRAIN STOPPED JUST LONG ENOUGH FOR us to board. It stopped again at Isleta Pueblo and two Indian ladies climbed on, lugging awkward bundles. In about two minutes Cordelia had them all chatting.

Maria and Francisca Chiwiwi were on their way to the Indian Building at the Alvarado. Francisca says her family is well known for their pottery, and she showed us an old photograph of them posing with huge pots balanced on their heads. Cordelia admired the heavy turquoise and silver necklaces they were both wearing. Maria called them "squash-blossom necklaces" and pointed out the dozens of silver "blossoms." She said they were made by her husband, a Navajo silversmith. I made sure to get their names

and to spell them correctly in my notebook. When the train pulled into the Albuquerque depot, the ladies collected their bundles and disappeared.

Red-roofed buildings and towers sprawl along the tracks, the depot at one end and the hotel at the other, connected by a long arcade. Indians had arranged pottery and jewelry on tables and blankets spread on the ground and were waiting for the first trainload of tourists to arrive. Just beyond the depot we found the Indian Building, with a moose head peering from one wall, a canoe hanging from the ceiling, Indian rugs laid out on the floor, and a jumble of pottery, baskets, jewelry, drums, hides, and weavings displayed on shelves, benches, and tables. Next to the museum, in the curio shop, Maria and Francisca had unpacked their pots and were busy talking with the manager.

"I'd love to have one of those squash-blossom necklaces," Emmy whispered as we passed.

"I bet she'd sell you one," Cordelia said. "For a month's pay."

"There's probably nothing here a Harvey Girl can afford," I said, and we moved on.

People sat on rocking chairs in the arcade, facing lawns and gardens on the street side. On the track side, courtyards and patios with fountains and lily ponds offered a magnificent view of the Sandia Mountains to the east. It's an oasis blooming in the middle of the desert.

Inside we discovered a grand dining room that Cordelia pronounced "baronial"; two elegant parlors, one exclusively for ladies; and a reading and writing room with a wall of books. A lounge with an enormous fireplace, like something you'd find in a Spanish castle, was furnished with colorful rugs and massive wooden tables and leather sofas.

Tea is served here every afternoon at four. I imagined myself ensconced in one of the comfortable chairs while a Harvey Girl in a Spanish costume filled my china cup from a silver teapot, offered me a choice of lemon or cream, and then passed me a plate of dainty sandwiches and biscuits. Gramma Blair would love this!

It was still early, but we decided to stop in the lunchroom. Not to criticize our own Harvey House in Belén, but it's just nothing like the Alvarado when it comes to elegance. Swiveling bronze chairs at the

U-shaped counter. Pies and bowls of fruit displayed in glass-shelved cases. Walls and columns covered in colorful tiles. We ordered coffee and pretended we were guests who'd booked splendid rooms where we'd spend a night or two on fine linen sheets and each of us would have our own private bathroom. It's been months since I haven't had to wait my turn to take a bath.

Cordelia and Emmy decided to sit in the courtyard, the main entrance for guests arriving by train. "Who knows, we might see somebody interesting," Cordelia said. "Somebody like Douglas Fairbanks or Mary Pickford."

But I wanted to find a spot in the reading and writing room and write something. I can see myself, someday in the future, scribbling away in this very place while the gentleman who will later take me to dine is having a shave in the nearby barbershop. (Is an aviator considered a gentleman?) The Alvarado is a place for entertaining fantasies.

I found a desk in a secluded corner, took out my notebook and pen, and had just settled into the role of *journalist* when a middle-aged lady in a rumpled suit and sensible shoes came in, accompanied by two silver-haired, well-dressed men, the kind with manicured nails who give off a whiff of expensive French cologne. If they noticed the girl in the corner toiling over a notebook, they paid no attention.

The men unrolled a set of large blueprints and

spread them out on the great oak table in the center of the room, but it was the lady who seemed to be in charge. The men addressed her as "Miss Colter."

I followed the advice William Allen White gave me back in Emporia. He told me I should learn to eavesdrop, that I'd find out a lot. As the conversation went on around the blueprints, I concluded that the gentlemen must be officials of the Fred Harvey Company. They were discussing plans for a new Harvey House to be built in Winslow, Arizona, one of the stops between here and Los Angeles. But who was Miss Colter?

"I'm going to tell you a story about an *hacienda*, and I want you to imagine the scene," she instructed the men. It was the way my high school English teacher, Miss Bratton, might have spoken—not loudly, but very clearly.

"Don Alfonso was the descendant of a noble Spanish family who arrived in the Arizona Territory early in the nineteenth century. He built a simple little adobe home, not much more than a *casita*, and began to establish an *estancia*, a ranch in the high desert. He passed it on to his sons, the ranch grew and prospered, and each new generation added lavish *salas*, even entire wings to the *casita*, until it had become the grandest *hacienda* in the area. The family called it *La Posada*—the inn."

I scribbled notes as fast as I could. Not sure about

the spelling of some of the words. A waitress tiptoed in and left a silver tray with glasses and a carafe of water on a side table. Miss Colter ignored it and continued to weave her story.

"At the end of the nineteenth century a great railroad was built that would connect the Atlantic Ocean with the Pacific. Steam locomotives drawing dozens of cars, freight trains and passenger trains, passed by the magnificent front doors of the *hacienda*. Visitors arrived from all over the country, from all over the world. They admired the beautiful gardens and the priceless collection of precious objects, slept in the exquisitely appointed guest rooms, and gathered around the bountiful table with the Don and his wife and children. But then came a tragic reversal in fortunes for this old and distinguished family. The fourth Don Alfonso was forced to sell everything. Everything!"

Miss Colter paused and leaned on the table, her voice dropping so low I had to strain to hear it. "The sons of Fred Harvey came to the rescue. They acquired La Posada, promising to operate it as one of the finest inns in America, inviting travelers to stop and rest, to marvel at the gardens and *salas*, and to enjoy the excellent cuisine created by the country's best chefs. And that vision, gentlemen, is what I offer you today."

She stepped back and folded her arms across her chest.

One of the men said, "Bravo, Miss Colter! You've

invented a history for a place that does not exist yet!"

The other said uneasily, "But, Mary, the cost."

"It will be phenomenal, of course! And worth every penny! Here, gentlemen, are the plans I've drawn up for the creation of La Posada. Please look them over at your leisure. I shall personally see to the acquisition of all the appropriate fixtures and furnishings and decorations, as I have here at the Alvarado and at the properties in the Grand Canyon. We can discuss the details later. Now I suggest we go into the dining hall and enjoy our lunch. I always begin with the Blue Point oysters on the half shell."

They were here for not more than twenty minutes, and now they are gone. It's as if I'd invented the whole thing, like Miss Colter's story of La Posada. But I wrote it all down.

Wednesday, September 15th

I'D BARELY FINISHED WRITING ABOUT MISS COLTER and her imaginary hotel when Emmy and Cordelia came looking for me, disappointed that they had not recognized a single celebrity. We debated whether to have lunch in the lunchroom, which seemed the sensible thing to do, or blow our tiny budgets on a first-class lunch in the dining hall. Cordelia argued that we had one special day, and we should treat ourselves especially well and eat in the grand dining hall. Emmy, no surprise, was concerned about what it was going to cost—she sends her pay home to her family and keeps only the tips for her own expenses. I was on the fence. I thought of Miss Colter's oysters. I'd never eaten raw oysters, but I wasn't sure I wanted to try them. In the end I tipped over to Emmy's side.

Louise, the Harvey Girl behind the lunch counter, has been at the Alvarado for several years and knows a lot about the place, so I asked her about Miss Colter. She said Mary Colter was hired by Mr. Fred Harvey years ago to decorate the hotels. "But she does more than that. She designed almost everything in the hotel, and the Indian Building, too." One of the men with her was Ford Harvey, Fred's son, who became the head of the company after his father died. Louise thought the other man might be married to Ford's sister, Minnie.

"Have you been to the Grand Canyon?" Louise asked, and we said we hadn't, but we hoped to go there one day. "Hermit's Rest and Bright Angel Lodge and Hopi House—they're all Miss Colter's work. It's incredible, what she's done. You won't believe it and you won't forget it."

"That lady designed all those buildings?" Emmy asked.

"She did. She's kind of a character," Louise said. "She wears trousers, although she's not allowed to wear them into the dining room. Mr. Fred Harvey would turn in his grave! And I've heard that she smokes cigars."

I ordered Creamed Shrimp Newburg on Toast for seventy-five cents, Cordelia had the Breast of Guinea Hen for ninety cents, and Emmy chose the Frankfurters and Hot Potato Salad, the cheapest item on the menu, for forty-five cents. We were lingering over cherry pie á la mode when there was a sudden noisy arrival of about twenty people dressed for country sightseeing.

"Indian Detours," Louise murmured. "The sightseers are called Detourists."

Two girls escorted the group, one in a dark red velveteen blouse and the other in dark green. Both were wearing walking skirts and boots, squash-blossom necklaces (not as bold as Maria and Francisca's), and soft felt hats.

"They're the Couriers, the tour guides," Louise said, and slipped us each a pamphlet.

The Couriers meet the Detourists at the depot in Las Vegas. They're driven in Packard touring cars called "Harveycars" to Santa Fe to spend the night, and the next day to Albuquerque, stopping at Indian pueblos along the way. After lunch, the Couriers escort them to Old Town Plaza in Albuquerque, then down to Isleta Pueblo, and back to the Alvarado in time for dinner and a private tour of the Indian Building. The Detour lasts three days. Tomorrow they'll be back on board the California Limited, headed to Los Angeles. According to the brochure, a Detourist can choose to travel in the opposite direction, starting out in Albuquerque, and after three days of sightseeing board the eastbound train in Las Vegas.

Emmy wondered what it's like to be a Courier, and Cordelia announced that she intended to find out.

"I'd certainly rather be wearing a velvet blouse and a silver necklace than a black-and-white uniform. I'm tired of looking like a pilgrim! Or a nun. Aren't you?"

Her plan was to stake out the ladies' toilet and casually start a conversation when one of the Couriers went to use it. She thought I was the perfect person to "interview" one of the girls in the striking uniforms. Emmy could go with me. Cordelia had spotted the drivers, sitting at a table by themselves, and she was going to "chat them up."

The plan worked, more or less. The Couriers were happy to answer my questions. The Detour service had started in May. You must be a college girl and able to speak Spanish plus another language. Magda, the girl in the red blouse, told me her father is from Hungary, and she speaks Hungarian fluently and manages some German and enough Spanish. They were trained for a month in Santa Fe by a lady who'd been running a tour business.

"You wouldn't believe all the history we had to memorize. And geology, so you know what kind of rocks your people are looking at, and the names of at least a dozen plants."

"It's no piece of cake," the second Courier said. Cars break down, although the drivers are good about fixing them. Detourists get cranky, especially if you're running late. "They can be awfully demanding," she said.

I jotted it all down, and the Couriers left to round up their Detourists. Cordelia was still engaged in charming the drivers. Minutes later Magda returned and informed the drivers that one of the Detourists was under the weather and would not be taking the trip to Old Town Plaza and Isleta Pueblo. So his driver, Leo, would have an empty seat in his car.

Leo had an idea. Why didn't one of us take that empty place? And then catch the train at Isleta Pueblo for Belén?

Emmy shook her head—no, thank you. But Cordelia was ready to jump at the chance. And, to be honest, so was I. An adventure!

Cordelia said we should flip a coin. Leo took a nickel out of his pocket, tossed it in the air, caught it, and slapped it on the back of his hand. "Call it," he said.

"Heads," said Cordelia.

It came up tails.

Cordelia was disappointed, I think, but she said she'd rather go guitar-shopping anyway. "Have fun,

Kitty. We'll look for you at the Isleta depot."

Three Harveycars had been washed and polished while the Detourists were at lunch. Magda and her driver were in one; the second courier, Dottie, and another driver were in the second; and I climbed into the third car with Leo. There was no courier in my car, but Magda and Dottie would take turns riding with us. The Harveycars drove down Central Avenue, past another hotel that wasn't nearly so grand as the Alvarado. We eventually arrived at the plaza in Old Town to visit the adobe church, San Felipe de Neri, the oldest surviving building in the city. It was named by the Spanish Duke of Alburquerque (the old spelling, which has lost an "r" along the way). The Detourists soaked up every word as Dottie explained the process of making adobes.

It was midafternoon when the Detour started toward Isleta. The unpaved road was terrible to begin with, and a recent rain had washed out parts of it. As the Harveycars navigated the washouts, I began to worry. What if I missed the train? I had no idea how I'd get to Belén.

One of the Harveycars slid off the road and into a shallow ditch, and the Detourists had to climb out and wait while a couple of the men helped the drivers to haul the car out of the ditch and back onto the road. It was regarded as a lark, part of the adventure. The second time it happened, they passed it off as a nuisance, but only a mile or two down the road when a car got stuck in a rut, the Detourists were plainly annoyed, and I was in a panic.

Somehow it worked out. The Harveycar left me at the Isleta depot, and the Detourists went off to tour the village, its whitewashed church standing out among the plain adobe houses and the stark brown earth. The station agent flagged down the southbound local, and Cordelia and Emmy greeted me with cheers when I jumped aboard. Cordelia brandished the guitar she'd found in a pawn shop. Emmy showed off her first store-bought dress, fifty percent off in a department store on Central.

We're already planning our next trip to Albuquerque. And Cordelia wants to spend the night there.

"Leave it to me," she says. "I'll figure it out."

Friday, September 17th

CORDELIA IS DETERMINED TO SIGN ON AS A COURIER when her six-month Harvey contract is up. It's all she talks about now.

"I thought you were going to California to play the piano in a swanky Hollywood hotel," I said.

"I can always do that later. Indian Detours are much more interesting."

"You have to be able to speak another language to be hired as a Courier."

"I'll practice speaking German with Viktor. Maybe Alicia will give me a few Spanish lessons. I can fudge it."

"You have to learn a lot of facts. Did you know there used to be another 'r' in Albuquerque? That the adobe church in Old Town collapsed after a rainstorm in 1792? That floors in adobe houses are made of mud and oxblood?"

Cordelia thinks she can fudge that, too.

They couldn't wait to tell me what I'd missed after I'd left with the Detourists. Louise showed them the rooms on the main floor of the hotel where the Harvey Girls stay. She made the life there sound exciting, they said. Celebrities are always arriving on the train—famous politicians, wealthy oilmen, glamorous movie stars—staying for days or even weeks, eating in the dining room, leaving big tips for waitresses and bellhops. And not just the rich and famous, but local people, too. The Alvarado is *the* place for dances and wedding receptions and dinner parties. Society types and ordinary people come to the Alvarado to stroll up and down the arcade, watch the trains, meet their friends. The pie served in the lunchroom is so popular that the swiveling seats at the counter are called "pie chairs." That cherry pie we had for lunch? Everybody orders it. They say it's the best in the world.

At Christmastime the mayor's wife gives a tea for the Harvey Girls. The girls get dressed up, put on hats and gloves, and take the electric streetcar to the mayor's house. It's a grand occasion, to have the wife of a judge or a doctor or the president of the bank asking if you prefer lemon or cream.

"But that doesn't mean you've arrived socially," Cordelia said. "Louise told us, 'Don't think you're ever going to date their sons. You're still just waitresses.'"

"But we're not just waitresses!" Emmy protested. "We're Harvey Girls!"

Monday, September 20th

THE MOOD IN THE LUNCHROOM USUALLY GOES UP WHEN our particular group of railroaders, the one that includes Gus and Tom Perkins, comes in for a meal or just a slice of pie and a cup of coffee. Gus smiles and winks when he catches my eye, as though we have a secret between us, and I don't know if it's that night I got dunked in the pond, or his confiding his dream of being an aviator.

This morning was different. The men were talking somberly about the death of a hobo called Wooly Sam. Hobos often ride in boxcars as a way of getting from one place to another in search of work, even though it's against the law and the guards always chase them away, and not gently. Jumping on a moving freight, even if it's going slowly, is dangerous. Late yesterday, Wooly Sam somehow missed his footing and fell under the wheels. Gus saw him and tried to rescue him, but it was too late—the hobo was already dead. The boss of the rail yard had the body taken away, to be buried somewhere in a pauper's grave.

Nick Mayfield, in town to take care of some business for the ranch, also happened to be in the Harvey House this morning, and he said that something ought to be done to give the hobo a decent send-off. Everybody thought that was a good idea, and even those of us who'd never met Wooly Sam or heard of him before said we wanted to be part of it, too. It's settled that next Sunday afternoon we'll drive out to Abo Canyon where Wooly Sam once worked for a while.

"It was Abo Pass that meant the most in Wooly Sam's life," Nick said.

Emmy is all for it, since Nick suggested it. At first Cordelia wasn't interested, but she changed her mind.

Before the railroaders left the lunchroom, Gus said loud enough for everyone to hear, "Kitty, you told me once you wanted to be a writer. We'd like for you to write an obituary for Wooly Sam. I'm acquainted with the editor over at the *Belén News*, and if you could write a nice piece about Wooly Sam and put your name to it, I believe I can get it printed."

The other railroaders were nodding. They'd tell me what they know, and I'd figure out what to do with the information.

"I've never written an obituary," I said. "I will do my best, but I don't have a typewriter."

"Take it to Miss Baca, over at the telephone company. She'll let you use hers."

THE DEATH OF A HOBO

by Katherine A. Evans

Nobody knows his real name, but the men at the rail yard where he died on Sunday, September 19th, called him Wooly Sam. He was a hobo.

With a long white beard that came down almost to the buckle on his worn leather belt, he was a familiar face around Belén. He came to be known as Wooly Sam because he worked on the sheep ranches, helping out at lambing time, or when the shearers came. Then he would disappear for a while, sometimes hopping a freight headed north for the summer and returning late in the fall for the *matanza*, when hogs are butchered for the winter.

Nobody knows why he happened to be here in mid-September.

Nick Mayfield, a foreman at John Becker's ranch, became friends with the old hobo who often came looking for work. "He caught the westbound," Nick said when he learned of Sam's death. "That's what they say when a hobo dies."

Some believe that hobos are too lazy to work and merely want a handout, but others, including those who knew Wooly Sam, disagree. Hobos are not tramps, his friends say. They want to work; they just don't want to be tied down to a steady job. Starting when they are young, they look for adventure—hop a freight, move on to the next town, and see what Lady Luck has in store.

Wooly Sam came to the area in '03, after John Becker and José Felipe Chávez, known as El Millonario, one of the richest men in New Mexico, persuaded the railroad to build a new line called the Belén Cutoff through Abo Canyon to Los Angeles. With dozens of other men, Wooly Sam camped along the route the line would take.

When the company ran out of money after six months, many left to find work elsewhere, but Sam stayed, and John Becker hired him to work on his ranch. When construction began again, he returned to pick-and-shovel work until the line was completed in 1908, and then went back to Becker's ranch.

But Sam did not stick to one thing for very long. If there was work and somebody would pay him to do it, he would stay for a while before moving on. He did that for years.

Nobody ever knew much about him—where he was born, how old he was. It seems he told everybody a different story: that he'd once panned for gold in California, been a cowboy in Wyoming, married a rich woman from Chicago, belonged to a band of outlaws in Oklahoma until he found religion and repented. Nobody believed any of these stories. Probably none were true.

His hair turned white and his beard grew long, but Wooly Sam stayed pretty much the same until the day he died, working hard and telling unbelievable stories. He will be missed.

Sunday, September 26th

It wasn't actually a funeral, because we didn't have Wooly Sam's body in a coffin, or a preacher to lead a proper service. But it was definitely a good send-off.

Nick Mayfield made the trip on his Indian, but Emmy declined to join him—too far to travel on the back of a motorcycle. She rode with Cordelia and me in the truck driven by Frank, the roast cook, who'd been giving handouts to Wooly Sam for years.

The dirt road headed south, following the train tracks through the grassy plain of the Rio Grande valley, and then turned east toward the Manzano Mountains. The truck began the long, slow climb in low gear through the foothills up to the pass. The rock formations were red sandstone, stark and beautiful and dotted with low-growing piñon and juniper.

Nick had already arrived and chosen the spot where we would gather to say good-bye to Sam. He spread a piece of sheepskin on a rock to represent the departed, and we gathered in a circle around it. But nobody had thought exactly what this memorial service was supposed to consist of. None of us had ever done one before. I've been to my share of funerals in a church with so many flowers the scent was enough to knock you over, and a coffin with the lid open so that you had to look at the waxy figure all through the formal prayers and try not to think about how dead that person was. This was different.

Emmy said, "I didn't know Wooly Sam, I don't think I ever saw him in the lunchroom, but if nobody else has an idea, I think we should recite the twenty-third Psalm."

We said it together as the September sun poured down on us like a blessing.

The Lord is my shepherd, I shall not want.

He maketh me to lie down in green pastures: he leadeth me beside the still waters.

He restoreth my soul: he leadeth me in the paths of righteousness for his name's sake.

Nick pulled a harmonica out of his pocket and began to play: *Amazing Grace, how sweet the sound . . .*

We all knew that one, too, and sang along:

. . . that saved a wretch like me.

I once was lost, but now I'm found,

Was blind but now I see.

It seemed we'd done what we could for the soul of Wooly Sam. Frank unpacked a lunch of deviled eggs, which, he recalled, were Sam's favorite food. He preferred them to fried chicken. Max had sent a devil's food cake.

"If it had some reference to the devil in it, Sam loved it," said Frank.

Gallon jars of iced tea were passed around. Every

few minutes a freight pulled by two locomotives crawled slowly up to the summit, crossed the canyon on several bridges, and eased down the westward slope. Oftentimes an eastbound would be waiting on the west side to use that single track through the pass.

"Someday," Gus said, "somebody is going to figure out a way to make a double track through that pass, so they can get the trains through quicker, without having to wait on a siding."

One of the men insisted it couldn't be done. Tom Perkins and a few others took Gus's side. They entertained themselves, arguing whether it was possible or not. I could tell they'd had this argument many times before. When they got tired of it, we packed up the sheepskin that represented Wooly Sam and prepared to drive back to Belén. Before long the five o'clock westbound would be making its way slowly through the pass, and we had to be there to serve the folks on board.

Gus reached over and squeezed my hand, but we didn't have much to say to each other. We didn't have to talk. I'm pretty sure we were both thinking about Wooly Sam and the odd life he'd lived.

Tuesday, September 28th

THE SUN IS STILL HOT, BUT MORNINGS ARE VERY CHILLY, now that fall is here. At home, Mother has had Betty Jane take down the sheer summer curtains and put up the heavy lace curtains and sateen drapes. The last roses have faded in her garden, and Daddy has stored the porch furniture in the garage. O'Reilly is looking for patches of sun to nap in. Gramma Blair is complaining about her knees. They're both getting old, both seem to be feeling their age.

Howie is back at college; his classes have started, and Daddy writes that my brother has a part in the Drama Club's fall production. Daddy hopes he'll stick it out. The classes I'd signed up for have also begun. I thought I'd be feeling blue, but somehow the idea of being in a freshman dormitory with girls who've never been much of anywhere or done much of anything now seems kind of *dull*.

I wrote to Mother a couple of weeks ago and asked her to send down my warm clothes. The box was delivered yesterday, mostly old school clothes that look really juvenile. She included a new sweater-and-scarf set with a matching hat and gloves. They're green, and she knows I never wear green. Ugly as sin! She must have found them on sale at McMeen's. Warm, though, and Mrs. McCreary says it gets cold here in winter. Belén Lake freezes hard enough for ice skating, and there is often snow. Surely no more than back home in Kansas.

Sometimes I wish I could be there, just for a day or two. Just to say hello to everybody, before coming back to Belén.

Wednesday, September 29th

GUTEN MORGEN, CORDELIA SAYS WHEN OUR ALARM clock rings. At bedtime as we turn out the lights, she says, *Gute nacht*. In between I'm treated to a lot of *Bitte* and *Danke*, "please" and "thank you," and such important phrases as the German for "Please take your belongings with you" and "Turn left at the end of the hall to the W.C."

The W.C.?

Cordelia says that in Europe the toilet is called the W.C., which stands for "water closet," and she needs to learn the correct term in German if she's going to become a Courier. She says the German she studied at boarding school is coming back to her, and Viktor has promised to help her practice.

"Don't you have to know how to speak Spanish,

too?" I asked, and she said, "That I'm *really* going to have to fudge. Maybe Alicia can teach me a few phrases, enough so I can get by."

Thursday, September 30th

MAGGIE DISCOVERED THE BOWLING ALLEY ON THE first floor of the Commercial Club building on Becker Avenue. "Pedro brought me here and taught me to bowl. We come here a lot. We can sit and talk and nobody pays any attention. Don't tell anyone—Susana doesn't know."

"Susana's going to make a lot of trouble for you if she finds out," Cordelia warned.

Maggie brushed it off. "I'm not worried about a salad girl," she said.

She's promised to teach Cordelia and me how to bowl. It doesn't cost much, and we can borrow the right shoes.

We went this afternoon, after the boys who work as pinsetters got out of school. Maggie showed us how to fit our thumb and fingers into the holes in the heavy ball and how to send it rolling down the alley with a kind of swooping motion that she executes very gracefully. Her ball knocked down several pins on the first try and a couple more on the second. When Cordelia tried, her ball rolled so slowly she was afraid it was going to stop, but she must have done something right because all her pins toppled over.

"Strike!" Maggie cried. "I can't believe it. You bowled a strike on your very first try!"

"Nothing to it," Cordelia said. "I'm a natural."

I'm not a natural. Every time I was up, the ball veered off either to the left or to the right, into the gutter. I had the distinction of not knocking down a single pin. I'm sure the pinsetters at the end of the alley must have been laughing.

Sunday, October 3rd

CORDELIA AND I HAD TALKED ABOUT GOING TO SEE A moving picture this afternoon, but we realized even before we got as far as the Central that it's Sunday, and of course the theater is closed. We walked by anyway, to look at the posters advertising coming attractions. Buster Keaton's *Battling Butler* is currently showing, but there was a big poster for *The Son of the Sheik*: NEXT WEEK, BACK BY POPULAR DEMAND! VALENTINO'S LAST FILM!

“I wonder how many times Opal and Pearl have come to see it,” Cordelia said. She says the sisters have a photograph of Valentino on their dresser. I probably saw it and didn’t know who he was.

We turned around and started back. Everything was shut down tight. A drowsy Sunday afternoon with nothing to do.

We were about halfway up Becker Avenue when a Model T roadster barreled past, going faster than people usually drive around here, raising billows of dust and barely missing a lazy old hound that had wandered into its path. Probably headed for the Harvey House—everything else in Belén might shut down on Sundays, but never the Harvey House. Anybody looking for something to eat or drink can always find it there.

“Idiot driver,” Cordelia snorted. “What’s the big hurry?”

We dawdled on, speculating on how Emmy was getting along on the back of Nick’s motorcycle—he’d taken her to Jarales to show her the ranch. We consider it a good sign that she isn’t still waiting for letters from Carl that never come.

The mud-splattered roadster was parked outside the Harvey House. Cordelia wrote “GO SLOW” with her finger in the dust on the driver’s door. She suggested stopping in the lunchroom for some iced tea before we went up to our room. It didn’t take a genius to figure out that she was curious about the driver of the Model T.

He was seated at the counter, and Gladys with her incandescent smile was taking his order when we came in. She saw us and gave us an odd look, her eyebrows rising almost up to her hairline. The man swiveled around to face us.

"Cordelia," he said.

Cordelia gasped and grabbed my arm. "Walter! What in heaven's name are you doing here?"

"I've just dropped by to say hello." He sprang up and came toward us, a wide grin pasted across his face.

So this was Walter Vogel! He's not bad-looking, I'll say that for him. If you squint, you could say that he looks a lot like the picture of Rudolph Valentino—dark hair parted left of center, deep brown eyes, nice mouth, chin chiseled out of granite. Dressed up in a cream-colored suit with dark blue pinstripes and a lemon-yellow necktie.

"You've certainly come a long way to say hello." Cordelia hung back. She sounded angry and a little frightened.

Walter loomed over us, so close I could smell his cologne. He glanced at me, probably wishing I'd go away, but Cordelia was clutching my arm. She was trembling. He stopped just a few inches away, still grinning.

"I came to persuade you to come back to Pennsylvania with me," he said, and suddenly he dropped to one knee, right there in the lunchroom. "Marry me, Cordelia!"

"Walter, stop this!" Cordelia hissed furiously. She

looked as though she was going to slap him.

Gladys, who'd been pretending to be cleaning the counter, filling the sugar bowl, anything to seem busy, stopped and stared. Half a dozen railroaders who'd avoided looking in our direction were now staring as well, pie forks hovering in mid-air.

Walter got up, took one long step forward, grabbed Cordelia's shoulders, and kissed her passionately. The customers put down their forks and applauded. They were rooting for Walter.

Cordelia wrenched herself away. "This is embarrassing," she growled. "Come outside, and we'll talk." She stalked out, Walter right behind her.

The other customers chuckled and murmured among themselves, Gladys went back to polishing the counter, and I stood glued to the spot, trying to decide what, if anything, I should do. Then I heard the motor turn over, and I hurried to the window in time to see the roadster take off down the street. Cordelia was in it.

A little later, Gladys came by our room and asked if I knew what was going on. I said I didn't.

Whenever one of us plans to take a half-day off—we're entitled to a half-day once a week—Mrs. McCreary figures out who will cover the station. Maggie was covering for Emmy today, but Cordelia's absence was unplanned. Maybe she'd rush in at the last moment, or not. She didn't show up by four o'clock when I went down to make sure everything was ready for the dinner train, so I had to say *something* to Mrs. McCreary.

"Cordelia is not feeling at all well," I said, forcing myself to look Mrs. McCreary in the eye. "A queasy stomach. I told her I'd take her station."

Mrs. McCreary regarded me thoughtfully, and I felt as though she could see it written all over my face that I was not telling the truth. But she just nodded. The telegraph operator at the depot who relays the number after the conductor does the count has notified Mr. Lawrence to expect fewer customers than usual, and most of them prefer to eat in the lunchroom. Cordelia's absence will not be a problem.

But where *is* she?

Later Sunday

THE DINNER TRAIN CAME AND WENT. GLADYS KEPT MUM and didn't say anything about Walter, or about Cordelia leaving with anyone. Everyone bought my story that she was in bed with a queasy stomach.

Around eight o'clock, when the shift was finished and I'd eaten my own dinner, even though I wasn't at all hungry, I went out to sit on the bench under the cottonwoods. It was dark, except for the bulb burning over the kitchen door. I'd be able to see the roadster when it drove up Becker Avenue, and I thought I could flag it down and somehow manage to smuggle Cordelia up to our room without Mrs. McCreary noticing that she wasn't actually sick.

Chef Viktor and the cooks and kitchen helpers came out from time to time to grab a smoke, nodded to me, and then went back inside. Nobody said anything, but I had a feeling that more people knew about the scene in the lunchroom than I'd thought.

Every few minutes I walked to the end of the street to see if I could spot any headlights coming up Becker Avenue. I nearly jumped out of my skin when a voice spoke from the darkness: "Looks like somebody's got a case of the heebie-jeebies."

Gus stepped into the pool of light. Any other time I'd have been happy to have him show up unexpectedly, but not tonight. "Want to tell me what's eating you?"

"It's Cordelia," I admitted.

He'd heard about Walter's appearance in the lunchroom. The railroaders who'd stopped by for their afternoon pie and coffee had witnessed it all—a ritzy-looking stranger arriving in a swell car and proposing to Cordelia on bended knee, her stomping off, him running after her, the two of them driving off in that car.

I told Gus as much as I knew: how Walter wanted to

marry her and had sent her a diamond engagement ring in the mail, and she'd mailed it back, telling him *No*. How her mother is mad at her but has gone right ahead planning the wedding and probably knows Walter has come all the way out to New Mexico to fetch her. Maybe Mrs. Hart even sent him.

I said I was worried she'd get back too late, and the doors would be locked and she'd be in trouble. She hadn't asked anyone's permission to leave.

Gus pointed out that a cook and one of the helpers are in the kitchen all night, in case a freight stops and the crew needs coffee and something to eat.

"The cook will let her in," I said, "but that's not the problem. The problem is Mrs. McCreary. She has ears like an owl and hears every little sound." I told him that the night I fell in Belén Lake and came home late, I tried to sneak up the stairs and Mrs. McCreary caught me.

Gus reached over and took my hand, rubbing my knuckles with his thumb. "So Cordelia gets caught breaking the curfew—is that the worst thing that can happen?"

The worst thing would be if Walter somehow persuaded her to go back to Pennsylvania with him. That would be the end of Cordelia's dreams of being a Detours Courier, or playing the piano in a swanky hotel in California, or seeing the Grand Canyon.

"Quit worrying, Kitty," he advised. "There's nothing you can do about it."

Of course I *know* that, but it was nice to have Gus there to talk to and to keep my mind off Cordelia. We heard the muffled roar of a motorcycle down the street. The roar died, and Nick and Emmy appeared. They stopped to talk for a few minutes before Emmy said goodnight and went inside and the Indian started up again. We listened until it faded away, and the only sound was the chirp of crickets.

Gus leaned close. "We have time for one more thing. That kiss I promised you."

He kissed me. Then he kissed me again. If Gus hadn't pulled out his railroad watch and checked it, there might have been a third time, and I would have missed curfew.

"Goodnight, Kitty," he said, and strode off into the darkness, while I ran up the stairs, marveling at what had just happened.

A few minutes ago, Emmy tapped on the door. "Where's Cordelia?"

"She's been gone for hours. She went off with Walter. I don't trust him."

Emmy perched on Cordelia's bed and we sat for a while, not saying anything. Emmy stood up to leave and then sat down again. "You'll never guess what happened."

I went to sit beside her. "Tell me."

"Nick kissed me. I'm not sure I should have let him."

I started laughing.

"What's so funny?" she asked.

"Gus kissed me," I said. "And I'm very glad he did!"

We talked for a while, waiting for Cordelia. Now it's an hour past curfew, Emmy has gone to her own room, and Cordelia still isn't back.

Monday, October 4th

CORDELIA CREPT IN ABOUT FIVE O'CLOCK THIS MORNING. Viktor opened the door for her, she avoided all the squeaky steps, and if Mrs. McCreary heard anything she must have thought Cordelia had just gone down to the kitchen for a cup of tea for her queasy stomach. Cordelia has all the luck.

I glanced bleary-eyed into the mirror as we rushed to get ready for the morning shift. "We both look like the wreck of the *Hesperus*," I said.

"The what?" Her voice was ragged.

"The Wreck of the *Hesperus*" is a poem by Henry Wadsworth Longfellow," I explained. "The *Hesperus* is a schooner, the captain takes his little daughter to sea, a storm comes up, the boat wrecks, and they all die. It means we look a mess."

We went down for breakfast. "I told Mrs. McCreary you were feeling sick," I warned her, and crossed my fingers that nobody would ask questions. Nobody did.

We struggled through the day, drinking lots of coffee and taking a long nap in the afternoon. It wasn't until this evening that she finally told me what happened.

I'm writing Cordelia's story here as the draft of a magazine article—something for the *Ladies' Home Journal*, maybe.

AN INCIDENT IN ALBUQUERQUE

On a bright October afternoon under a cloudless New Mexico sky, Walter Vogel stepped off the train in Albuquerque. He checked into the luxurious Alvarado Hotel, asked the manager to hire a car for him, and completed the last leg of his journey across the country from Pennsylvania. Following narrow, unpaved roads, he drove to a picturesque village with a Spanish name: Belén, meaning "Bethlehem."

This was not a simple vacation jaunt for twenty-seven-year-old Walter. He was on a mission: to persuade Cordelia Hart to marry him. Cordelia, twenty years old and a former student at a conservatory of music in Philadelphia, had left a promising musical career to be trained as a Harvey Girl. She had become a waitress of the highest order, employed by the Fred Harvey Company in one of their famously attractive eating houses along the Atchison, Topeka & Santa Fe Railroad.

Walter's earlier attempts at persuasion had met with failure: his proposal rejected, his diamond-and-sapphire engagement ring refused. Now he would press his suit in person. In the lunchroom of the Belén Harvey House he waited for Cordelia's return from a Sunday afternoon stroll, surprising her and rendering her almost speechless when she found him there.

He agreed that the Harvey House meals were superlative, the best he'd eaten anywhere. He allowed that the scenery of the Southwest was grand indeed. He admitted that the service performed by the Harvey Girls was impeccable, although why any young lady wished to work so devilishly hard for so little reward, when other options were available, was unfathomable.

"Enough is enough, Cordelia," he said. "Your mother, your stepfather, and I all agree that it's in your best interest to return to Pennsylvania, settle down, and live the sort of life that is appropriate and expected of you by your family."

He told her gently that he was willing to forgive her petulant return of the engagement ring and the accompanying letter, which he found dismissive. [Author's note: I asked Cordelia if she'd told him someone else—me—had written it for her, and she said of course not.] *He told her how much the ring had cost. He said that he'd found a delightful little bungalow for their home. He reminded her that her mother had taken care of all the arrangements for a June wedding—tentatively booking the fashionable church, reserving the country club for the reception, and hiring a caterer, a florist, and a dressmaker for the wedding gown and trousseau. All that was lacking was Cordelia's approval of the wedding date.*

For now, Walter would drive her to Albuquerque, where they could discuss their relationship in privacy at the fabled Alvarado Hotel.

Cordelia hesitated. Although she had grave misgivings, she finally agreed to accompany him. Foolishly, perhaps, she assumed that she would return to Belén before the curfew. For nearly an hour and a half Walter urged the automobile over rough roads until at last they arrived at the Alvarado, its picturesque towers and arched arcades welcoming passengers as they arrived by train from east and west.

Cordelia and Walter strolled through the long arcade. From rocking chairs they gazed at gardens decked in glorious fall colors. They were in no hurry. Without telling her, Walter had reserved a room for Cordelia, and there was plenty of time to explore. They toured the Indian Building, admired the enormous fireplace in the lounge, and peered into the parlors. Cordelia told Walter about Belén and the Harvey House. She did not mention that this was not her first visit to the Alvarado. For his part, Walter had little to say about Reading, Pennsylvania, and the cement plant.

A reserved table with a bouquet of fresh flowers awaited them in the baronial dining room. A little velvet box containing the ring had been placed next to the flowers.

Walter's plan was to relax there for a while before the two of them boarded the eastbound train and returned to Pennsylvania. Lorenzo, Cordelia's stepfather, had given Walter leave "to take care of our little girl." Perhaps they might spend a few days in Santa Fe, if she liked. Or continue on west and visit the Grand Canyon. Would she prefer that? Walter had been keen to see the Grand Canyon, ever since he majored in geology at Princeton. They could arrange to have someone pack her clothes and ship them. She could buy whatever she needed in the meantime. Lorenzo would foot the bill.

Cordelia promised Walter that she would think about all of this—a trip to the Grand Canyon, his proposal of marriage. Then, saying that she was tired and wanted to rest, she excused herself and took the key to her room. She left the ring in the velvet box next to the flowers. She had brought nothing with her—no change of clothes, no nightdress, no toothbrush. She called down to the manager, who promised to send one of the Harvey Girls with whatever she needed. Cordelia requested that he send Louise, the Harvey Girl who had been the lunchroom waitress on her earlier visit.

Louise recognized her immediately. Cordelia explained that a certain friend of the family was insisting on taking her back to Pennsylvania against her will. "I am desperate to get away from him," she said.

Louise was sympathetic. A southbound local left Albuquerque early each morning and stopped in Belén, and Louise promised to have the bellhop awaken Cordelia in time to be on that train. Cordelia composed a note to Walter, telling him that she had not changed her mind: she would not marry him, and he was to return to Reading and inform her mother of her decision. If he dared to show his face in Belén again, she would have the law on him. Adiós, Walter!

Then she lay down on her bed and tried to sleep.

In the wee hours of the morning, Cordelia slipped the note under Walter's door, left the Alvarado, and caught the early train from

Albuquerque. Just as the first rays of the sun rose over the Manzano Mountains, Cordelia was back in Belén.

That's as far as I've gotten with the story. I'm not sure how it's going to end—and neither is Cordelia.

Wednesday, October 6th

FOR THE FIRST COUPLE OF DAYS AFTER WALTER'S VISIT, Cordelia was constantly looking over her shoulder, half-expecting him to jump out from behind a tree or pop up on the other side of the lunch counter with some new scheme to lure her back to Pennsylvania. She left word downstairs with Mr. Lawrence and Enrique, the newsstand manager, as well as Mrs. McCreary and the chefs and cooks, that if a tall, well-dressed stranger comes looking for her, she is not to be found. So far, so good—there's no sign of him.

I don't believe he'll let her go quite so easily, not after making such a long trip all the way across the country. And what about her mother? If ever there was a woman not used to taking no for an answer, it's Mrs. Hart. I'm still afraid she and Walter will find a way to lasso Cordelia and haul her off to the altar, kicking and screaming.

This morning Mrs. McCreary summoned Cordelia to the telephone. Mrs. Hart was calling. Not long after we arrived in Belén, almost three months ago, she'd called and ordered Cordelia to return home, threatening to cut her off without a cent if she didn't obey. Cordelia had refused. Now Cordelia pleaded with me to take the call and speak to her mother, but I protested that her mother didn't want to talk to me and I had no idea what to say.

"Please, Kitty," Cordelia begged, and steered me to the telephone in the office. "You're good at this! Just put her off somehow."

I picked up the receiver and lowered my voice, trying to sound mature. "This is Katherine Evans, Miss Hart's supervisor. Miss Hart is unable to take your call at this time. May I help you in some way?"

Cordelia silently applauded.

Her mother's angry voice sounded tinny and far away. It was not a good connection, but I caught "Walter" and "Mr. Vogel" and "immediately."

I cleared my throat loudly and interrupted. "Miss Hart has informed Mr. Vogel that she is refusing his proposal and that she wishes to hear no more from him." Cordelia bobbed her head up and down, egging me on. I forged ahead. "Any further interference from him at her place of work or her place of residence will be promptly reported to the local authorities and his removal requested from the premises as an infringement on her privacy."

Without waiting for an answer from her mother, I said good-bye—courteously, I thought—and hung up.

"Kitty, you were wonderful! Have you ever considered being a lawyer? Or maybe even an actress?"

"Not a chance," I said. "I'm going to be a journalist, and that's that."

"'Going to be'"? Cordelia said. "I'd say you already are one."

Thursday, October 7th

STILL NO WORD FROM WALTER. I THINK THAT'S A GOOD thing, but Cordelia isn't so sure.

Yesterday she telephoned Louise at the Alvarado and asked her to find out if Walter Vogel had checked out of the hotel and, if he had, where he was headed. She instructed Louise to call her collect as soon as she had any information.

Today Louise called. Cordelia came back from the office looking stunned. Walter is gone, and nobody seems to know where he went. The problem is, he ran up quite a bill and then skipped out without paying. If Cordelia knows of Walter Vogel's whereabouts, the manager of the Alvarado would be most grateful for any information.

"That skunk!" Cordelia raged. "That louse! To embarrass me like this! How can I ever go back and ask for a job as a Courier? He's ruined my reputation! If I ever hear from him again, it will be too soon!"

Cordelia says she won't relax until she's positive that Walter has left the state and is out of her life, once and for all.

Tuesday, October 12th

A LETTER ARRIVED FROM CORDELIA'S MOTHER IN TODAY'S mail. Cordelia was in no hurry to open it.

"Aren't you even curious?" I asked, because I surely was.

"It's going to be another lecture," she said, and tossed it aside. "Walter probably went back to Reading with a made-up tale, and now they're blaming me for everything."

"Went back without paying his hotel bill?"

"He no doubt cooked up some excuse for stiffing the hotel," Cordelia grumbled, but still she didn't open the letter.

We were taking our afternoon break, trying to decide what, if anything, we'd do for the next couple of hours until it was time to go back to work. I looked forward to reading the book I'd just bought at the newsstand.

I went down to the garden with my novel, *Seventeen* by Booth Tarkington. I'd barely begun the story of William's infatuation with Lola Pratt, the kind of girl you want to hate, when Cordelia dashed out, clutching the letter and looking deathly pale. She sank onto the bench beside me and handed me the four pages of scrawl.

"Go on," she said. "Read it."

Dearest Cordelia, I have the most awful news for you concerning Walter.

I read through the letter slowly, to make sure I understood. Mrs. Hart writes in fragments of thought divided by long dashes, with no particular order or logic. This is the gist of it:

Walter is a humbug. He has deceived just about everyone, embezzling funds from Lorenzo's cement factory and running the business into the ground. He had also been involved in Lorenzo's contracts to build a stadium and other big projects, siphoning off thousands upon thousands of dollars.

Betting on the horses, Mrs. Hart had written. *Big bets, big losses.*

He must've thought he was going to marry the boss's daughter and everything would work out in the end. But then Cordelia refused to marry him, and now nothing was working out. Lorenzo had loaned Walter the money to buy the engagement ring and given him an advance against his salary to pay for the trip to New Mexico. That was Walter's last chance.

Bad for Walter, but even worse for Lorenzo and Mrs. Hart. The cement business was in trouble. *Declaring bankruptcy—might have to sell the big house, move into one of the small rental houses Lorenzo owns—or used to own. Resigned from the country club—too humiliating to go there, see old friends. What wretchedness.*

Cordelia sat with her elbows on her knees and her head buried in her hands.

I folded the letter and slid it back in the envelope. "Maybe your uncle in Leavenworth can help them," I suggested, thinking of the rich relative she'd been visiting when I first met her.

"Mummy is too humiliated to ask Uncle Cam," Cordelia murmured. "So, as it turns out, Lorenzo couldn't have afforded to let me go back to the conservatory after all. Why did it take him so long to figure out what was happening? Working as a Harvey Girl isn't just a lark anymore. I actually do need a job!"

And the big question still isn't answered: *Where is Walter?*

Wednesday, October 13th

I WAS STRUGGLING WITH THE ONEROUS CHORE OF ironing the starched white collars and cuffs of my uniform during our afternoon break. Cordelia had gone to the bank to talk with Mr. Dalies about her account. She's thinking of paying her portion of the bill that Walter ran up at the Alvarado—half the expensive dinner and her room. "How can I ever get a job with Indian Detours if they think I'm a deadbeat?"

She's been depositing her monthly pay into an account that's in her name and her mother's, the same account where Mrs. Hart or Lorenzo has been sending her monthly allowance. When tips are good, Cordelia puts some aside in her bureau drawer as "mad money" and deposits the rest. She hardly ever writes a check and never bothers to balance her checkbook. Mr. Dalies would help her decide what to do about the Alvarado.

Mrs. McCreary came looking for her. "Cordelia has a visitor," Mrs. McCreary said. "A male visitor."

Walter, I thought, and nearly dropped the iron.

"Is he still there? Did he give his name?"

No. And no.

I asked what he looked like. An older man, Mrs. McCreary said. He was carrying a violin case.

He said he'd come back another time.

That didn't sound like Walter. But who could it be? I finished my ironing and waited for Cordelia to come back.

She was in quite a state when she did. Her mother and Lorenzo put money into her account, but they can also take money out. She hadn't realized that. Now most of it is gone. "If Mummy needed it and took it, that's one thing. Most of it was hers to begin with. But if Walter somehow got his hands on it, I'll—well, I don't know what I'll do!"

Then I told her about the mysterious visitor with a violin, and that took her mind off her money problems. "Tell me again what Mrs. McCreary said."

I repeated the message word for word.

Who could it be? she wondered. Maybe one of the drivers for the Indian Detours—Leo, for instance? *An older man*, Mrs. McCreary had said, but Leo is no more than thirty, probably younger. And why would he be carrying a violin?

We went to find Mrs. McCreary. "He's about fifty, I'd say," she reported. "Tall and thin. Very neat and clean but rather shabbily dressed. Needs a haircut. Well-spoken. Looks like anybody you'd see getting off the dinner train, except for the violin case. And he asked specifically for you."

"A mystery!" Cordelia said. Suddenly she stopped, a stricken look on her face. "What if he's a private detective and he's looking for the person who skipped out on the bill at the Alvarado!"

"And carries a violin case?"

"Part of his disguise!" Finally Cordelia laughed. "All right. I guess I just have to wait and see, don't I?"

Saturday, October 16th

THE WEDNESDAY DINNER TRAIN WAS CROWDED; THE dining room was full, and the lunchroom, too. Travel is heavy at this time of year, with clear sunny days that aren't too hot and cool nights, perfect weather. Cordelia and I kept an anxious eye on the front entrance for any customer who might turn out to be the mysterious stranger. But the train left, the usual dinner customers arrived, and no stranger appeared.

It was the same on Thursday and Friday, a nerve-wracking couple of days. Hardly anything rattles Cordelia, but she was plainly rattled.

Then today at lunchtime a man came in carrying a battered violin case and a worn valise. I didn't recognize him, and neither did Cordelia. He asked for a table in the dining room. He wasn't wearing a jacket, and Mrs. McCreary explained the coat rule and brought him a jacket from the closet. He sat at a table for two and stood the violin case on the empty chair.

We had a good number of customers today, regulars mostly—Mr. John Becker was there, as usual; his nephew Paul Dalies from the bank; Mr. Brower, the editor of the newspaper—but something about the stranger, besides the violin, grabbed my attention. I couldn't say exactly what it was.

Maggie was waiting on that table, and she offered the gentleman a menu. He took it but kept glancing around the dining room, as though he was looking for someone. He was as Mrs. McCreary described him: middle-aged, baggy suit, frayed shirt-cuffs, and he did need a haircut. A traveling salesman, maybe. Now he was studying Cordelia, taking in the blond hair, blue eyes, creamy skin.

Their eyes met, and the gentleman smiled and rose slowly, his napkin in his hand. "Cordelia?"

She moved closer to the table, warily. "Yes, sir?"

"Cordelia," he repeated, a smile lighting up his weathered face like sunshine. "Yes, it is you! I haven't seen you since you were a little girl, and here you are, all grown up! A beautiful young woman."

Cordelia stared uncertainly. Then she gasped, her hands flew up to her mouth, and she cried, "Daddy?"

Even though no professional Harvey Girl ever does such a thing, she threw her arms around his neck and buried her face on his shoulder. Everybody stopped reading, talking, eating, and serving to watch the scene unfolding in front of us.

Cordelia stepped back, struggling to regain her composure. “We can talk when I finish my shift,” she said shakily. “Maggie is your waitress. She’ll take good care of you.”

Cordelia was trembling, but somehow she managed to greet her customers, take their orders, and hurry to the kitchen, performing smoothly in the Harvey Way, once again a well-disciplined Harvey Girl. But she did come over to ask me if I would be willing to switch tables with Maggie.

“It’s my father. I haven’t seen him since I was eight years old,” she whispered. “I can’t imagine what he’s doing here or how he found me. Kitty, you’re such a good judge of people. I’d appreciate it so much if you’d wait on him. Will you?”

I said I would. Mrs. McCreary, who as usual was keeping a sharp eye on the situation, quickly agreed, and Maggie and I made the switch.

I set down the bowl of cauliflower soup he’d ordered and introduced myself. “I’m Cordelia’s roommate. We were hired on the same day, and we’ve been together ever since.” I explained that we were not supposed to carry on personal conversations with customers but assured him that Cordelia was looking forward to spending time with him soon. In the meantime, I would be happy to bring him whatever he liked. Another roll? Was the soup to his satisfaction?

Cordelia has her father's eyes, deep blue and intense. The nose is different, but the mouth is the same, dimples that appear and disappear, and an expression that says he knows something amusing but can't let on. Her father's hair might have been blond once, but now it is faded and streaked with gray. And I noticed his hands and his long, tapering fingers.

On the other side of the dining room Cordelia was carrying on with her duties as though nothing unusual had happened, as though her life had not just suddenly been turned upside down *again*. Her father ordered chocolate custard, drank another cup of coffee, and pulled a worn leather wallet out of his pocket.

"Please tell my daughter I'll wait for her in the garden," he murmured, paying his bill, and I said I would. He hung the borrowed jacket over the back of his chair, picked up the violin case and his valise, and left. There was a dime under the saucer.

Cordelia is down there with him now. I can see them from the window at the end of the hall. They're sitting on the bench together, talking animatedly. I can hear the lilt in Cordelia's voice and occasional quiet laughter. It's that lilt I recognized in her father's voice that sounded somehow familiar. They must have a lot to catch up on, after all these years, and I'm dying of curiosity. Where did he come from? Where has he been? Why has he not seen Cordelia for more than twelve years?

Monday, October 18th

TODAY IS CORDELIA'S TWENTY-FIRST BIRTHDAY. SHE asked Max to make her a baked Alaska: a sponge cake topped with ice cream, then covered with meringue and put in a hot oven just long enough to brown the meringue without melting the ice cream. Max took it as a challenge and promised to rise to the occasion.

Cordelia's father—his name is John Paul Sidney—was here.

Mr. Sidney is staying at the Belén Hotel and eating most of his meals at the Cutoff Café, to spare Cordelia the discomfort of having him come to the Harvey House when she's working. She's spent most of her free time with her father since he arrived, sitting under the portal facing the tracks or taking long walks together. When it's time for her to go back to work, he goes down to the AT&SF Reading Room and reads the newspapers.

After the lunch crowd left today, the usual gang of railroaders gathered at the lunch counter, waiting for the appearance of the birthday cake. John Paul Sidney slipped in quietly just as Max carried in his masterpiece with one big candle stuck in the middle. After we'd all sung "Happy Birthday" and Cordelia had blown out the candle, Mr. Sidney opened his violin case, lifted out his fiddle, as he calls it, and began to play "Beautiful Dreamer."

What sweet music he coaxed from that fiddle! It filled the lunchroom and floated out into the dining room. Enrique left the newsstand to listen, and Mr. Lawrence and Mrs. McCreary, as well as Viktor and every single one of the cooks and kitchen helpers, who normally ignore what's happening on the other side of the kitchen doors unless it has something to do with the food, stopped whatever they were doing and came to listen. But the big surprise was Tom Perkins, who began to sing along in a husky tenor voice that blended perfectly with the mellow sound of the violin.

Beautiful dreamer, wake unto me

Starlight and dewdrops are waiting for thee . . .

It was as if the two had been performing together for ages. Cordelia's eyes filled with tears, and she is definitely not a weeper. She wasn't the only one wiping her eyes by the time their song ended. I was, too.

The audience clapped and called for more. Mr. Sidney played "Old Folks at Home" and Tom joined in for that one, too:

Way down upon the Swanee River, far far away . . .

“Stephen Foster wrote those songs,” Mr. Sidney said when they’d finished. “He was from Pittsburgh, you know. Like me.” He proceeded to give us a lesson on the history of the man he said was the father of American music. “Foster wrote over two hundred songs and died a penniless alcoholic in the Bowery of New York. A sad, sad life,” he said, tenderly laying his violin in the case. He saw me watching. “Lovely, isn’t it? Just look at the grain in that wood! Not quite a Stradivarius, but it is Italian, and it is very old. It’s my most prized possession, as dear to me as a close friend. You don’t get sound like that from just any violin.”

We finished up Cordelia’s fancy dessert, and her father launched into another history lesson, this one on baked Alaska. “It was created in New York by a French chef to commemorate the purchase of Alaska in 1867.”

Cordelia rolled her eyes. “There’s not much he doesn’t know,” she said, but she wasn’t able to disguise her pride.

Mr. Lawrence had been listening from the doorway, and now he wondered aloud if the railroaders and the people of Belén might not enjoy an evening of violin music over at the Reading Room one night soon, if perhaps Mr. Sidney planned to remain in town for a while longer? Mr. Sidney agreed that he could arrange a suitable program.

Cordelia broke into a wide smile, we all applauded, and the Harvey House staff went back to work.

As Gus was about to leave, he pulled me aside and handed me an envelope. "I was asked to deliver this," he said.

Inside was a note from Mr. Brower, the editor of the Belén News:

Your piece on Wooly Sam will run in Thursday's paper. Nice work. I'd like to see more of your writing.

Enclosed was a one-dollar bill.

My piece accepted and my first pay as a journalist, with the possibility of more! I felt as though I'd taken a giant step toward my future.

I showed the note to Gus.

"Congratulations, Kitty!" he said, grinning. "You're on your way!"

I feel like celebrating, but the five o'clock is due any minute, so for right now I'm still a Harvey Girl.

Tuesday, October 19th

LAST NIGHT AFTER CURFEW, CORDELIA AND I LAY IN our beds and she told me about her father. It's a long story, she said, and she's been piecing it together a little at a time.

John Paul Sidney was born in Pittsburgh, where his

father worked in the steel mills. He first got his hands on a violin when he was eight or nine, and soon he'd figured out how to play it. A few years later he left home, moving from job to job, none of them having anything to do with music but earning enough money to pay for lessons from any violinist with something to teach him.

He was playing with a dance band in Reading when he met Dorothy Fuller. Dorothy's father was a textile manufacturer who never approved of John Paul—didn't think a fiddler could ever amount to much. They married anyway, and Cordelia was born in 1905. But in a few years the marriage had soured, partly because John Paul was often traveling, making whatever living he could eke out as a musician and teacher. Also, he was "overly fond of spirits," Cordelia's mother told her, when she said anything about him at all.

"He says Mummy told him to go away and not come back, and he took her at her word."

Dorothy married Lorenzo Hart and changed Cordelia's last name from Sidney to Hart. Cordelia didn't see her father again. John Paul Sidney disappeared, and stayed disappeared until a few days ago.

But he never forgot her birthday, he told her, and made up his mind to find her when she turned twenty-one, legally an adult. Her mother would no longer have any control over her. Mr. Sidney went back to Reading and started asking questions. Her mother refused to speak to him, but he still had a few friends there. Someone mentioned that Cordelia had studied at a conservatory in Philadelphia. Someone else heard that she'd gone to visit her mother's brother in Kansas.

It took him months, but he made it as far as Kansas City, playing in smoke-filled speakeasies and private clubs and working at odd jobs to make ends meet. He remembered that Cordelia had a cousin named Violet, and once he'd managed to speak to Violet alone, away from Cordelia's Uncle Cam, she told him about the Harvey Girls. Mr. Sidney paid a call on Miss Steele, who, once she was convinced that this actually was Cordelia's father, directed him to Belén.

"Mummy never once mentioned that my father was trying to find me!" Cordelia said.

"He's a regular Sherlock Holmes," I said.

"Elementary, my dear Kitty."

Cordelia told her father a few stories of her own, about her two years at the conservatory and her dreams of being a pianist. And the whole saga of Walter Vogel, the engagement ring she refused, the wedding that won't happen, Walter's recent visit, and the ruination of Lorenzo's business.

It was very late when we finally turned out the light. "Happy birthday, Cordelia," I said, yawning, my eyes already closing.

"Happiest ever," she replied.

Thursday, October 21st

"The Death of a Hobo" appears in today's paper with my byline, "by Katherine A. Evans." Cordelia thinks I should write under the name "K. A. Evans" or "Kit Evans," so it won't be so obvious that I'm a female journalist, because, she says, it's easier to break into newspaper work if you're a man. Maybe she's right, but for now I've decided to stay with my given name.

Also in today's *Belén News* is this advertisement:

> The public is cordially invited to
> **A SPECIAL MUSICAL PROGRAM**
> featuring renowned violinist
> John Paul Sidney
> performing compositions by Mozart,
> Bach, and Paganini
> as well as such popular composers as
> Stephen Foster and George Gershwin
> Saturday, October 23rd, 7:30 p.m.
> AT&SF Railroad Reading Room

Monday, October 25th

I DELIVERED THE FOLLOWING ARTICLE THIS AFTERnoon to Mr. Brower at the *Belén News*. A skinny man with a big bow tie and owlish eyeglasses, he sat at a rolltop desk, making corrections on a news story with a blue pencil. While I fidgeted, he read over my article. He didn't have anything to say about it, good or bad, but he fished a fifty-cent piece from a drawer and handed it to me. My article will appear in the next issue, this coming Thursday.

Miss Baca at the telephone company let me use her typewriter again, but she says from now on I need to make other arrangements.

TOURING VIOLINIST DAZZLES LOCAL AUDIENCE

by Katherine A. Evans

The Reading Room of the Atchison, Topeka & Santa Fe Railroad was filled to overflowing last Saturday evening with music lovers who turned out en masse to enjoy the virtuosic performance of violinist John Paul Sidney. Many of those unable to gain admittance crowded the porch, enduring a chilly evening to listen to music of breathtaking beauty.

Mr. Sidney, of Pittsburgh, Pennsylvania, received an enthusiastic response to his elegant rendering of solo violin compositions by the world's most acclaimed composers. He opened his program with Mozart's "Adagio and Rondo," followed by "Chaconne" by J. S. Bach, and "Caprice" by Paganini.

The enthusiastic audience rose to its feet when in the second half of the program Mr. Sidney played his arrangement of music by George and Ira Gershwin from their musical comedy Broadway success, *Lady, Be Good*, including the popular "Fascinating Rhythm." He followed this with a medley of songs both soulful and gay by the American composer Stephen Foster. Between numbers he informed his rapt listeners with stories of Mr. Foster's life and work and his premature death.

The evening ended with sustained applause and a standing ovation, acknowledged modestly by the outstanding performer.

Wednesday, October 27th

Mr. Sidney is leaving. He's told Cordelia that today is his last day in Belén.

His concert on Saturday night was a great success. Everybody was there—the entire Becker family, Alicia and a good part of her family, the railroaders who heard him play at Cordelia's birthday party at the Harvey House, even several of the cooks and kitchen workers. Sally and Tom were there, and Gus was sitting with them. Mr. Sidney made money with his performance. The railroad paid him twenty dollars, and although there was no admission charge, members of the audience were encouraged to leave a contribution in a basket placed by the door. Many did—even just a quarter apiece adds up, and some placed dollar bills in the basket.

He looked very handsome, for an older man. He'd gotten a haircut, shave, and shoeshine at the barbershop and had his suit pressed, and Cordelia bought him a new shirt at Becker's because his only two shirts were both in ruins. Mr. Lawrence loaned him a necktie and gave him a nice introduction at the Reading Room. A number of ladies in the audience fussed over him after the concert, which he seemed to enjoy.

He has spent the past few days roaming the dirt

streets and coaxing children to sing their favorite songs for him. Miss Delgado, the teacher at the grade school, attended the concert, and she asked him to come into her classes and play for the children. In return, they sang for him and taught him their songs. Their favorite seems to be *"La Cucaracha,"* which means "Little Cockroach."

I asked Cordelia if she thought he'd stay around for long, and she said she had no idea. "He's kind of a troubadour, going from place to place, making music, learning new songs wherever he goes."

Then today Mr. Sidney came into the lunchroom carrying his violin and valise. Cordelia asked why he'd brought them, and that's when he told her he's leaving.

"I think I've stayed in Belén long enough," he said. "You've got your work and your life here, and there's not much for me to do, now that I've had my concert. I'm ready for a change of scenery." He's going up to Santa Fe to see if he can earn some money there.

"But you'll be coming back, won't you?" Cordelia asked, and I could hear the threat of tears in her voice.

Her father took her hand and held it. "Of course, but not right away. I know where to find you, and I see that you're all right. That's all I set out to do." He said he was sorry to hear about that rat, Walter, and the bad trick he pulled. "I'm afraid I can't help you much, but I certainly don't want to be a hindrance. So I believe it's time to move on."

Mr. Sidney made the rounds, shaking hands, saying good-bye, thanking Mrs. McCreary and Mr. Lawrence for being good to his daughter, even sticking his head into the kitchen to wish Viktor and the cooks and kitchen helpers well, telling them it was the best food he'd ever had.

Cordelia is out on the platform with him now, waiting to see him off on the next local train headed north.

I've come to feel very close to Cordelia, almost like she's my big sister, and it makes me sad that Cordelia is sad. Still, I think her father made the right decision, and I'm betting she'll soon see it that way, too.

Monday, November 1st

THE RAILROADERS ARE ELECTRIFIED BY THE NEWS. THE Atchison, Topeka & Santa Fe is inaugurating a new high-speed train between Chicago and Los Angeles. It's called the *Chief*, and it will make the run in sixty-three hours. It starts in two weeks.

"That's nine hours less than three days, which is amazing when you think about it," Tom Perkins informed anyone who would listen at the lunch counter today.

The disappointment to our boys is that the *Chief* will go through Albuquerque over the Raton Pass, and not through Belén by the Belén Cutoff. They won't have the privilege of servicing it in our roundhouse.

For more than thirty years there has been one luxury passenger train making the run from Chicago to Los Angeles, the *California Limited.* When it started, the trip took three and a half days; they finally got it down to sixty-eight hours. It's expensive, but it's been the best way to travel across the country. During the summer sometimes as many as two dozen sections of the *Limited* left the Chicago station in a single day. The *Chief* will be faster than the *Limited* by five hours.

"Someday that trip will take a lot less than sixty-three hours," Gus said. "Someday people will cross the whole country in less than a day."

"And how do you think they're going to do that?" Tom scoffed. "On a rocket ship?"

"On an airplane. They're already carrying sacks of mail, flying from St. Louis to Chicago. Pretty soon they'll be taking passengers, too."

The railroaders laughed, thinking that was a great joke. Gus took their ribbing good-naturedly, but he caught my eye and winked. *He's not kidding*, I thought. *He really believes he's going to be flying one of those mail planes.*

But here was big news for the Harvey Girls: Mrs. McCreary said a huge celebration is planned at La Castañeda when the trains meet in Las Vegas the next day. Because of the different time zones, the westbound will leave Chicago on the morning of Sunday the fourteenth, and the eastbound will leave Los Angeles Sunday evening. If all goes according to plan, they'll both arrive in Las Vegas around six p.m. Most of the passengers will be executives of the railroad, of course, and the governors of California and Illinois and New Mexico and maybe the states that the trains pass through. Their wives, too, Mrs. McCreary said, and some congressmen and *their* wives. Possibly even President Coolidge and the First Lady!

They'll celebrate with the usual speeches, followed by a five-course banquet. Some of the passengers will elect to stay the night at La Castañeda, and the rest will board the eastbound or westbound *Chief* again and continue to their destination.

"With all those people, the Castañeda is going to need extra help for a couple of days, and the manager has asked me to send up a few Harvey Girls, if I can spare you. So if any of you are interested, please let me—"

But we didn't let Mrs. McCreary finish. Every one of the Harvey Girls raised their hands and volunteered to go.

"I'll let you know who's been picked," our head waitress said. She says La Castañeda is smaller than the Alvarado, but just as luxurious.

Thursday, November 4th

It's been almost three months since Emmy decided to stop writing to Carl until he wrote to her. So far she's heard nothing. Then there it was today: a letter from Carl.

It's about time, I thought, but I didn't say anything, and now I'm glad I didn't.

She tore open the envelope and pulled out a single sheet of paper. It took her only seconds to read it, and then to read it again. Her face was as white as that paper.

"He's getting married," she said. "To Clara Mae Dobson, my best friend from Sunday school. On the thirteenth." She refolded the letter and carefully placed it back in the envelope. "He says he hopes I'm not too mad at him."

I didn't know what to say—*I'm sorry,* or *You're better off without him*—so I put my arms around her and gave her a hug.

"I am sort of surprised," she said. "But I think I'm also sort of relieved. Clara Mae's a nice girl. She'll be good to him." She wiped her eyes with the back of her hand. "Now I won't feel guilty if I let Nick kiss me again. He's been wanting to for the longest time."

Monday, November 8th

Still no word on who will be allowed to go to Las Vegas for the celebration.

I've made myself a promise. If I'm picked, or even if I'm not, I'm going to buy a typewriter. I asked about them today at Becker's, and Miss Lucie showed me an advertisement for an Underwood Portable model that comes in its own carrying case. "Better than the big one," she said, and she's right, because I don't know where I could ever put a standard-size machine. "But we have to order it from the company."

It costs fifty dollars. That's as much as I earn in a month, plus tips. She says I can pay it off little by little—ten dollars a month.

I promised to think it over. Fifty dollars is such a lot of money!

Wednesday, November 10th

We found out this morning who is going: Opal and Pearl, Maggie and Emmy, Cordelia and me. We'll take the early train on Sunday, help with the setup at La

Castañeda, serve the banquet, stay over Sunday night, and come back to Belén on Monday in time to set up for the five o'clock train.

As soon as I found out, I went over to the office of the *Belén News* to speak to Mr. Brower. I found him stooped over a big table, laying out the next issue that comes out tomorrow. He was cutting up and rearranging long columns of type, and pasting them down with rubber cement, just the way Phil Rayburn and I used to paste up the *Patriot* when we were in high school. That feels like about a hundred years ago.

Mr. Brower pushed back his green eyeshade and peered at me over his glasses. "You have something for me, Miss Evans?"

"I have an article in mind that you might like," I said. I was nervous. I'd never done this before.

"Ah, you want to pitch a story!" he said and straightened up. "Well, make it snappy then. Tell me about it in one sentence."

One sentence? My mouth went dry. "Two new cross-country Santa Fe trains will make their first run on Sunday, one leaving from Chicago and the other from Los Angeles, and they'll meet in Las Vegas for a banquet with speeches by important people."

The editor scratched his chin. "Bad sentence, but not a bad idea. Harvey Girls going up to Las Vegas?"

I said we were.

"The *Las Vegas Optic* will cover it, but your take on it could be interesting. Bring me five hundred words," he said. "By Tuesday."

He went back to pasting. Katherine A. Evans has an actual assignment from the editor of a real newspaper.

On the way back to the Harvey House, I stopped at Becker's and told Miss Lucie I'd be back tomorrow with a down payment on that typewriter.

Monday, November 15th

WE TOOK THE LOCAL THROUGH ALBUQUERQUE TOWARD Santa Fe, following the west side of the Sandia Mountains. The train doesn't pass through Santa Fe, because of the rugged mountains, but stops several miles east in the little town of Lamy. A young couple boarded who spent their honeymoon in the tiny El Ortiz Hotel. "So charming, almost like a private home," the wife said. "Only eight guest rooms and a dozen chairs in the dining room."

Another of Miss Mary Colter's ideas, the husband said.

"What a perfect place for a honeymoon," sighed Pearl. Weddings seem to be much on her mind recently, and on Opal's, too. Things must be getting serious with the ranchers in Mountainair.

It was almost noon when we arrived in Las Vegas. We were met on the platform by Miss Nelly Nelson, the head waitress of La Castañeda, and told that as soon as we'd had lunch we would be put to work polishing silverware.

The silverware had come from the Montezuma, which used to be famous as a grand health resort. When the Montezuma closed in 1903 due to economic conditions, most of the furnishings were sold, but the silver—place settings, serving dishes, sugar bowls and cream pitchers, trays and serving pieces—was stored at La Castañeda.

Now that silver was waiting for us, and there was an awful lot of it.

Polishing silverware has always been part of a Harvey Girl's job. We did it almost every day in Emporia when we were greenhorns, still struggling to memorize the cup code and remember to empty the great coffee urns every two hours. The other girls thought it was mindlessly boring, like folding dozens of starched napkins, but I enjoy small tasks where you can see an immediate result: black tarnish on the polishing rag that shows you've done the job, the glow of a finished piece.

We tied smocks over our clothes and set to work with flannel rags and jars of silver cream, working our way through chests of flatware and piles of trays with ornate handles, covered platters, footed ewers for ice water, domed butter dishes, and filigreed nut baskets.

It was a dirty job that went on for most of the afternoon—it did seem that the silver polishing had been left exclusively to the girls from Belén—while we talked and laughed and became acquainted with some of Las Vegas girls who stopped by to chat. One of them was Franny K., the girl with the Czech accent.

"I wanted the Alvarado when I left Emporia," she said, "but honestly, this is great. I'm thrilled to be here. Maybe next year or the year after, I'll get to the Alvarado."

Late in the afternoon a marching band began practicing to greet the trains as they pulled in—they must have played "You're a Grand Old Flag" and "The Stars and Stripes Forever" a half-dozen times—and an eight-piece orchestra set up their instruments in the grand dining room. A local printer delivered the programs for the evening. A company from Albuquerque carried in vases of fall flowers for each table, upsetting the owner of a Las Vegas flower shop who had expected to have the business.

The Las Vegas Harvey Girls rushed around, setting the tables with china from the old Montezuma, snatching up the gleaming flatware, making sure each place setting was precisely half an inch from the edge, crystal water goblets were at the tip of each knife, and starched linen napkins stood crisply at each place.

Miss Nelson marched back and forth among the troops, issuing an order to one group, barking a command to another, like a general preparing for battle. "That's the Harvey Way," she repeated irritatingly.

One of the local Harvey Girls—her name is Vivian—came to pick up a huge urn that Cordelia and I had just finished. She was ready to hoist the urn and carry it off when Cordelia exclaimed, "Vivian, where did you get that ring?"

Vivian proudly held out her left hand, sporting an engagement ring with an enormous diamond surrounded by tiny sapphires. "Isn't it beautiful? My fiancé gave it to me when we got engaged."

I recognized that ring. Emmy's mouth opened and closed; Maggie's, too. We all knew about the ring, but we didn't say a word.

"Congratulations," Cordelia said through clenched teeth. "It's lovely. But can you tell me where your fiancé might have bought it?"

"My Charley won it in a poker game!" Vivian said. "He is just so lucky."

A few weeks ago a fella who said his name was Robert Smith came through town—well dressed, pin-striped suit, yellow necktie—on his way to Chicago to open a business. Said his girl had thrown him over. Charley and some of the boys started a poker game and invited him to join. Robert did all right in the beginning, but then he started to lose. Pretty soon he'd gone through his whole bankroll. The only thing he had left was this ring, still in the velvet box. He put it on the table, and the game went on. People gathered around to watch. Then the last hand was dealt, and Robert lost.

"He looked pretty broken up about losing that ring," Vivian said. He was gone the next day, on the train north. "He left without paying the bill. The manager is furious."

Nobody said anything. Cordelia looked as though she might faint. But just then Miss Nelson swooped down on us, squawking like a crow, telling us to get a move on, there was still a lot to do before the *Chief* came in.

Now I have the ending for my story about Cordelia and Walter—a much more startling one than I could have ever made up.

LAS VEGAS WELCOMES THE *CHIEF*

by Katherine A. Evans

A half-dozen Belén Harvey Girls brought a special shine to the inaugural celebration of the new AT&SF luxury train, christened *Chief*, when the east- and westbound trains met for the first time in Las Vegas, New Mexico, last Monday.

The #3 left Chicago Sunday morning, November 14th; the #4 departed Los Angeles late the same day; and both arrived in Las Vegas in time for a festive dinner the evening of the 15th. La Castañeda Hotel pulled out all the stops to prepare for the arrival of their distinguished guests.

Waitresses on loan from the Belén Harvey House were entrusted with the job of restoring the luster to the priceless silverware from the Montezuma. This historic Harvey House, built in 1882, burned to the ground two years later, and was then rebuilt and claimed to be completely fireproof. Four months after reopening, the "fireproof" Montezuma burned down a second time and was rebuilt a second time. The grand resort that played host to President Ulysses S. Grant and President Rutherford B. Hayes shut its doors for the last time in 1903, but the silverware, stored in a vault at La Castañeda, is brought out for special occasions like this one.

As seven o'clock neared, a crowd gathered at La Castañeda and the AT&SF depot next door. Electric lights flickered on along the length of the station platform. The mayor of Las Vegas moved through the crowd, shaking hands. The president of the railroad paced anxiously. A. T. Hannett, governor of New Mexico, glanced over his prepared remarks. Inside La Castañeda, the six Harvey Girls from Belén and those from Las Vegas gathered by the windows for a glimpse of the twin trains.

Alerted by a telegram from up the line, the band began a medley of patriotic songs. Whistle blowing and bell clanging, the westbound *Chief* pulled into the station, drowning out the band's best efforts. Another twenty minutes passed until the band signaled the approach of the eastbound *Chief* by playing "You're a Grand Old Flag" and other pieces a second time.

The mayor of Las Vegas welcomed the *Chief*, the railroaders, the passengers, and everyone who had anything to do with the new train. The president of the railroad thanked all those same people for their support. Governor A. T. Hannett, who was defeated for re-election earlier this month, surprised his audience by scarcely mentioning the new trains. Instead he spoke at length about the section of road he has ordered to be constructed, starting December 1st, as part of Route 66, the new east-west national highway. Rumors immediately began circulating that the governor deliberately laid out the new section to bypass Santa Fe, where his political rivals do business.

There was some disappointment that President and Mrs. Coolidge had not made the journey.

Following the speeches, invited guests enjoyed a meal that began with Oysters Rockefeller, continued with Roast Venison, and ended with Peach Melba, served by the Harvey Girls of Las Vegas and Belén. (TOTAL WORD COUNT: 498)

Wednesday, November 17th

My Underwood Portable typewriter has not yet arrived, but Miss Baca agreed, reluctantly, to let me use hers one last time. I delivered my article about the *Chief* to Mr. Brower yesterday and pointed out that I'd written two fewer words than the five hundred he'd assigned. He grabbed his blue pencil and began making corrections.

"'Pulled out all the stops' is a cliché," he said. "Just say 'prepared for the arrival.' Also, I have no doubt that the guv will do anything to get even with his enemies, but you can't report a rumor. It was a nasty thing for him to bring up when he was supposed to be celebrating the new train."

I received a dollar for this one and a compliment: "More interesting than the piece the *Optic* sent me. I'll run them both."

Low clouds had moved in and a cold wind sliced through my ugly green sweater. I hurried along with my cap pulled down over my ears. In front of the Cutoff Café I ran into Gus. He was blowing on his hands to warm them.

"You look just about frozen, Kitty," he said. "Let's go in here, and I'll buy you a cup of coffee."

The Cutoff is a gloomy, rundown-looking place, but if Gus had offered to take me rowing again on Belén Lake in the middle of a blizzard, I'd have jumped at the chance.

Gus led me to a wooden booth with one small yellowish lamp glowing on the varnished table, the dim light making it feel more like nighttime than midafternoon. "It was a cantina before Prohibition," Gus said. "Now coffee is about all you can get to drink here. And I guarantee you that Cash doesn't dump the coffee every two hours and make a fresh batch. Sometimes it tastes as though it's been there for a week."

A man with a white apron wrapped around his big belly came to our booth and made a few swipes at the sticky table with a damp rag. "What'll it be?" he asked.

"Cuppa joe," Gus said. "Make it two, and some of your special doughnuts."

Cash left to get our order, and Gus laughed at the expression on my face. "You can have pie or cake or a fancy French pastry at the Harvey House, but never a greasy doughnut and stale coffee like the Cutoff's."

Cash was back with two coffees and two doughnuts. You didn't need a bright light to notice the stains on his apron. Gus watched me stir sugar into my coffee, pour in cream, add more sugar. At least it was hot. Gus dunked his doughnut and asked about the celebration in Las Vegas.

I told him about polishing all that silver and then serving a dinner that went on for three hours. Then I told him about the diamond-and-sapphire engagement ring, Vivian's story of Walter Vogel (alias Robert Smith), and how he'd skipped out on his bill in Albuquerque and again in Las Vegas, using a different name. "Vivian says he told anyone who asked that he was on his way to Chicago. But nobody really knows."

"What a con man!" he said. "Poor Cordelia!"

Gus finished his doughnut, and I pushed the rest of mine across the table for him. "The coffee may be bad," Gus said, "but it's not like meeting at the Harvey House, where everybody knows what you're doing. My shift changes, but I get afternoons off sometimes. I'd like it if you'd meet me here when you can. If you want to."

If I want to!

He'd lay a penny on the lunchroom counter when he had time off, and I'd pick it up if I could meet him and push it back if I couldn't.

Cash waved as I went out the door, calling, "Come back soon, miss!" I said I would, and hurried to the Harvey House, hardly noticing the cold.

Sunday, November 21st

I WAS STILL AWAKE LAST NIGHT WHEN I HEARD SHOUTING in the hall and ran out to see what was going on. Doors were opening up and down the hall, Opal and Pearl were peering out, Gladys had just come out of the bathroom, and Mrs. McCreary was at the top of the stairs, looking madder than a wet hen.

The cause of the ruckus was Maggie, sneaking in two hours past curfew. She'd been with Pedro, and Susana knew it and was waiting for her downstairs.

Maggie has continued to flirt with Pedro, the kitchen helper, right under Susana's nose. It was foolish. Everybody knew they'd been meeting at the bowling alley.

Alicia asked me to talk to Maggie. "She's teasing a

mountain lion. Susana is going to get her fired, if she can."

When I mentioned it to Emmy, Emmy said she'd already tried to talk to her, but Maggie wouldn't listen. Then I tried, but she wouldn't listen to me, either.

"Pedro says he's broken off with her. If he'd rather be with me, there's nothing Susana can do about it, and that's just the way it is," Maggie said. "It would be better for everybody if she'd just quit. It can't be fun for her to keep working in the kitchen with Pedro right there, and knowing he wants to be with me."

Susana vowed to Alicia that she'd fix Maggie and win Pedro back, but so far nothing had happened—until last night. Maggie went out with Pedro, and as usual she wasn't in by curfew. The cooks are good about unlocking the back door and letting in any of us who are late. If you can make it up the creaky stairs past Mrs. McCreary's room without getting caught, you're home free. Maggie was an expert at that.

But last night Susana set a trap. Pedro's friend José was working the night shift, and Susana talked him into letting her into the kitchen. When Maggie tapped on the door around midnight, Susana slipped out of sight, José unlocked the door, and Maggie hurried inside. She made it halfway up the stairs, remembering which steps creaked, keeping close to the wall or to the railing and avoiding certain steps altogether.

Susana jumped out from the shadows, yelling,

"Maggie! Wait! I want to talk to you!"

Maggie froze. "Are you crazy, Susana?" she hissed. "Shut up!"

"No, I'm not going to shut up!" Susana shouted. "Not until you promise to stay away from Pedro!"

Mrs. McCreary burst out of her room at the top of the stairs. "Quiet, both of you," the head waitress growled in a voice like a rusty gate. "Susana, go home. You have no business here. And you, Maggie, come into my room. Now."

The outcome was predictable. Susana triumphed: Maggie has been fired. She came down for breakfast with her eyes red and swollen from crying. Her bags are packed. Nobody quite knows what to say to her. We all feel terrible, even Cordelia. Maggie can really get under your skin, but she is also bubbly and fun. All of us secretly admire the way she always tries to get away with as much as she can—like ignoring the curfew and any other rules she feels like breaking—and then we are relieved that it isn't us when she gets caught.

She's told everyone how sorry she is; that she loves being a Harvey Girl, she's happy here, and she doesn't want to leave. "Maybe if you all went to Mrs. McCreary and put in a good word for me, she'd reconsider. I promise I'll never break curfew again! And I'll stop seeing Pedro. It's not that I'm in love with him—he's just fun to be with, and Susana is—well, boring old Susana.

Just look what a silly fit she threw! As though that will get Pedro back!"

Opal and Pearl avoided looking at her, Cordelia glanced at me and rolled her eyes, and Emmy sighed, "Oh, Maggie, I warned you so many times, and you wouldn't listen!"

But Mrs. McCreary won't change her mind.

Maggie said she doesn't know what she'll do now, but she confided to Emmy and me that she planned to stop in Vaughn and see if her old manager there—the one Mrs. McCreary thinks is too lenient—will overlook the little fact that she's been fired and rehire her. "I brought in a lot of customers," she said. "Ranchers from the area were always coming by."

She was to leave on the noon train. Susana, looking smug, was in the kitchen making salads as though nothing had happened, and Pedro kept his head down and went on frying fish and making omelets for the lunch crowd. Mrs. McCreary and Mr. Lawrence shook hands with Maggie solemnly. When we heard the eastbound pulling in, Emmy and I stepped out to say good-bye. Gus and Tom and a few other railroaders looked surprised to see her on the platform with her bags.

"I'll send you a postcard," Maggie said, climbing aboard, her defiant chin up, and that was the last we saw of her halo of wild, rust-colored hair.

Monday, November 22nd

My Underwood Portable typewriter arrived today! Miss Lucie Becker had it delivered to me, along with a package of typing paper, two sheets of carbon paper, an extra ribbon, and an eraser, which I'll probably wear out fast. I'm not much of a typist.

Emmy says I can keep it in her room. There's plenty of space, now that Maggie is gone. And Mrs. McCreary says I can use the table in the employees' lunchroom in the evenings when nobody's there.

The first thing I plan to do is type a letter to Daddy and Mother, to show them that I really am becoming a journalist.

Tuesday, November 23rd

Opal and Pearl are officially engaged, with Mr. Lawrence's blessing, to those two ranchers they've been dating. The brothers, Ed and Albert, also operate a filling station in Mountainair, and they work as carpenters in the off-season. Each girl got a ring with the birthstone for which she's named—Opal for her birthday in October, Pearl for hers in June—and their fiancés have promised to fix up their ranch houses just the way the girls want them.

One of the terms of the Harvey Girl contract is that we're not allowed to marry. The sisters' contracts will be up at the end of December, but although they like the idea of having steady beaux, they're in no hurry to get married. They want to stay on as Harvey Girls for another six months, save some money, and have a June wedding and a real honeymoon.

But Ed and Albert don't want their sweethearts to spend even one more week working at the Harvey House. The brothers say that waitressing is low-class and waitresses, even Harvey Girls, are on the bottom rung of the social ladder. They even had the nerve to tell Opal and Pearl *it's a well-known fact* that many waitresses are "ladies of the evening."

"They told us we have to quit. The school in Mountainair is looking for teachers, and we can teach until the wedding. After that, there will be enough for us to do as ranch wives." Opal shook her head and sighed.

"Those boys were so sweet when we first started dating them," Pearl said. "They didn't say a thing then about Harvey Girls being low-class."

Emmy added her two cents. "When I told Carl I was going to work as a Harvey Girl, he acted the same way. The preacher had everybody convinced I was falling into sin and I'd end up going to hell. Carl just wanted me to stay home and get married. Then he turned around and married somebody else. If you want my opinion, I think you should do whatever you want to do, and let those boys figure it out for themselves."

There have been several arguments and quite a few tears. With Maggie gone and nobody taking her place until new Harvey Girls are sent here, we gathered in Emmy's room, sat on the empty bed, and discussed the situation.

Cordelia thinks Opal and Pearl should tell Ed and Albert to go jump in the lake. Walter cured her of any interest in men, although she still enjoys flirting, and her German lessons with Viktor do seem to take up a lot of her free time.

"It's not that I *dislike* men," Cordelia said. "I just don't want to get married for a long time. As soon as a man is sure of you, he thinks he can tell you what to do. I promise you, *nobody* is going to boss me around."

"What kind of advice do you suppose Maggie would have?" Opal wondered, and Cordelia answered, "Not to mess around with Susana's boyfriend."

Pearl snorted and looked over at me. "You haven't said a word, Kitty. What do you think?"

"If you tell them to jump in the lake, you better find one that's deeper than Belén Lake."

By now even Pearl and Opal were laughing, remembering some of the fixes Maggie got herself into. We all wonder if she's talked her old boss into hiring her back, or if she's gone home to Ogallala.

Then somebody suggested we go down to the kitchen and see if any of Max's sticky buns were left over, because they're a sure way to cheer you up, no matter what's got you down.

Wednesday, November 24th

Dear Mother and Daddy,

Tomorrow is Thanksgiving, the biggest day of the year at the Belén Harvey House.

That's all the further I got.

There will be Blue Point oysters and two kinds of soup. The main course is a choice of either Roast Turkey with Chestnut Dressing, or Roast Prime Rib of Beef, with broccoli hollandaise, baked squash, and mashed or sweet potatoes. But the menu will not include Lobster en Cassolette—whatever that is—or the Braised Sweetbreads with Truffles Perigord, all of which Viktor says will be featured at the Alvarado. Glasses of Punch Maraschino will be presented between courses. Desserts will include mince pie with hard sauce, pumpkin pie with whipped cream, and Nesselrode ice cream made with candied chestnuts, but no English plum pudding or fruitcake. "They're for Christmas," Viktor says.

It's a tradition for many Belén families to come to the Harvey House for their Thanksgiving dinner, and all the railroaders will be treated to a free meal by the railroad. Mrs. McCreary and Mr. Lawrence are planning for three sittings in the dining room, sixty-four people at each sitting, for which reservations are required. The lunchroom, with places at the counter for forty-five, will be open for people who decide to come at the last minute, no reservations needed, and they'll be served as spaces become available. Based on past years' experience, Mrs. McCreary says, we can expect close to four hundred people. Obviously nobody will have the day off. Without Maggie, who was the speediest of all the waitresses, we'll be working even harder, running even faster.

If I were back home in Leavenworth we'd go to Gramma Blair's for the huge meal that Josephine started preparing three days ago. Aunt May and Uncle Hal and their boys will be coming down from Atchison. I won't have any time to think about my family and to miss gathering around Gramma Blair's big mahogany table. And I surely won't miss the arguments that always erupt between Uncle Hal and Daddy over politics, until Mother and Aunt May make them stop.

Friday, November 26th

THANKSGIVING IS OVER, AND I'M THANKFUL FOR THAT. Usually we work a split shift, but yesterday we worked straight through. The railroad crews still came in for breakfast, and then the grand Thanksgiving Dinner began. I have no idea how many turkeys were roasted and carved and how many potatoes had to be peeled and mashed and how many gallons of Punch Maraschino (which turned out to be a cherry drink) were mixed, but

I can say that I ran my legs off all day with no chance to take a break.

My mood soured when Gus showed up with Tom and Sally and an elderly lady in an old-fashioned bonnet who must be the Auntie Gertrude they all live with. The boys were dressed up in jackets and neckties, and Sally sported a smart little hat with a pheasant feather. They ate in the lunchroom. I was assigned to the dining room, and I was glad I didn't have to serve them. I might have accidentally dropped a bowl of cranberry sauce in Sally's lap. Or thought about doing it. Gus winked, and I pasted on a smile.

Two long tables had been set up to serve the entire John Becker family at the last sitting, and four of us—Cordelia, Emmy, Gladys, and I—were assigned to wait on that table: Beckers and Dalieses and Vielstichs and all the various nieces and nephews. I'd seen most of them before, but now there was somebody new, a ruddy-faced lady in a big hat, sitting beside old Mr. Becker.

"That's Ina Innebickler, the housekeeper," Gladys whispered on one of our dashes to the kitchen. "Soon to be the next Mrs. Becker. Hans and Lucie Becker are probably gritting their teeth."

Mrs. Innebickler spotted Auntie Gertrude and waved. Auntie Gertrude waved back. Tom and Sally and Gus went over to say hello to the Beckers.

John Becker tapped on his water glass, and all

conversation in the dining room stopped. "Our young friend, Tom Perkins, has agreed to honor us with a Thanksgiving hymn."

Tom stepped forward and, without any accompaniment, began to sing. I recognized the tune we sang at our church back home—*Praise to the Lord, the Almighty, the King of creation!*—but he sang it in German. The Becker clan was wreathed in smiles, as though they'd just heard an angel singing.

"He knows German?" I whispered to Gladys.

"Probably learned it from Auntie Gertrude," Gladys whispered back.

After the last of the guests had gone, we were allowed to sit down to our own dinner—cooks, kitchen helpers, Harvey Girls. And not in the employees' lunchroom where we normally eat our meals on the run. This time we ate in the main dining room, with fresh linens and perfectly set china and silverware. Each of us took a turn serving part of the meal. It felt almost like a family.

Gladys and Pearl and I brought out the mince and pumpkin pies and passed around bowls of hard sauce and whipped cream. Even before we'd laid down our forks, Viktor coaxed Cordelia to fetch her guitar.

She started off with a quiet piece, "Drifting and Dreaming," followed by "Peg o' My Heart." Then one of the kitchen boys hollered, "Hey, Cordelia! Play 'Somebody Stole My Gal'!"

She obliged, and everybody sang along.

People were calling out the songs they wanted to hear, and then a couple of them got up, pushed aside a table, grabbed the closest girls, and started dancing.

Our jaws dropped when stuffy Mr. Lawrence took prim Mrs. McCreary by the hand and the two performed a little fancy footwork. Mrs. McCreary, a widow with an eight-year-old daughter who lives somewhere with Mrs. McCreary's mother? Mr. Lawrence, a bachelor and never married, as far as any of us knows? I couldn't have been the only one to notice that Mrs. McCreary's usually pale face was flushed, and her eyes sparkled, and Mr. Lawrence actually displayed the glimmer of a smile. Emmy is convinced that something is going on between them, but Cordelia says Emmy has turned into a hopeless romantic.

Saturday, November 27th

IN TWO WEEKS, DECEMBER 11TH, OUR SIX-MONTH contracts will be up—mine, Emmy's, and Cordelia's—and we'll get thirty days off and train passes to go home to visit our families. We don't get paid for the time off, but we can sign up for another six- or nine-month contract, even a year if we want it.

We can ask for new assignments, but the chances of getting the Alvarado or La Castañeda or the Grand Canyon are nonexistent. We haven't been Harvey Girls long enough to work our way up to one of those plum assignments. Cordelia dreams about the Indian Detours, but she'll have to dream about that for a while longer.

So we'll all tell Mrs. McCreary that we want to come back here for six more months.

In the meantime, I invited Cordelia and Emmy to come home with me to Leavenworth. The three of us can take the streetcar to Kansas City, eat at the Harvey House in Union Station, and stop by to say hello to Miss Steele and show her how well we're doing. Cordelia can visit her Uncle Cameron and her cousin, Violet, if Violet isn't still mad at Cordelia for getting hired as a Harvey Girl. Emmy can stop off in Topeka for a few days to see her folks on the way back.

The more we talked about it, the more excited we became.

Then this afternoon Gladys raced upstairs to tell us we were wanted down in the dining room. She didn't say why, but her electric smile was turned all the way up. It was too early to start setting up for the dinner train. We asked if we should put on our uniforms. Not necessary, she said; just come.

"Is it only the three of us?" I wondered aloud. Opal

and Pearl had left in the morning to spend the day with their sweethearts.

"Let's hope they're going to tell those dumb ranchers to jump in the lake," Cordelia had said after they'd gone. "There must be a deep-enough lake somewhere."

"They were all dolled up when they left," Emmy had said. "You don't dress up like that when you're planning to tell somebody to jump in the lake."

Emmy was right. They got married by a judge at noon today.

On a table in the dining room was a fancy wedding cake with two tiny brides and two tiny grooms on top. Max, sworn to secrecy, had baked it for them. Gladys mixed a batch of Punch Maraschino and poured us each a glass. Mr. Lawrence offered a toast to the brides and grooms, and they ceremonially cut the cake. Cordelia and I pretended to be happy for them, and Gladys beamed as though she really was.

The salad girls snitched a bag of rice from the pantry and doled out handfuls to toss. The two couples climbed into the car Ed and Albert had borrowed to drive one block to the Central Hotel for their wedding night. They plan to leave for Mountainair after breakfast. They'd already packed their things. They won't be back.

We helped Mrs. McCreary clean up the punch glasses and cake plates. "Girls, I need your help," she said. "Opal and Pearl are gone. Maggie is gone. And the three of you are ending your contracts in two weeks. Are you intending to sign up for another six months?"

When we assured Mrs. McCreary that we were staying, she looked relieved. She's asked for new Harvey Girls to be sent out from Topeka, but it's always hard to recruit in the month before Christmas. So, she asked, would we consider staying on through Christmas and New Year's and taking our leaves beginning in January?

We looked at each other. I'd been planning how we'd spend Christmas in Leavenworth, putting up the tree, hanging the big wreath on the front door, inviting friends for Mother's special eggnog and fruitcake, hanging stockings by the fireplace—I'd make sure there were stockings for Emmy and Cordelia. Maudie would come over, and I'd invite Jimmy Bedwell to meet my friends. Howie would be there, of course.

I didn't realize how much I'd been looking forward to the time off and to the fun we were going to have. And now Mrs. McCreary was saying we were needed here. She promised us extra time off when we come back. We'd be able to go up to Albuquerque once a week, if we wanted to.

Cordelia spoke up first. "It's fine with me," she said. "It might be very interesting to spend Christmas here in Belén. A new experience."

"Me, too," said Emmy. "The salad girls have been telling me about the local traditions."

I hesitated. I could go to Leavenworth without them. Mrs. McCreary would have the help she needed, and I could go home and do all those things I'd been looking forward to, and come back after Christmas.

Mrs. McCreary and Emmy and Cordelia were waiting for an answer.

"I'll stay," I said. "I'll let my parents know that we'll be there in January."

Monday, November 29th

I HADN'T BEEN TO THE CUTOFF CAFÉ SINCE BEFORE Thanksgiving. Gus had stopped by the lunchroom a couple of times for morning coffee, but we hadn't had a chance to talk without everybody hearing every word. This morning Gus left a penny on the counter, as we'd agreed, and I picked it up. We'd meet this afternoon.

I remembered to ask Mr. Lawrence's permission. "It's not really a date," I said. "We're just having coffee at the Cutoff Café."

I was anxious to tell Gus about the change of plans—that I'd be staying in Belén through Christmas.

He was waiting for me, and we sat in the same booth we'd shared before. Cash brought coffee and doughnuts without being asked. I was just starting to tell Gus about Opal and Pearl when the door flew open and a blast of cold air blew in, accompanied by Sally Perkins.

Sally rushed straight to our booth. She looked terrible, hair a mess, nose red, eyes puffy.

Gus was plainly surprised. "Sally?" he said. "What in heaven's name?"

"Oh, Gus!" she cried. "Thank God I found you! Tom's been hurt, and it's real bad!"

"Tom's hurt?" Gus jumped up, and Sally threw herself into his arms, sobbing.

There'd been an accident at the rail yard. Tom was doing something, coupling cars, uncoupling them, she didn't know what, and he somehow got caught between them, and he was in awful shape. "You've got to come!"

"All right, Sally," he said quietly, and pushed back a straggle of hair from her face. "Tell me where he is."

Sally explained in disconnected bits and pieces that they'd taken Tom to the clinic, where Doc Wilkinson, the doctor for the railroad, was working on him. The doctor's wife had driven their automobile to Becker's store to tell Sally, and Sally had come to find Gus. Mrs. Wilkinson was waiting outside to take her to the clinic.

"You've got to come with me!" Sally sobbed.

Gus dropped a half-dollar on the table, mouthed that he'd see me later, and guided Sally out the door with his arm around her shoulders.

I sat there stunned, not sure what to do. Finally I drank part of my coffee and handed Cash the fifty-cent piece. He gave me the change, a dime that I put under my saucer. As I was leaving, he asked if I wanted to take the doughnuts with me. I shook my head.

I walked slowly toward the Harvey House. It had started to snow lightly, the flakes stinging my face. I wasn't ready to talk to Cordelia or anyone, and I veered toward Belén Lake. It's a stark and lonely place now, the rowboat upside down in the weeds, a skin of new ice on the water. Enrique says it will freeze solid by Christmas and be thick enough to skate on. I walked all the way around it, remembering Tom singing in his husky tenor at Cordelia's birthday party and again last week at the Thanksgiving dinner. I thought of the fear in Sally's eyes and the concern in Gus's and said a prayer for Tom. Then I headed home.

Cordelia glanced up from filing her nails. "What happened, Kitty? You look like the wreck of the—what? Some kind of boat?"

"The wreck of the *Hesperus*," I said, and told her as much as I knew about Tom.

Wednesday, December 1st

TOM PERKINS'S ACCIDENT IS ALL ANYONE TALKS ABOUT in the lunchroom. Nobody knows exactly what happened that resulted in his leg being broken in three places, his arm broken and his shoulder dislocated, and a mass of cuts and bruises.

Whatever the circumstances were, railroaders found him, improvised a stretcher, and carried him to the railroad clinic. Dr. Wilkinson—everyone calls him "Doc"—recognized the seriousness of Tom's injuries and sent his wife to ask for help from Dr. Radcliffe, Belén's regular family doctor, and then to fetch Sally and Gus. When they reached the clinic—it's in the Wilkinsons' house on First Street—the two doctors were working to bandage the cuts, set the broken bones, and apply plaster casts. Tom had been knocked unconscious, and he woke up to find himself helpless, barely able to move.

Gus and Sally are taking turns staying at the clinic. Gus spends the night on a cot near Tom's bed and lets Sally go home to sleep. The railroaders stop by often to inquire about Tom's condition and try to cheer him up. Cordelia has organized the Harvey Girls to visit Tom every afternoon. She and I will go tomorrow.

Thursday, December 2nd

Poor Tom! He's miserable, lying flat on his back, immobilized in casts. He wants to go home, but he may have to stay at the clinic for a few weeks. The pain pills make him goofy. Sally hovers around him. She says Gus is figuring out a way to set up a bed for him at home, as soon as Doc Wilkinson gives the word. "Maybe by Christmas," she says.

Cordelia brought her new guitar, which I thought was a great idea, and asked Tom what he wanted to hear. He requested "Five Foot Two, Eyes of Blue." Cordelia played it, and Sally sang along. She does have a nice voice.

But it didn't cheer Tom up. In fact, a couple of tears rolled down his cheeks. "I may never be able to dance again," he said, and turned his face to the wall.

We all reassured him that of course he will, he just has to be patient, he's young and strong, he'll be out there dancing the Charleston in no time, just like he used to.

"Maybe that wasn't such a good idea," Cordelia said as we walked back to the Harvey House. "What if he's right, and he won't ever dance again! How awful!"

We decided that the next time we visit, she'll play something different. Hymns might be a good idea.

Monday, December 6th

It's been a week since Tom was hurt. Gus stops in at the lunchroom almost every day to give us news of Tom's progress, gulps down whatever he orders, takes a piece of pie for Tom that one of us has wrapped up, and rushes off to spend an hour or so at the clinic. "It makes Tom feel he's still part of things," Gus said.

Gus and I finally met today at the Cutoff. He says it's going to be a long haul until Tom's leg is mended. The break in the arm is not as serious and should heal faster. "We talk about what's going on at the roundhouse," Gus said. "But I think he's just as interested in Harvey House gossip."

He promised to tell Tom about Opal and Pearl being saved from ruined reputations by Ed and Albert.

"You railroaders will have to wait a while until any new Harvey Girls arrive for you to size up," I said, and explained that the departure of Maggie and the two brides left Mrs. McCreary shorthanded. "I was planning to go home for Christmas, and Cordelia and Emmy were going to come with me, but that's changed. We'll stay through the first of the year to help out."

"I'm glad you'll be here," Gus said, and squeezed my hand.

I believe him. But I can't help wondering about Sally, and somehow I don't know how to ask.

Wednesday, December 8th

Mother and Daddy are upset that I won't be coming home for Christmas. I received my usual Sunday letter from Daddy today, and I'm surprised at how upset they are—especially Mother.

Daddy says, "It won't be much of a Christmas here without you," but Mother makes it sound as though not having me there is going to ruin everyone's holiday, and says I'm being very selfish. "We've always been together for Christmas," Mother wrote in the note she added at the bottom of Daddy's letter.

In my letter to my parents—typewritten!—I'd explained that I'd planned all along to come home and I'll miss them very much, but I'm badly needed here because, due to an emergency, we're understaffed. I liked that word, "understaffed." I thought it sounded very mature.

Mother wasn't persuaded. "Your family should come

first," she'd written. "Never forget that."

She hadn't wanted to bring it up, but Gramma is getting old—her memory isn't what it once was. I'm only seventeen, she said, much too young to be out on my own like this, and now it just goes to show that I'm too easily influenced, too likely to fall under the sway of people who will manipulate me for their own devious ends. She'd been afraid all along that this would happen.

I showed the letter to Cordelia and to Emmy.

"You're only seventeen?" Emmy asked. "I thought you were nineteen. Weren't there nineteen candles on your birthday cake?"

"I lied about my age," I confessed. "Otherwise I wouldn't have gotten hired."

"Seventeen is old enough to know what you want to do," Cordelia said. "And I can assure your mother that you're not at all easily influenced. I've been trying for months to manipulate you for my own devious ends, and you've always thwarted me."

Of course I laughed. "But do you think I'm being selfish?"

"You *are* needed here," Emmy reminded me. "People are counting on you."

I wrote back, telling my parents that as much as I want to be with them, it is *my duty* to stay here. Then I stamped the letter and mailed it before I could wobble.

Saturday, December 11th

Tom has been allowed to leave the clinic and go home. The doctors agree there's nothing more they can do; only time will heal him, and the care he'll get at home will be just as good. "Better," Gus says. "Auntie Gertrude will be at his beck and call. She dotes on him."

Gus and the other railroaders have rearranged Auntie Gertrude's parlor to accommodate a bed for Tom, and they hired a truck from Wilson Brothers Rapid Transit to haul him there this afternoon, bed and all. Sally, who has been taking time off to stay with him at the clinic, can go back to her job at Becker's, and Tom can give up the cot at the clinic and sleep at home in his own bed.

More good news: Cordelia has been invited to give a concert at the Reading Room on the Sunday before Christmas. Word got around that she's a real musician and plays the piano just as well as she does the guitar and the ukulele. The concert was Mr. Lawrence's idea, and the railroad executives gave their approval. Cordelia is thrilled that she's been asked to play, but the problem is that there is no piano at the Reading Room. There's been talk of moving the old upright from the employees' lunchroom, but she says it's badly out of tune, and where can a piano tuner be found on such short notice?

Monday, December 13th

This afternoon Cordelia and I visited Tom at Auntie Gertrude's, a pretty little Victorian cottage on Dalies Avenue. Auntie Gertrude loves to do needlework. Consequently, her parlor is decorated with crocheted doilies on every table and embroidered antimacassars on the arms and back of every chair.

The old lady bustled in and out, insisting that we must have a cup of tea and sample her gingersnaps, before settling down with her crocheting. We just wanted a chance to talk to Tom, but Auntie Gertrude had no intention of leaving two Harvey Girls alone with her poor, helpless boy. Tom rolled his eyes, and we tried to think of a polite way to get rid of her. Then, among all the chairs upholstered in scratchy material, whatnot shelves crowded with china figurines, and tables buried under bric-a-brac, Cordelia found a treasure.

"Look at this!" she cried. "A parlor organ!"

The small organ had been given to Auntie Gertrude as an engagement gift from her dear departed husband, Mr. Goebel, and she'd brought it with her all the way from Germany as a young bride. She found a hymnal and a couple of battered old music books and invited Cordelia to try it out.

Cordelia sat down on the twirly little stool and began to pump the two large foot-pedals that worked the bellows. The keyboard had four octaves—thirty-two keys—and a row of knobs to change the sound.

"This is the diapason," Cordelia said, pulling out one of the knobs, and played a couple of full, rich-sounding chords. "And here's the piccolo"—a piping note, like a flute—"and the vox humana, most like the human voice." A lever next to her knee controlled the volume.

Hoping to get on Auntie Gertrude's good side, Cordelia started off with some German hymns that made the old lady smile, and the Bach "Fantasia in C major," which seemed to be her special favorite. After a while the old lady's eyelids began to droop, and Tom could hardly keep from laughing when Cordelia slipped in Brahms's "Lullaby." Soon his auntie was snoring softly, her crochet work in her lap.

"I think you've found the solution to your problem," Tom said. "You can move the organ to the Reading Room for your concert. I'm sure she'll be happy to loan it to you."

Auntie Gertrude snoozed on. By the time she woke up and it was time for us to leave, Tom had it all figured out. We'd hire Wilson Brothers Rapid Transit to haul the organ in the same truck that brought Tom home from the clinic. And they could take Tom to the Reading Room, too.

Tuesday, December 14th

Almost every night a different group holds a special holiday dinner here, and it's a mad rush to keep up with them.

Bowling is a popular sport in Belén, and the clubs get together once a year for their traditional dinner. The men's teams always order steaks, shrimp cocktail, and chocolate cake. Mr. Lawrence personally made sure the steaks were cooked exactly the way the men wanted them, from rare to well done, and brought them to the table still sizzling. The lady bowlers, who had their own table, preferred breast of guinea hen and charlotte russe.

After the bowlers came the basketball team from the high school, and after the basketball team came a group of Lutheran ladies, who were here on the same night as a men's club that meets every Thursday to play cards. Between now and the first of the year we will host the people who work at Mr. Becker's bank and the employees at his various businesses—the flourmill, the ice plant, the mercantile, the ranch. There will be a quilters' club and the choir from the Lutheran church. Viktor makes up a special menu for each party.

I'm counting the days until I can get on that train and go home for a few weeks, but right now people are entering into the holiday spirit, and tips are good. My pre–New Year's Resolution: to pay for my Underwood Portable by the start of 1927, much sooner than I thought.

Wednesday, December 15th

SNOW AND FREEZING COLD! CORDELIA HAS BEEN lamenting that her muskrat fur coat is in Pennsylvania, packed in mothballs.

"I can't ask Mummy to ship it," Cordelia said. "Apparently she's not speaking to me. I haven't heard from her since I opened a bank account in my own name, after the money in the old one disappeared."

Then today she got one of Mrs. Hart's rambling letters, one long sentence broken up with lots of dashes. "Mummy, complaining as usual," she said.

"Upset because you're not going home for Christmas?"

"That, too."

Cordelia didn't show me the letter. She doesn't seem to want to talk about it.

The announcement for her Christmas program at the Reading Room will appear tomorrow in the Belén News. She's been going over to Auntie Gertrude's every afternoon to practice and to decide what she's going to play on Sunday.

Why do I have a hunch that practicing on the parlor organ isn't the only reason she's been spending so much time there?

BELENITES ENJOY CHRISTMAS PROGRAM

by Katherine A. Evans

It was standing room only on Sunday afternoon at the AT&SF Reading Room for a program of Christmas music presented by Miss Cordelia Hart. Miss Hart performed a selection of traditional carols on an antique parlor organ loaned by Mrs. Oscar Goebel.

Mrs. Goebel is the beloved aunt of Mr. Thomas Perkins, who is recovering from injuries sustained earlier this month in an accident at the rail yard.

Miss Hart began with keyboard variations on the Latin hymn "Adeste Fideles," and then invited everyone to join in singing the English words, "O Come, All Ye Faithful," which they did enthusiastically.

The program continued with such familiar carols as "Hark, the Herald Angels Sing" and "Joy to the World."

Mr. Gustav Becker, who is remembered for his lively recitation of "The Shooting of Dan McGrew" at the Central Theater in September, brought smiles with his rendering of "A Visit from St. Nicholas," the beloved poem that begins: "'Twas the night before Christmas."

Lovers of classical music particularly enjoyed Miss Hart's rendition of "Fantasia in C major" by J. S. Bach.

A most pleasant surprise was the unexpected arrival of Mr. John Paul Sidney, who impressed all who heard his excellent performance on the violin at the Reading Room this past October. At Miss Hart's invitation, he honored his audience with a solo rendition of the beautiful French Christmas song, "Cantique de Noël," bringing a reverent hush to the crowd.

All present then joined Miss Hart and Mr. Sidney in singing several more carols: "It Came Upon the Midnight Clear" and "The First Noël." Mr. Sidney coaxed the children, some of whom had taught him "La Cucaracha" during his previous visit, to join him now in singing "Away in a Manger." The children charmed him by singing the carol in Spanish.

Mr. Perkins, who attended in a wheelchair, brought the listeners close to tears by singing

"O Holy Night," accompanied by Miss Hart. His fine tenor voice was obviously unaffected by his recent injuries.

The concert concluded with organ, violin, and audience joining in a quietly reverent "Silent Night," sung first in English, and finally in German.

A social hour followed, with mulled cider and *biscochitos* provided by the Harvey House.

Tuesday, December 21st

I WADED THROUGH FRESH SNOW TO DELIVER THE article to Mr. Brower yesterday for this week's paper and waited while he read it, wincing every time he wielded his blue pencil.

"Nice work, Kitty, but don't list all the carols sung by the audience. Keep it tight." He glanced at me over the tops of his eyeglasses as he reached into the cash drawer. "I was there. Tell Miss Hart I enjoyed it."

There was actually a lot I didn't include in that article.

The sudden appearance of Cordelia's father in the lunchroom on Friday was a total surprise. He didn't know she was giving a concert; he'd just decided to come to

Belén for a Christmas visit. He's been traveling around New Mexico, he told Cordelia. In Taos he met a number of writers and artists, as well as some rich people who hired him to play at their parties. He stayed in Santa Fe for a while, too, and met more interesting people there.

A further surprise: he's traveling with a lady friend. Her name is Millicent Morgan, and she's a photographer. "Destined to be famous one of these days," he says. She wears her dark hair in a chignon, and she showed up dressed in trousers. I hope she's also brought a skirt, or she won't be allowed in the dining room.

Cordelia was shocked. "Is that *Miss* Morgan, or *Mrs.*?" she asked.

"Just call me Millicent," the lady friend answered with a big smile.

They're planning to stay at the Central Hotel until the day after Christmas and then take a train to Arizona. Millicent wants to photograph the Grand Canyon in the snow.

Also not in the *Belén News* article: When Cordelia went to Auntie Gertrude's to practice on the organ, she convinced Tom he could sing just as well from a wheelchair and rehearsed "O Holy Night" with him until he felt confident. The Wilson brothers refused payment for moving the parlor organ, and Tom and his wheelchair, too.

Cordelia also claims responsibility for persuading

Gus to recite "A Visit from St. Nicholas." He was wonderful, but I didn't get to tell him that on Sunday. He was busy tending to Tom, and Sally never seemed to be more than three feet away.

After the concert Mr. Lawrence and Mrs. McCreary personally served mugs of hot cider and passed plates of *biscochitos*, anise-flavored cookies. (I mailed a box of them to Mother and Daddy, and a little pot from Isleta Pueblo made by Maria Chiwiwi.)

Emmy remains convinced that the manager and the head waitress have something going between them.

"I wouldn't be surprised if they're secretly married," she says.

Cordelia doubts they are, and I agree with her. But I do wonder about Mr. Sidney and his lady friend, although I haven't mentioned that to Cordelia.

Thursday, December 23rd

John Becker had a shipment of Christmas trees and wreaths brought into Belén by freight and sent a spruce to Harvey House that's so tall it nearly reaches the ceiling. We were busy all evening, but after the last party cleared out—a group of war veterans—the kitchen boys moved a table away from a corner of the dining room to make room for the tree. We decorated it with colored glass balls, cardboard angels and Santas, and ropes of sparkly tinsel. Chef Viktor climbed a ladder to put the star on top.

Mr. Sidney and Millicent asked if they might stay and help. He'd brought his violin and needed no coaxing to play. The salad girls took over the kitchen and came out with *empanaditas*, little turnovers filled with mincemeat.

Dinner on Christmas Eve will be a lot like the Feast of Our Lady of Belén—not many people coming here to eat, because so much else is going on. A skeleton staff is staying to take care of stragglers and train crews unlucky enough to have a run on Christmas. The rest of us are to go out and enjoy ourselves.

Alicia insists that we must not miss the nativity play, *Los Pastores*. Her uncle, the Harvey House gardener, plays San Miguel, the archangel. Enrique is Demonio, the devil. Marie says her *abuelo*—her grandfather—always takes the part of Bartolo, the lazy shepherd. He's been doing it for decades. Every year a different girl and boy are chosen for the roles of Mary and Joseph, and there's a special doll that's always used as the Holy Infant.

"One year Susana and I were picked to be Mary and Joseph, if you can believe that," Pedro said, and Susana giggled and swatted him. Those two seem to have patched things up now that Maggie is gone.

Mrs. McCreary has announced a midnight curfew, with special permission until one o'clock for those attending Midnight Mass.

Cordelia asked if we'll get to sleep in.

"Only if you're willing to skip breakfast," Mrs. McCreary said. "And Max has promised to make his special French toast. Right, Max?"

"Worth getting up for," said Max.

Cordelia is not so sure. She says she'd give a lot to have just one morning to sleep.

Saturday, December 25th—Christmas

It's past midnight, already Christmas Day.

Cordelia raced up the stairs a few minutes ago. She'd spent Christmas Eve with her father and his lady friend, and she was practically on fire.

"I have terrific news!" she crowed. "You will never guess!"

It turns out that Millicent is a good friend of the lady in charge of Indian Detours. Not only did Miss Erna Fergusson organize the Detour Service, but she does all the hiring and training of the Couriers, and Millicent promised to introduce them when Cordelia goes up to Santa Fe to visit. Millicent told her not to worry, that if she knows a few phrases in German and can pronounce the Spanish names correctly, she'll do fine.

"I simply have to pay off that bill at the Alvarado," Cordelia said. "Otherwise I won't be able to look them in the eye."

I'm to go to Santa Fe with her, because not only does Miss Fergusson run the Detours and train the Couriers, but she's also a well-known author who writes articles for magazines and has plans for a couple of books.

"You'll have so much to talk about!" Cordelia enthused. "I'm sure she'll have excellent advice for you." She peeled off her clothes, dropped them on the floor, and collapsed into bed. "Oh, lord, I am completely done in," she said. "Did you have fun at *Los Pastores*?"

But she was asleep before I could answer.

Los Pastores started off at the railroad depot and gathered shepherds as it moved in a loose procession down Becker Avenue toward the church of Our Lady of Belén. A group of us left the depot together, but we were soon separated, buoyed along in the river of people making its way toward the church. San Miguel was trying to lead the shepherds to the newborn Christ child, while Demonio used every possible way to get the shepherds to follow him instead. Emmy's friend Nick had brought a pile of sheepskins, and a dozen little kids had bundled themselves up in the warm fleece, hollering *baa, baa* as they capered along. Musicians—a harmonica and a guitar and a violin—accompanied the crowd. Singers sang, all in Spanish. I didn't understand a word, but it didn't matter.

Warm yellow light spilled out of the Cutoff Café as we passed by. I was thinking of Gus when, as if my thoughts had conjured him up, I spotted him in the crowd. At the very same moment, he spotted me. We worked our way toward each other.

"*Feliz Navidad*, Kitty," he said, drawing me into a hug. "Merry Christmas. Did you know that your nose is red?"

We linked arms so we wouldn't get separated, and Gus began pointing out the main characters in the play. He knew them all. There was Alicia's uncle, Epifanio Chávez, the gardener, dressed in the dazzling costume of the archangel. Enrique García, the newsstand manager, looking suitably demonic in a red suit with horns and a pitchfork. Lurching along at the side of the crowd, Felipe Castillo, Maria's grandfather, was the perfect embodiment of Bartolo. The comical lazy shepherd was everybody's favorite, offering his empty flask to anyone who caught his eye.

The beautiful old adobe church isn't large enough to accommodate everyone, so we were ushered down one side-aisle to the altar to honor Mary and Joseph and the Infant in the manger, and quickly ushered up the other side-aisle and out.

"Let's walk," Gus said. "You should see all the *luminarias*. You'll like it."

We turned away from the lights of Main Street and Becker Avenue, onto the quiet side streets. At every house, dozens of paper bag lanterns held lighted candles to guide the Holy Family to a resting place. It was a dark night, no moon—it might snow again—and the glow of the *luminarias* was magical.

"Warm enough?" Gus asked. "Your nose is still cold." He pulled me close and kissed me. His arm around me, we strolled on, more or less in the direction of the Harvey House, pausing often.

He asked when I'm leaving for Kansas. The third of January, I told him, and he said that he wants to see me as much as he can before I leave. We agreed to meet Wednesday afternoon.

The light above the kitchen door is too bright. Gus grinned, touched my cold nose with his lips, and said again, "*Feliz Navidad*, Kitty."

A full half-hour before midnight I came into the steamy kitchen where Viktor had already begun preparing the Christmas feast. I must have been floating several inches above the ground, because Viktor looked at me sharply.

"*Frohe Weihnachten*," he said. "Now go to bed. You'll be working very hard tomorrow."

Sunday, December 26th

I was up in time for Max's French toast yesterday morning. It was scrumptious, but worth getting up early for? I'm not sure. Cordelia skipped it, but Emmy was there, showing us the turquoise necklace that Nick gave her. We're not permitted to wear jewelry, so she has it on under her uniform, and every now and then she reaches up to touch it through the cloth.

The early part of the day was slow. Not many people come for breakfast on Christmas, except a few railroaders who have to work and are rewarding themselves with French toast or the little orange pancakes that are a Harvey House specialty.

From noon until evening, we had to fly to keep up. Oysters Rockefeller were on the menu for the first course. Then a choice of Turkey with Chestnut Stuffing, Leg of Lamb with Mint Jelly, or Prime Rib of Beef with Yorkshire Pudding. For dessert Max baked three kinds of pie, two kinds of cake, and a plum pudding. "In Vienna we set it alight with brandy and bring it to the table in flames, but not here," Max grumbled. "Prohibition. No brandy, no flames."

Sally, Gus, and Auntie Gertrude, maneuvering Tom in his wheelchair, came to an early sitting and ate in the dining room to accommodate the wheelchair. I had to fight down my usual attack of jealousy and smile graciously. Twenty-four hours earlier Gus had kissed me, not once but several times, and now he sat next to Sally, who looks at him as though he *belongs* beside her. Or as though she thinks he does.

Halfway through their meal I got a drop of gravy on my white apron and had to rush upstairs and change. I've never done that, and I blame it on Sally. I should have asked to switch places with Cordelia, as we did at Thanksgiving, and let her be their waitress. That would surely have pleased Tom. He hardly takes his eyes off her. I'm sure he has a huge crush on Cordelia, and I'm also sure she's aware of it. How she feels about Tom, I can't say.

Two girls had come down from the Alvarado to help out for the day, but we didn't have a minute's rest. At the very last sitting, when I thought my legs would not hold up much longer and I'd just crumple onto the floor, Mr. Sidney arrived with Millicent and asked if Cordelia and I could be permitted to join them for dinner. But we were having a "Harvey Family Christmas Dinner," like the one we'd had at Thanksgiving, and Mr. Lawrence invited *them* to join us. "As a way of thanking you for providing us with so much fine entertainment."

There was more of that fine entertainment. When we finished eating, Mr. Sidney brought out his violin again and played whatever was requested. Tom sang, accompanied by the violin, and he and Sally even sang a couple of duets. By the time Mr. Sidney closed his violin case, Christmas day was almost over, possibly the merriest I've ever spent.

Tuesday, December 28th

CORDELIA IS FEELING BLUE. I THOUGHT AT FIRST IT WAS because her father and Millicent left this morning for Arizona, but that doesn't make sense, because she'll likely see them again in Santa Fe. Then she told me she's gotten another letter from her mother. This time she showed it to me.

Mrs. Hart wrote that Lorenzo has been suffering from heart pains, brought on by the failure of his business and Walter's betrayal. Because of all this, her nerves are bad, she can't sleep, she suffers from headaches and dizziness, and everything was made so much worse because Cordelia didn't come home for Christmas. Only a thoughtless, ungrateful daughter would deliberately stay away at a time like this.

I tried to make her feel better. My parents were upset, too, and Mother said I was being selfish, but they got over it, and now they're delighted that the three of us are coming to Leavenworth next week. Daddy wrote that they're making all kinds of plans to entertain us.

"We'll probably be exhausted and glad to get back to the easy life of being a Harvey Girl," I said. I thought that would make her laugh, or at least smile. It didn't.

Wednesday, December 29th

All morning I kept one eye on the clock, wishing the time would go by faster until I could change out of my uniform and go to meet Gus at the Cutoff. It's been more than three weeks since our last time there—three weeks and two days, to be exact.

When we're together everything is fine, but it's hard to find time because Gus works odd shifts, and my split shifts don't give me much time off. Still! If he wanted to see me, we'd figure something out. I blame Sally—again.

Gus was waiting for me when I got there. I made sure not to arrive early. That would have made me look too anxious. He helped me off with my coat. My eyeglasses were steamed up, and he lifted them off, wiped them with his handkerchief, and set them back on my nose. "Better?" he asked, and I said it was fine.

Cash brought the coffee and doughnuts without being asked.

I told Gus about Mr. Sidney and Millicent. We talked about how much better Tom is doing, although it will still be a long time until the casts come off and he can handle crutches.

"He's lucky to have you there at Mrs. Goebel's to help take care of him," I said.

"It's Sally he's lucky to have."

That wasn't exactly what I wanted to hear, and I suppose I didn't quite disguise that.

He looked at me intently. "You're thinking about Sally, aren't you?" he asked, and I admitted that I was.

Gus reached across the table and took my hand. He and Sally have known each other for a long time, he explained. He has been a boarder at Auntie Gertrude's since he first came to Belén, and he and Tom have been close since Day One. The three of them have often done things together, like performing "Dangerous Dan McGrew." The problem, Gus said, is that since Tom's accident he and Sally have spent even more time together, looking after Tom. They used to be like brother and sister. Now things have changed on her side. Sally's begun to have certain expectations, suggesting that he might have in mind to settle down with a wife, a home, children, all those things, and that she'd be part of that picture.

My hand was starting to perspire, the way it does

when I'm nervous, and I pulled it away. My mouth felt dry. I didn't say anything.

"I made it plain that she and I aren't sweethearts, but I'd like to stay friends." What he hasn't told her, though, is that there's someone else—me—he's begun to care about. "I don't have the heart to tell her now," he said. "She's so worried about Tom. I don't want to make her feel worse."

I could feel my stomach twisting. *So when is he going to tell her?*

"Kitty, you and I have dreams. I want you to know that it sure would be nice to have you close to me while we're dreaming." He smiled, a smile that made my knees go weak. "Before you come back from Kansas, I'll tell Sally about you. I promise. And after the first of the year I'll have a new schedule. We'll have more time together. I promise that, too."

Friday, December 31st—New Year's Eve

WHEN I CAME BACK TO OUR ROOM AFTER BEING WITH Gus at the Cutoff, I found Cordelia's trunk, two suitcases, valise, and hatbox taking up every inch of available floor space. Her clothes were strewn over both beds.

I stood in the doorway, gaping. "I don't understand," I said. "We don't leave for Kansas until Monday, and we'll only be gone for three weeks. You won't need all those clothes. Especially not the summer ones."

"I'm going home," she said. "Back to Reading, P-A." Her eyes were red, and she kept wiping her nose with the back of her hand.

I crawled over an open suitcase and cleared a place to sit. "You're going to Reading? What happened?" I asked.

She'd been thinking about it, she explained, after that second letter from her mother. It was one thing to decide to spend Christmas away from home, but something else to sign a contract for another six months—or nine, as she'd been considering.

I tried to make some sense of what she was saying. "We told Mrs. McCreary we'd come back at the end of January."

"I'm not coming back, Kitty," she said. "My Harvey Girl days are through."

By then we were both crying. I was sobbing that she couldn't just quit like this, why would she do this? And Cordelia tried to make me understand that she feels she has to go home and help her mother. "Mummy is going through a very bad time."

I said I didn't think she could do much about that, and she replied, "Kitty, she's my mother."

"But maybe you'll come back," I said. "You can spend

three weeks in Reading, get everything straightened out, and come back. It will all work out!"

Cordelia looked at me sadly. "Please don't make it any harder for me, Kitty."

It was getting late. The Harvey House was hosting a big New Year's Eve celebration for the volunteer firemen and the county sheriff's deputies and their wives. Viktor had built a brick oven behind the Harvey House and was roasting a half-dozen suckling pigs. We had to put on our uniforms and go downstairs to start setting up. It was going to be a big night.

"Are you coming?" I asked Cordelia, because if it were me, I think I'd just sit there and cry.

"Of course," she said. "I'm still a Harvey Girl until I'm not anymore." Then she added, "I think I'll wear lipstick tonight, in honor of the occasion. Mrs. McCreary can't fire me!"

Sunday, January 2nd, 1927

EVERYONE WHO KNOWS CORDELIA HAS TRIED TO convince her that she must come back. Mr. Lawrence and Mrs. McCreary both had long talks with her, asking if there's anything that can be done. Emmy and I tried to get her to agree to at least *think about* coming back in a few weeks. She just shook her head. "Maybe someday."

But we did extract a compromise: Cordelia will spend a few days with us in Leavenworth. Then on January 10th, the same day Emmy heads to Topeka to visit her family, we'll put Cordelia on the train to Chicago. From there she'll go on to Reading.

She made us promise that we won't bring up the subject again and try to change her mind. Secretly I'm hoping she'll change it anyway.

She went to Auntie Gertrude's to say good-bye to Tom. The news stunned him. I think he's become fonder of her than he'd realized.

Monday, January 3rd—On the eastbound train

GUS WAS AT THE DEPOT THIS MORNING TO SAY GOOD-BYE. Nick was there, too, holding Emmy's hand. I asked Gus to take a picture of the three of us—Cordelia, Emmy, and me—with my camera, in front of the Harvey House. As we waited for the train, Gus put his arm around me and drew me aside.

"I've talked to Sally," he said quietly. "She wasn't at all surprised—about us. She said she already knew I was falling for you, and anyone who isn't blind could see it, too."

The train was pulling in, making the usual racket that drowned out conversation, but I know the grin on my face told Gus how I felt.

Gus and Nick helped us get Cordelia's considerable baggage on board, her guitar case on top. Gus hugged me, whispering, "See you in a few weeks, Kitty. I miss you already."

"I miss you already, too!" I called out as he swung down, and blew him a kiss as the conductor called "B-o-a-a-rd!"

The train began to move, slowly at first and then picking up speed. Cordelia gazed out the window until Belén had disappeared behind us. Then she turned to Emmy and me and snapped her fingers. "Don't look so gloomy! We're going to have fun! Who knows what will happen next."

She pulled out her guitar and began to play, singing softly:

Pack up all my care and woe,

Here I go, singing low,

Bye, bye, blackbird!

By the time we crossed the Rio Grande, Cordelia was standing in the aisle, fingers flying over the guitar strings. First Emmy and then everybody in the car was singing along with her—*Blackbird, bye, bye!*—as the train rolled steadily toward home.

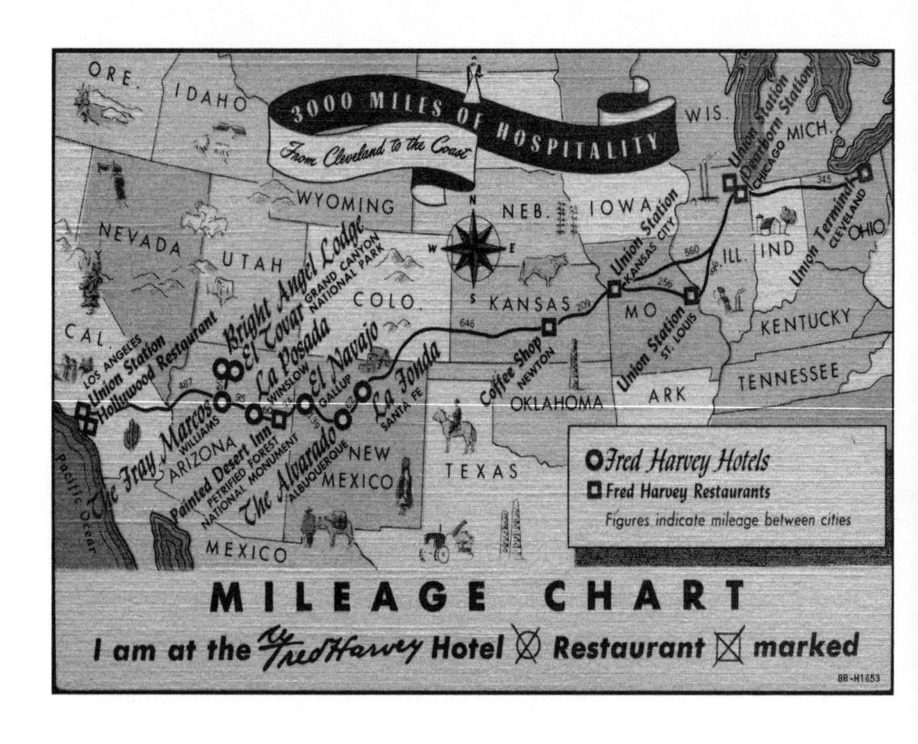

Friday, June 8th, 1951—
The Alvarado, Albuquerque

TWENTY-FIVE YEARS AGO TODAY—ON JUNE 8TH, 1926—Cordelia and Emmy and I met by chance at the Fred Harvey office in Union Station, Kansas City. Two days later we found each other again on a train bound for Emporia, Kansas, to begin our training as Harvey Girls. In July, Cordelia, Emmy, and I were sent to Belén; Maggie joined us there. It was Maggie's idea to get us all together here at the Alvarado for a twenty-fifth reunion.

Now, a quarter-century later, the world is a different place. We survived the Great Depression and World War II. The Harvey Girls have changed, and so have we.

I knew a little about the history of the Harvey Girls when I was one of them, but after I fulfilled my dream of becoming a journalist, I did some research and learned a lot more.

Our story actually began almost a hundred years ago when a fifteen-year-old British immigrant named Fred Harvey arrived in New York and took a job as a dishwasher. By the 1870s, Fred was working for the railroad, traveling a lot, and eating horrible food along the way. His solution was to open a restaurant. The first Harvey House, in the depot at Topeka, was so successful that Fred opened more restaurants and brought in first-class chefs to run the kitchens.

In 1883, when he learned that Harvey House waiters in Raton, New Mexico, had gotten into a drunken brawl, Mr. Harvey decided to hire girls instead. He dressed them in those severe black uniforms and white aprons and trained them in "the Harvey Way," rules guaranteed to drive us crazy until they became second nature. Within a few years, dozens of Harvey eating houses and hotels—and thousands of Harvey Girls—were providing excellent food and efficient service in towns along the railroad from Kansas City to California. The company was thriving, and we thrived with it.

But things were about to change for all of us.

After that visit to my family in Leavenworth in January of '27, Cordelia went home to Pennsylvania. Emmy stopped to see her family outside of Topeka, and then both of us returned to Belén. Maggie, meanwhile, had managed to talk her way back into a job in Vaughn.

Charles Lindbergh, probably the most famous man in America after his solo flight across the Atlantic in 1927, experienced an engine failure a year later and landed his airplane in the desert outside of Vaughn. He had to wait for several days for the parts to come in. Maggie sent us a postcard: *Lindy ate every meal here. We fought to be the one to serve him.*

Cordelia and I corresponded often at first, then less often. Her mother was driving her crazy, and Cordelia, to keep her sanity, served as a church organist and played the piano at the country club where she'd once learned to play golf. "One of these days," she wrote, "I'll be back."

It was no surprise when Emmy married Nick Mayfield and went to live on John Becker's sheep ranch in Jarales. Opal and Pearl and their husbands stopped by the Harvey House now and then with their growing families. Maggie's old rival, Susana, married Pedro, but we heard that it was an anything-but-peaceful marriage. Alicia became a nurse and moved to El Paso. She came home often, and I always found her at the annual fiesta.

I stayed on at the Belén Harvey House, and Gus and I saw each other as often as possible. When Charles Lindbergh designed an airport in Winslow, Arizona, for the company he and Amelia Earhart formed with Transcontinental Air Transport, Gus landed a job with the railroad in Winslow and started taking flying lessons. And when La Posada, Mary Colter's beautiful new hotel, opened in Winslow in 1930, I transferred there. By then Gus had his pilot's license and flew the mail, and I worked as a Harvey Girl. It was an exciting life.

The stock market crash of '29 marked the beginning of the Great Depression, and that changed everything for everybody. Jobs dried up. We began to see freight trains rolling through, loaded with people desperate for work. But Gus and I were in love, and in 1932, after going together for five years, we were married. We spent our honeymoon at the Grand Canyon. I was thrilled to finally see it.

The smaller Harvey Houses were suffering. In 1935, the Belén Harvey House closed; so did many others. Gus and I had a baby girl, Carrie Mae, and I wondered what her life would be like. The Depression dragged on. Back in Leavenworth, Daddy lost his business. Both he and Howie were looking for work. Maudie married Jimmy Bedwell and kept his family's lumber business afloat somehow. I stayed home with Carrie Mae and wrote short stories on my faithful

Underwood Portable—stories that nobody wanted to publish—but I also began writing articles for magazines, which brought in a few dollars and allowed me to keep thinking of myself as a real journalist.

Then, on December 7, 1941, the Japanese bombed Pearl Harbor, and four days later President Roosevelt declared war on Germany. World War II had begun. Gus enlisted before Christmas. The Winslow airfield was being used as a training base for pilots, and Gus was stationed there until he was sent overseas. We heard that Tom tried to enlist but was turned down because of his bad leg, and ended up as a radio announcer in Oklahoma. Sally, who married a railroader, moved to Texas after Auntie Gertrude died. My parents wanted me to move back to Leavenworth with Carrie Mae, but I decided to stay in Winslow.

Troop trains rolled across the country, carrying soldiers to California before they were sent to the Pacific. Harvey Houses that had been closed now opened up again and began serving thousands of meals each day to "Private Pringle," the Harvey name for the servicemen. Maggie went to work at La Castañeda, which had also been scheduled to close but stayed open during the war to feed the troops.

Winslow was the largest troop stop on the AT&SF. I made arrangements for a neighbor to look after Carrie Mae, and became a Harvey Girl again. In one month alone in 1943, we served close to thirty thousand men. We were always shorthanded.

During those hectic years, who should turn up but Cordelia! She'd married a doctor during the Depression, "a lovely man," she said, who enlisted in the Navy. His ship was sunk in the Pacific, and she packed up and came out West again. The Indian Detours had been suspended, but Cordelia joined the Harvey Girls at the Alvarado, feeding Private Pringle.

Gus made it home safely when the war ended and is now a pilot for Trans World Airlines. Cordelia stayed in Albuquerque, earned a degree at the university, and teaches music in San Francisco. Maggie works at the Kachina Room at the Albuquerque Airport, dressed in a multicolored skirt and a white peasant blouse and as much Indian jewelry as she can manage. No more staid black-and-white outfits! The look suits her well.

Trains still stop in Albuquerque, but most people who come to the Alvarado now arrive by car. Blame it on Route 66, the highway that now stretches from Chicago to Los Angeles. Americans do most of their traveling by car, although Gus keeps telling me—and I believe him—that in a few years everybody will cross the country by airplane. Maggie, out at the handsome new airport, agrees.

Although the Alvarado doesn't have as many movie stars and celebrities stepping off the trains that used to come through here, it's still the center of social life in Albuquerque. Maggie made the arrangements, and here we are.

For the past couple of nights, the four of us sat in rocking chairs on the arcade, remembering the heyday of the Harvey Girls and talking until the moon was setting and we couldn't stay awake any longer. Tomorrow Emmy will go back to the ranch in Jarales, and Cordelia will visit her father in Santa Fe. He plays his violin once in a while at La Fonda, one of the few remaining Harvey House hotels.

"What about you, Kitty?" Cordelia asked. "Are you still writing in your diary?"

I said I was.

"You should write a book about the Harvey Girls," she said.

"A novel of romance and adventure," Emmy suggested.

"A book about us," Maggie insisted.

I promised them I'd think about it.

AUTHOR'S NOTE

THE ERA OF THE HARVEY GIRLS FLOURISHED FOR OVER seventy years. In that time more than one hundred thousand young women left home and headed west, ready for a different kind of life.

But eventually that era and the popularity of Harvey Houses came to an end. La Posada closed in 1957 and was converted into offices for the Santa Fe Railway. In 1997 it was purchased, restored, and reopened.

Despite passionate efforts of Albuquerque civic groups to save it, the Alvarado ended its days in 1969 and was torn down. A busy transportation center now occupies the site. City buses come and go, long-distance buses pull in farther down the street, and beyond the fake-adobe building meant to mimic that beautiful old hotel, the local commuter train sounds its regular arrivals and departures. Around noon the blast of a horn announces the departure of Amtrak's eastbound

Southwest Chief on its way to Chicago; the #3 comes through late in the afternoon, bound for Los Angeles. Native Americans from nearby pueblos are there to greet passengers with displays of jewelry and pots.

I've lived in New Mexico since 1978, except for a five-year stint next door in Texas, but only in the past few years have I become aware of the Harvey Girls and their rich story. The more I heard about them, the more fascinated I became—especially when I moved into an apartment across from the site of the Alvarado. I visited the Belén Harvey House, rescued from demolition and now a museum, and stayed for a couple of nights at the beautifully restored La Posada in Winslow, Arizona. Mary Colter would be proud! I poked around the remains of La Castañeda in Las Vegas, New Mexico, which I'm happy to report has been bought with plans to restore it to its former glory.

Diary of a Waitress is a work of fiction, and most of the characters—Kitty, Cordelia, Emmy, and their friends—are my inventions. A few characters are real: Fred Harvey and his family (his home in Leavenworth, Kansas, is now a museum); Alice Steele, who interviewed and hired Harvey Girls in the 1920s; William Allen White, editor of the *Emporia Gazette*; Mary Jane Colter, who designed the interiors of many Harvey House hotels and restaurants; Belén businessman John Becker and his family (except for Gus, who is fictional);

the two doctors, and even the Wilson Brothers who moved the (fictional) parlor organ; and the two Isleta Pueblo potters, Maria and Francisca Chiwiwi. All of them are people Kitty Evans might have met.

Carolyn Meyer
Albuquerque, New Mexico

SELECTED BIBLIOGRAPHY

Berke, Arnold. *Mary Colter: Architect of the Southwest.* New York: Princeton Architectural Press, 2002.

Burr, Baldwin G. *Belen.* Charleston, SC: Arcadia Publishing, 2013.

Fried, Stephen. *Appetite for America: How Visionary Businessman Fred Harvey Built a Railroad Hospitality Empire that Civilized the Wild West.* New York: Random House, 2010.

Poling-Kempes, Lesley. *The Harvey Girls: Women Who Opened the West.* New York: Marlowe & Co., 1991.

Melzer, Richard. *Fred Harvey Houses of the Southwest.* Charleston, SC: Arcadia Publishing, 2008.

Myrick, David F. *New Mexico's Railroads: A Historical Survey.* Albuquerque: University of New Mexico Press, 1970.

PICTURE CREDITS

Arizona State Library, Archives and Public Records, History and Archives Division, Phoenix, #01-4548: 64–65.

Courtesy of Jim Sloan: 118–119.

© **Lake County Museum/CORBIS:** 336.

Library of Congress, Prints & Photographs Division: LC-USZ62-118086: 18–19; LC-DIG-ppmsca-09507: 137; LC-USZ62-97656: 209; LC-USZ62-116105: 211; LC-USW3-015590-E: 296.

TEXT PERMISSIONS

"Bye Bye Blackbird"
Lyrics by Mort Dixon
Music by Ray Henderson

"I Love You Truly," lyrics and music by Carrie Jacobs Bond, the Lorenz Corporation.